Christmas Stalkings

TALES OF YULETIDE MURDER

Christmas Stalkings

COLLECTED BY

CHARLOTTE MACLEOD

THE MYSTERIOUS PRESS

New York · Tokyo · Sweden · Milan

Published by Warner Books

 A Time Warner Company

Library of Congress Cataloging-in-Publication Data

Christmas stalkings : more tales of Yuletide murder / collected by
    Charlotte MacLeod.
        p.   cm.
    ISBN 0-89296-437-5
    1. Detective and mystery stories, American.   2. Christmas sto-
ries, American.   I. MacLeod, Charlotte.
    PS648.D4C48   1991
    813'.08720833—dc20   91-10306
                                                                CIP

Contents

Christmas
Stalkings

It was in 1978 that Professor Peter Shandy introduced me to Balaclava Agricultural College and its traditional Grand Christmas Illumination . . . at which he behaved disgracefully, as anyone who has read Peter's and my first collaborative venture, Rest You Merry, *can attest.*

Since that time, I've served as Peter's Ms. Watson in seven other adventures, but I'd never been invited back to Balaclava at Illumination time until this odd situation cropped up. I did expect the dauntless agronomist and the possibly even more dauntless President Thorkjeld Svenson would have got all the bugs worked out by now, but it seems that the best-laid plans of mice, men, and even the Illumination Committee can still go agley.

CHARLOTTE MACLEOD

COUNTERFEIT
CHRISTMAS

Deck the halls with boughs of holly,
"Fa, la la la la, la la, la la."

Professor Peter Shandy of Balaclava Agricultural College found the carolers' injunction as superfluous as that inane string of meaningless syllables tacked on after it. Every house on the Crescent was already as bedizened as it could get, for Yuletide was rife and the annual Grand Illumination was not only heard all over campus and down in the village but could also be seen, smelled, touched, and even tasted, if you got close enough.

During most of the year, the open space encircled by eight faculty dwellings, including Peter's, was placid enough; merely a grassy sward kept in seemly order by the trusty men of Buildings & Grounds and appropriately bedded out here and there with flowers of spring, summer, or fall, depending. Came the holiday season, however, and the usually by then snow-covered Crescent erupted into a festive welter of illuminated Christmas trees and quaint gingerbread

3

houses cut from plywood and assembled by the trusty screwdrivers of brawny students, who then donned oversized elf suits and flung themselves joyously into the time-honored Yankee pastime of turning an honest buck.

From some of the gingerbread houses, bonny lasses in frilly mobcaps and brave lads in stovepipe hats and home-grown chin whiskers purveyed artifacts ranging from apple-head dolls to woolens woven from fleece donated by the college sheep. Others hawked mulled cider, hot coffee, hot chocolate, and hot peppermint tea. Cold switchel had been tried one year but hadn't caught on. Homemade doughnuts kept warm in imitation stoneware Crockpots whose electric cords were cunningly hidden from the customers' view were a big item, though. So were hot dogs with festive garnishes of red-and-green piccalilli from the college kitchens.

Popcorn balls and taffy apples never failed to sell, as did more exotic comestibles. Foremost among these latter was a sort of antic sweetmeat made of shredded coconut, molasses, melted chocolate, and a number of other things that Professor Peter Shandy, the Crescent's least Yule-minded resident, preferred not to think about. Years ago, some coarse-minded wag had noticed the resemblance between these biggish, flattish, brownish, whiskerish confections and a certain bovine by-product familiar to every animal-husbandry student. Coconut cowpats he'd dubbed them, and coconut cowpats they'd remained. They sold even faster than hotcakes, and Peter Shandy thought them obscene.

But then, Peter thought most things about the

Illumination obscene. For the first eighteen years of his residence on the Crescent, he'd been the self-appointed faculty Scrooge. Despite endless nagging by the Illumination Committee, he'd allowed not so much as a Styrofoam candy cane or a wreath of lollipops to sully the simple dignity of his small old rosy brick house. Then one year, goaded to fury by the Illumination chairperson's attempt to foist off on him a poinsettia fashioned from pieces of red detergent bottles, he'd gone hog-wild.

In a burst of uncontrollable fury, Peter had hired decorators to transform his premises into a veritable Walpurgisnacht scene of garish blinking light bulbs, life-size plastic reindeer, and hideous Santa Claus masks that lit up and leered. Then, fleeing the ire of his neighbors, he'd gone off on a cruise, got shipwrecked as he well deserved to be, and slunk home to find the Illumination chairperson's body stiff and stark behind his living-room sofa.

Oddly enough, Peter had emerged from this deplorable incident not only with a whole skin but with a wife. Under the benign influence of his delightful Helen, the renegade bachelor had been transformed into a relatively civilized husband. Even his next-door neighbor said so in her mellower moments, of which it must also be admitted she didn't have many. By now, Peter had gentled down to the point where he didn't even put up much of a squawk when Helen gently but firmly insisted on doing in Balaclava as the Balaclavans did.

Fortunately, Helen's instincts were for the tastefully simple as opposed to the more-is-better. There had been one unfortunate experiment with topiary trees made from fresh-cut boxwood that stunk the place up like a houseful of tomcats, but on the whole she'd done fine. This year, Helen's decorations were particularly charming.

Eschewing the excesses of her neighbors, she'd made low arrangements of evergreen twigs for all the front windows upstairs and down, and trimmed them with a few small rose-colored baubles and velvet bows to complement the aged brick walls. In the middle of each arrangement she'd set a real candle, protected by a glass hurricane-lamp chimney so that it could be lighted after dark without setting fire to the house. On the front door she'd hung a fat balsam wreath tied with a larger bow of the same rosy velvet. To the wreath was fastened an old brass cornet that Peter had tooted in his high school marching band, salvaged from the attic and shined up till it dazzled the eyeballs. Peter had pretended to scoff but been secretly tickled. He'd even taken pains to wire the cornet to the door, lest it be pinched by some souvenir hunter among the multitudes.

For multitudes there were. Balaclava's Grand Illumination had been going on ever since the bleak Depression years of the early 1930s. Photographed and written up in newspapers and magazines, talked about on the radio and even shown now and then on television, the event had become a New England tradition, attracting visitors from far and wide to this rural Massachusetts community.

Fairly far, anyway, and reasonably wide. Wide enough to keep Police Chief Fred Ottermole and his force, which consisted mostly of Officer Budge Dorkin, oftentimes hard-put to keep the traffic unsnarled.

Fortunately the college had its own larger and better-equipped security force, so there was seldom any trouble about maintaining law and order.

The college, of course, was squarely behind the Illumination, and with good reason. Its student body was not rich; most of the kids were working their way, and here was a welcome source of tuition money. A fair number of students willingly forwent part or all of their Christmas holidays for the greater good of hustling the tourists. Peter could admire their self-sacrifice and respect their motives; he just didn't see why in Sam Hill they couldn't maintain their blasted tradition someplace else.

Out beyond the pigpens, for instance. At this very moment, a disgusting youth in a just-purchased Viking helmet with plush moose horns on it was unwrapping a coconut cowpat and throwing the paper on the trodden snow. Peter was glaring balefully down at him through the upstairs front window and wishing it were the second week of January when he heard a thump at the door.

Some keen-eyed visitor must have managed to sort out the knocker from the balsam, or else a miscreant tourist was trying to swipe his cornet. Normally Peter would have flung open the window and stuck out his head to settle the matter with a lusty bellow, but he was loath to disarrange Helen's artistically disposed greenery and even loather to smash the hurricane lamp. There was no use even trying to bellow, he'd never be able to make himself heard over the general hullabaloo. He bowed to the inevitable and went downstairs. It might be his old friend and neighbor Professor Ames, at loose ends between semesters, looking for a game of cribbage.

No, by George, it was about the third from the last person he'd have expected. Moira Haskins, the college comptroller, was a pleasant woman and a neighbor on the Crescent, but not one with whom he and Helen were on dropping-in terms. Peter had an ominous foreboding that Moira was after something.

As so often happened, Peter was right. When he indicated a readiness to divest her of her storm coat and call Helen down from the den where she was wrapping presents, the comptroller shook her head.

"Thanks, Peter, but I can't stay. I just wanted to show you this and see what you make of it."

Moira's "this" was a twenty-dollar bill. It looked to Peter like all the other twenty-dollar bills he'd been shelling out with unaccustomed abandon during this expensive season, until he put on his reading glasses and studied it closely. Then he began to chuckle. Where he'd have expected the grim and lowering portrait of President Andrew Jackson, he saw instead the even grimmer and far more lowering visage of President Thorkjeld Svenson.

"My God! Where the flaming perdition did this come from?"

"One of the gingerbread houses, I assume. It was in with the rest when Silvester Lomax brought me last night's cash pickup. I was sitting at my desk just now, counting the money for this morning's deposit, when I did a double take and almost freaked out. What do you think, Peter? You don't suppose somebody got to doodling around on the bill with a drawing pen or something and—"

"Not on your life. Jackson's head is long and skinny. It might have been managed with Ulysses S. Grant, I suppose, if they could have got the beard off. Just a second, I think I've—" He fished in his wallet and pulled out a fifty, marveling that he did in fact still have one. "See, Grant had a heavy, squarish face like the president's. Rather as if he'd been hacked out of Mount Rushmore."

"Yes, I see," said Moira. "Then why didn't they use a fifty instead of a twenty?"

"Probably because fifties are less common and therefore more apt to be given close scrutiny. Is this the only such bill you've found?"

"So far. The only one that's been caught, anyway. We're into the fifth day of the Illumination, you know, and we've taken in an awful lot of money. There's no telling how many may have slipped through."

"Not all that many, I shouldn't think. This is a remarkably good likeness."

"Frighteningly good." Moira shuddered slightly despite the storm coat she hadn't taken off. "But President Svenson's so much more presidential than most presidents. If those kids in the booths did happen to notice, they'd take it for granted he belonged there. Most of them have probably never heard of Andrew Jackson anyway. I wonder what Dr. Svenson's going to think of this."

"He'll think it's funny, provided we don't get stuck with a whole flock of them. As for this one—" Peter kept hold of the startling counterfeit and handed Moira a genuine twenty taken from his wallet. "Fair swap?"

"No, really, Peter. Why should you stand the loss?"

"What loss? This bill's a collector's item, it's worth far more than the alleged face value. I'm probably gypping the college worse than the counterfeiter did.

Drat it, Moira, this is a fantastically expert job. Look at the workmanship. Can you tell me why anybody with the talent to pull off such a magnificent fake would waste his time on a practical joke that could send him to jail?"

"Well, no, I hadn't thought of that. It doesn't make sense, does it?"

"It might, I suppose, though I can't think how. Look, Moira, let's keep this between ourselves for the time being. There could be something more than meets the eye here. I'd like to check around a bit before we spread the word. Let me know if you get any others, will you?"

"All right, Peter. I certainly don't want to involve the college in anything shady, especially at Illumination time. You know how stories get blown up and stretched out of proportion. You're quite sure I shouldn't go to the president?"

"You can't right now, he's gone off skiing. I tell you what, Moira: I'll have the security guards pass on to the students a general warning about being on the alert for funny money. A big event like this, run by young amateurs, creates an ideal situation for the passing of counterfeit bills. I'm surprised the Illumination's never been hit sooner, now that I think of it. Anyway, we'll cope. Thank you for coming, Moira."

"Thank you for listening, Peter. I'm sorry to be dumping on you, but then everybody does, don't they?"

That was true enough. Peter had been Balaclava's unofficial private detective ever since that great debacle at the earlier Illumination, when President Svenson had confronted him with the dire consequences of his ill-judged prank and saddled him with the job of catching the murderer.

Peter knew he'd get stuck again anyhow, so he might as well get to work right away, not that he had the remotest idea where to start. He let the comptroller out and went back upstairs with the aberrant twenty-dollar bill in his hand.

"Helen, what do you make of this?"

"Of what?" his wife replied somewhat testily. "Stick your finger on this knot, will you? I don't see why it's always the woman who gets landed with wrapping the parcels. I'll bet Margaret Thatcher doesn't wrap presents."

"Couldn't you have had them gift-wrapped at the stores?"

"Of course not. You have to stand in line till your feet kill you, then they charge you an extra dollar for a piece of fancy paper and a stupid little bow. You can take your finger out now."

"No, I can't, you've lashed it down."

"Oh, Peter!" Sighing, Helen freed the captive digit and yanked tight the knot. "All right, now what am I supposed to look at?"

"Behold."

Peter handed her the note. She stared blankly for about a quarter of a second, then burst out laughing.

"Where in heaven's name did you get that?"

"From Moira Haskins. She was here just now."

"Why didn't you call me?"

"I offered to, but she said she couldn't stay."

"Then why did she come? It's not like Moira to be showing silly jokes around."

"She wasn't joking. This thing turned up in last night's Illumination takings."

"Are you saying somebody actually succeeded in passing Thorkjeld's picture off as legal tender?"

"That appears to have been the case. Unless some student worker stuck it in as a joke. Which, I must say, seems a bit subtle for purveyors of coconut cowpats."

"I see what you mean." Helen picked up the magnifying glass she used for studying ancient documents from the college's historic Buggins Collection, of which she was curator. "You know, Peter, this likeness to Thorkjeld is quite a piece of work. I think it's actually a pen-and-ink drawing, but it reproduces the steel-engraving technique so expertly that I can't tell for sure. As a guess I'd say the artist, and I'm not using the word loosely, may have photocopied a real twenty, cut out the medallion on the front, inserted his drawing of Thorkjeld Svenson in place of Andrew Jackson, and run it off again. You could do that easily enough if you had access to a copier that does color work."

"Having made his own paper?"

"I expect this is simply a very-good quality rag-content bond that's been dipped in tea or something and wrinkled up to make it look more authentic. It doesn't have quite the feel of real currency, but I can see where an inexperienced student clerk with cold hands and fourteen more customers clamoring to be served might not notice, especially at night with all those colored lights around. It would have been simply a matter of picking the right time and place. But why Thorkjeld?"

"Moira suggested it could be because the students would assume he belonged there."

"She's probably right. How many of these have been turned in?"

"Just this one so far, that Moira knows of. She's going to let me know if she gets any more. I'm wondering whether I ought to take this along to the state police, in case the bills are being passed elsewhere."

Helen shook her head. "That seems hardly likely, don't you think? To me, this looks more like somebody having a quiet little snicker at the college's expense."

"It also looks like one hell of a lot of work for a secret snicker," Peter replied, "but I have to admit that's how it strikes me, too. Can you think of anybody on the faculty who knows how to draw and goes in for being inscrutable?"

"Dr. Porble enjoys a private joke"—Porble was the college librarian and Helen's alleged boss—"but he can't draw for beans. He can't even doodle. He simply writes down the Dewey Decimal Code for whatever he happens to be thinking about but isn't going to tell you; then he smiles that sneaky little smile of his and scratches it out."

"You don't happen by any chance to have a pen-and-ink portrait of the president in the library files that Porble might have used?"

"We have a few mildly scurrilous caricatures, but nothing that could even remotely pass for a steel engraving. You know what, Peter? I'll bet you a nickel this was copied from the photograph on that program the art department got up to celebrate Thorkjeld's twenty-fifth anniversary as president of the college."

"The one Shirley Wrenne took, that makes him look like Zeus hunting for a likely target to hurl his thunderbolt at? By George, Helen, I think you're right. What happened to that program? We had a copy of it around here somewhere, didn't we?"

"Yes, but I took ours over to the library. The one we had in the files disappeared."

"How long ago?"

"I couldn't say. That particular file doesn't get much attention as a rule. If the program had been a bunch of hog statistics, Dr. Porble would have been on it like a hawk. Want me to go over and get our copy back?"

"No, don't bother, I have to go out anyway. I promised Moira I'd speak to Security about issuing a general ukase on keeping an eye out for counterfeit money, for whatever good that may do. Are we dining at home, or would you like some handsome and dashing he-man to sweep you off your feet and take you out for a pizza?"

"La, sir, I'm just the bundle-wrapper; you'll have to ask the butler's permission. Let's see how we feel when the time comes."

Helen didn't abominate the Illumination the way Peter did, she couldn't be feeling the same frantic urge as he to get away from the crowd and the racket. Well, what couldn't be cured must be endured. There was always the faculty dining room to fall back on, provided its staffers weren't all off catering a marshmallow roast or some other unspeakable orgy. Peter gritted his teeth, put on his old mackinaw and his rubber-soled boots, and went forth to brave the surging tide of festivity.

The security office was up toward the back of the campus; Peter would have enjoyed the stroll if he hadn't been constantly beset by husky students in those infernally whimsical elf suits, giving rides to bundled-up tourists on bright-red hand sleds with curlicues on their front runners. He managed to find both sanctuary and Silvester Lomax inside the small brick building, showed Moira's find, and explained his errand. Silvester permitted himself one quick snort of glee, then buckled down to composing a stern memorandum.

In the face of such efficiency, Peter didn't feel disposed to loiter making small talk; so he went back to the library and satisfied himself that the portrait on the bill could in fact have been drawn from the photograph on the program. There'd only been about five hundred of them printed, he supposed, and not more than half of those taken home and tucked away wherever people were wont to keep their useless junk. That would limit the field, but not by much.

He fiddled around the library for a while, dropped in at the greenhouse to check on some experimental seedlings, then moseyed back to the Crescent. He found some gratification in the sight of Purvis Mink, one of Silvester's henchmen, passing out memos to the kids in the gingerbread houses; but little consolation at watching the harried kids give them cursory glances and stick them back among the piccalilli jars. He might as well go home and see if Helen had any more knots to be tied.

The next morning, Moira Haskins was on his doorstep betimes, looking fussed and bothered. "It's happened again, Peter."

"You've found another?"

"No, two. You did speak to Security?"

"I did, and Purvis Mink passed out notices. Whether the guards came around again later to warn the kids on the evening shift, I couldn't say, but I expect they did. There was an awful mob last night, though, as usual. Short of setting a guard at each booth to examine every bill as it comes over the counter, I don't see how in Sam Hill we're going to catch the passer."

"It does look like just one person, doesn't it? I don't know whether that makes the job easier or harder. Talk about needles in haystacks! Well, I must get down to the bank. Do you think I should speak to the manager?"

"I don't know, Moira. I'll talk with the guards and get back to you."

"Thanks, Peter. It's good of you to help. Oh, your cat's going out."

"That's all right, she won't go far; Jane's not one for getting her feet wet. Besides, she hates the crowds even worse than I do."

No visitors were about this early. Students were still picking up yesterday's litter, resanding the iced-over paths, replacing burned-out light bulbs on the over-worked Christmas trees, taking care of the myriad details that must be seen to before the onslaught began anew. It was oddly peaceful. Peter stood for a moment watching the small tiger cat pick her dainty way down the front walk, stopping every few steps to give each white-stockinged paw an angry shake. She wouldn't stay out long. She never did. He went into his tiny first-floor office and began correcting exam papers.

Helen had gone up to the library; the phone didn't ring once; the sounds from outside hadn't started to build. Working along in semi-silence, Peter found his task only mildly tedious. He must have been at it for upward of an hour before it occurred to him that tourists were arriving, but that Jane was not. Where in tunket had she got to? Surely he'd have heard if she'd asked to come in, Jane had her family well-trained. In some perturbation, he got up and went to the door.

Jane was not on the stoop, nor yet on the walk. She, the dedicated house cat, was over on the green. She, the snob who shunned all lesser felines, the timid soul who wouldn't even go back across the Crescent to visit her own mother at the Enderbles', was leading a squad of raucous felines in a concerted attack on the third gingerbread house.

Oddly enough, this wasn't the stand that sold the hot dogs and hamburgers, which might have made some sense. It was the one that dispensed the gingerbread men, the taffy apples, the popcorn balls, and the coconut cowpats. Even as Peter watched, nonplussed by the cats' frantic clawing and scrambling, a grandmotherly-looking woman picked her way among them and purchased three coconut cowpats, one for each of the two moppets who clung to her coat, and one that she stowed in her capacious handbag, perhaps to take home to Grandpa. The little girl slipped hers out of its waxed-paper wrapping, took an experimental nibble, rewrapped it, and stowed it carefully in the pocket of her snowsuit. The little boy ripped the paper off his and took a large bite.

Peter shuddered. So, oddly enough, did the boy. He made a terrible face and dumped the rest of the cowpat on the ground. Immediately the cats pounced on it, gentle Jane the first to spring. This was too much for Peter. Hatless and coatless, he dashed across to sort out his own cherished pet from the yowling, scratching heap, getting himself rather lavishly lacerated in the process, but managing to secure a fragment of what the little boy had thrown away. The fragile flower of felinity did not take rescue kindly, she wanted that cowpat.

Jane fussed all the way home, but quieted down once she got in the house and went off in a corner to sulk. Peter took his so painfully obtained fragment into the kitchen, laid it out on the saucer, pulled it apart with a couple of toothpicks, and studied it carefully. The texture was fibrous, as he'd expected, and not all the fiber was coconut.

He worked loose a fragment of the alien substance, sniffed at it, tasted it with utmost caution. He was not surprised by what he discovered. He applied healing ointment to his more spectacular wounds, tried to placate Jane, who only spat and growled, and went back to the third gingerbread house. The other cats were still fighting over the crumbs, a few were trying to climb up on the counter and being shooed down. The few early visitors were gawking in wonder, the workers were looking nonplussed.

"I don't know what's got into them," stammered the youngest student, a young woman whose eyes were wide and whose mobcap was sadly awry. "They've never acted like this before."

"I expect they've never had occasion to," said Peter. "Who brought in the latest batch of cowpats?"

The girl stared at the pile on the counter, her two workmates stared at her. Peter looked at all three. Balaclava was not a large college. Faculty and students got to know each other pretty quickly; if not by name, at least by sight.

The chap in the stovepipe hat was one of Peter's

own seniors. He came from Maine, lived in the dorms, and worked in the greenhouses when he wasn't in class or peddling cowpats. The other young woman, also a senior, was majoring in botany. She also lived in the dorms, her botanical notebooks were works of art. She was possessed of a comfortable trust fund and she was engaged to the chap in the stovepipe hat. According to Mrs. Mouzouka of culinary arts, she was congenitally unable to boil water. She must be here because she'd wanted to stay with her fiancé or because she didn't want to go home, or both. She might have done the drawing of Dr. Svenson. She could easily have supplied the plant material. She could never in God's world have baked the cowpats.

All Peter knew about the girl with the big round eyes was that she was a freshman, she was studying culinary arts, and she didn't live in the dorms. Since there were very few rental apartments around town, and those few all grabbed up by faculty, she must either be living with her own family or boarding with somebody else's. Peter's face grew as stern as he could make it with one of the Enderbles' half-grown kittens crawling up his pant leg.

"All right, you three, come clean. Whose idea was it to bake those cowpats?"

"C-cowpats?" stammered the freshman. "I don't know what you're talking about."

"This critter does." Peter set the young cat on the counter; it headed straight for the oversized compote that held the cowpats. "You might as well give him one. You can't sell them, you know."

The male senior reached for one of the cowpats, smelled it and took a gingerly nibble. "It does taste—

Kathy, this isn't funny! You could get us all pinched and the Illumination shut down."

"Gerry, what are you talking about?" snapped his fiancée. She grabbed the cowpat, nibbled, made a face, and burst into laughter. "You idiot, don't you know cannabis from catnip? Clarice, have you any thoughts on the matter?"

Clarice had no thought but burst into tears. Peter reached over and touched her arm.

"I think you'd better come along with me, Miss— er—"

"S-s-s-sissler. Am I under arrest?"

"Not at all. I have no authority to arrest anybody, we just need to talk. Miss Bunce"—he'd finally remembered the senior woman's name—"perhaps you'd be good enough to come with us. Can you manage alone for a few minutes, Pascoe?"

"I guess so, Professor," the male member of the group replied. "If you wouldn't mind impounding the evidence, maybe those cats would go away. I think this kitten's about to throw up on the counter."

"An excellent suggestion, Pascoe. I assume you have something to put the cowpats in. Come on, kitty, I'd better take you home. Are you ladies ready to go?"

"K-kathy doesn't need to c-come," sniffled the wretched Miss Sissler. "Sh-she didn't do anything."

"That's all right, Clarice," said Miss Bunce. "I don't mind."

"Well, I d-do."

"All right then, if that's how you feel."

With a toss of her mobcap, Miss Bunce began rearranging the counter. Followed by a number of disappointed cats, Peter delivered the kitten to Mrs. Enderble, then led his weeping semi-captive away to the nearest dumpster and thence to the faculty dining room. He wasn't about to take a young female student into his own house now that she'd refused a chaperone, not with Helen gone. He'd assumed the dining room would be all but deserted at this hour, and it was. Nobody was around, except a student waiter who came somewhat reluctantly out to take their order.

"Now then, Miss Sissler," said Peter, "what would you like? Tea? Coffee? Hot chocolate?"

"S-strychnine, please."

"Come now, it's not that bad. Two coffees, please, and a couple of muffins. Just plain ones, not your holiday specials." Peter didn't feel up to snippets of red and green candied cherries this morning.

Neither of them said anything more until after the waiter had brought their coffee and corn muffins and gone back to whatever culinary beguilements awaited him in the kitchen. Peter waited until the lachrymose freshman had creamed and sugared her coffee and taken a timid sip.

"Now then, Miss Sissler, would you care to explain?"

She shook her head frantically. Tears welled again in the big round eyes. "I can't, Professor Shandy. Truly I can't."

"Young woman, are you by any chance trying to be a heroine? Here, have a muffin and tell me whom you're covering up for. Is it your boyfriend?"

"No!"

"Is somebody blackmailing you into trying to wreck the Illumination?"

"No."

"Then can you tell me why in Sam Hill you pulled

such a stupid stunt? Did you think it was marijuana you were putting in those infernal objects?"

"Y-yes."

"Where did it come from?"

"I f-found it."

"Where?"

"Hanging up."

"Hanging up where?"

"In the k-kitchen."

"Whose kitchen? Not the college's?"

"Of course not! Mrs. Mouzouka wouldn't—"

"No, I don't suppose she would. Come on, Miss Sissler, let's get this over with. I have exams to correct. And you have a fresh batch of cowpats to bake, strictly according to the standard recipe, disgusting though it may be. The college is counting on you, drat it. Where do you do your cooking? You don't live in the dorms, do you? Where are your people?"

"In F-florida. I'm staying with my great-aunt, here in Balaclava Junction."

"She being—?"

"Miss Viola Harp. You know her. She calligraphs the college diplomas."

"Does she indeed? I'm afraid I can't quite place her."

"Nobody can! Nobody cares. That's why she—"

Miss Sissler essayed another sip of her coffee, and choked on it. As Peter watched her coughing into her napkin, a great light dawned. He took the three bogus twenties out of his wallet and spread them on the table.

"That's why she got sore enough at the college to do this?"

Yet once more, Miss Sissler fell to sobbing.

"All right, Miss Sissler. Would you kindly explain why your aunt's venture into counterfeiting inspired you to perpetrate an even more harebrained machination? What did she do it for, anyway? Is she desperately hard up?"

"She has enough to get by on. Just about. But that's not why. She did it because nobody pays any attention to her. Nobody ever has. She's been calligraphing the college diplomas for twenty-seven years, and not once, not one single time, has anybody ever come up to her and told her what a lovely job she did. She drew that little picture of the administration building for the college stationery, and nobody even said how nice it was. And it is nice! It's just lovely! And I think you're a bunch of old pigs and I don't blame her one bit, and it serves you right. And I was on the booth last night when she came up, and I stood right there when Kathy took the money from her and didn't notice it wasn't real, and I didn't say one word. And I'd do it again! Again, do you hear me!"

"I hear you, Miss Sissler. Is Miss Harp planning an again?"

"S-she said she'd go on till somebody noticed, no matter what. Aunt Viola's determined to get some recognition for her work, even if she has to go to jail for it. And I don't blame her! I'll go with her. Go ahead, Professor Shandy, arrest me!"

"Sorry, Miss Sissler, I've already explained that I'm not a campus cop. To repeat my question, what made you decide on the catnip cowpats? And what made you think your aunt would have marijuana in the house? Does she smoke it?"

"Of course not, she'd rather die. I just thought—oh, I don't know what I thought. A kid in Florida had some pot once and I thought maybe Aunt Viola had picked some by accident. She likes to pick things and hang them up to dry; she thinks it looks picturesque. The stuff was there and I used it. All right, so I flunked botany. It's the college's fault, not mine. I never wanted to take botany in the first place. You and your dumb old curriculum!"

"Very well, Miss Sissler, I'll accept full culpability on behalf of the college if you'll tell me what gave you the bright idea of hurling yourself into the breach."

"It was that notice they sent around yesterday from Security, about watching out for counterfeit money. I knew then that Aunt Viola's work had been noticed, and they were out to get her. And it was all very well for her to say she wouldn't mind going to jail, but she'd hate it really. Aunt Viola's not young, you know, and she—well, she likes things nice. She'd miss her canary and her goldfish and I just think she'd die! And I do love her so. So I thought if I put marijuana in the cowpats it would make a stink and take Security's mind off the counterfeit bills."

"It never occurred to you that you yourself might get caught? Or that your being arrested might be even harder on your aunt?"

"Oh, no, why would they have arrested me? I mean, lots of people bake for the Illumination, they're always bringing stuff. It could have been anybody. Well, maybe not just anybody. Anyway, I was going to make up this story about this mysterious stranger wearing a ski mask who—I guess I wasn't very smart, was I? So what are you going to do, Professor Shandy?"

"I'm going to finish my coffee and pay the check."

"And then what?"

"Trust me, Miss Sissler. You may wish to do something about your face before we go. Your aunt will be at home this time of day, will she?"

"No! Oh my God, I forgot! She'll be coming up here to pass another bill. She said she was going to try it in broad daylight this time, because nobody's noticed the last two times and she thought it might be on account of the dark and all those crazy colored lights. Come on, we've got to head her off!"

Pausing only long enough for Miss Sissler to dip her napkin in her water glass and mop the tear streaks off her face and for Peter to leave some money on the table, they rushed forth into the by now fairly thickly touristed Illumination area. The cats were all gone, but a small, slight figure in an outmoded dark-green winter coat with a black astrakhan collar and a black felt hat that Peter vaguely recalled having seen around the village off and on for the past couple of decades was just coming up the walkway, her eye fixed grimly on the third gingerbread house.

"There she is!" cried Miss Sissler. "Hurry!"

He travels fastest who travels alone. Peter left the mobcapped freshman to struggle through as best she might, and plunged straight through the mob, abandoning gentility in the interests of alacrity. He reached the small, slight figure about two elbows' lengths before she'd got to the fateful counter.

"Miss Harp?" Peter was again the gentleman, his hat raised, his countenance affable. "My name is Shandy. I was on my way to call on you, on behalf of the college. I expect this is a bad time to come asking a favor, but I'd be very grateful if you could spare me a moment. Ah, here's your niece. Miss Sissler, would you join us? I wonder if you'd both do me the honor of stepping over to my house? It's that little red brick one over there. I'm not sure whether my wife's at home, but I know she's been wanting to meet you. She's a great admirer of your work, as are we all."

"Really?" Miss Harp wasn't too dumbfounded to forget her grievance so easily. "I don't recall anyone's ever having said so."

"M'well, Miss Harp, if the college's having depended on you for twenty-seven years in a row to calligraph its diplomas doesn't demonstrate our appreciation of your talents, I'd like to know what does. Which brings me to my purpose in seeking you out. Mind the step here, it may be a bit slippery. Would you care to remove your coat?"

"Why, I . . ."

Peter didn't press her. Miss Harp was like a canary herself, he thought, tiny and fragile and easily fluttered. When she unbent far enough to loosen her top button, he wasn't at all surprised to see that she wore an old-fashioned lace collar, pinned with a small gold locket-brooch that had a pressed violet inside. Of course a frail creature like this couldn't go to jail, he'd better get down to business before she started beating her wings at the windows.

"Perhaps we'll go into the dining room, if you don't mind. It will be easier for you to write at the table. I'm going to ask for your autograph."

"My-my autograph?"

"If you'll be so kind." Peter took the three twenties from his wallet and laid them out in front of her.

"As I'm sure you realize, Miss Harp, these three bills are going to be valuable collectors' items. We do appreciate your kindness in contributing them to the Illumination, but we'd have been ever happier if you'd signed them first. Could I prevail upon you to do it now? One will be for the college archives, one a Christmas gift for President Svenson, and the third, I must confess, will go into my own private collection. If you wouldn't mind? Perhaps here, above the 'Treasurer of the United States'? I hope I have a suitable pen."

Miss Harp was not too flustered to start digging in her handbag. "Oh, that's quite all right, Professor Shandy. I have my own."

It was a slim mother-of-pearl fountain pen with a gold tip, dating probably from the nineteen twenties, like its owner. With sure, deliberate strokes, Miss Viola Harp added her own tiny, perfect signature to those of the Treasurer of the United States and the Secretary of the Treasury.

"There you are, Professor Shandy. Is that what you want?"

"That's exactly what I want, Miss Harp. And now for the big one. What we're particularly hoping is that you'll sell us your master drawing, which is indeed masterful. We want to have it framed, in gold if that can be managed in time, and present it to the president and his wife at a reception which will be held on"—he sneaked a quick glance through the door toward the kitchen calendar—"the eighteenth of February. We'd want the drawing signed, of course, and we further hope that you yourself might consent to attend the reception and make the presentation as a tribute to your artistry and your long association with the college. We—er—don't know what price you've put on the drawing. Would a thousand dollars be—er—adequate?"

Miss Harp was sitting up very straight now, happy as a canary with a brand-new cuttlebone. "A thousand dollars would indeed be adequate, Professor, but I should prefer to donate the portrait. This will be my return to the college for its faith and trust in me down through the years. And, yes," she added with a proud toss of her head, "I shall be pleased to attend the reception. After so many years of having seen my work presented to others by others, it will be a refreshing change to make the presentation myself. I shall deliver the portrait to you as soon as I have it properly signed and mounted."

"How remarkably good of you, Miss Harp. The committee will be delighted. We'll be getting back to you, then, with full particulars about the reception and presentation."

As soon as he and Helen had managed to think up a reasonable excuse to hold the event, settle the details, and whomp up a suitably impressive guest list. The actual reason need never be told, except of course to the president, his wife, and maybe Moira Haskins. Surprisingly, the increasing volume of revelry from the Crescent was no longer jarring on Peter's ear.

"Thank you again, Miss Harp, and a very merry Christmas to you. Miss Sissler, I expect you'd like to see your aunt safely home. I'll drop over and explain to Miss Bunce and Mr. Pascoe that you've gone home to finish your baking."

"But they won't understand!"

"They'll understand. Merry Christmas, Miss Sissler."

After one last sniffle, the freshman managed a watery smile. "Merry Christmas, Professor Shandy."

Arm in arm, the great-aunt and the great-niece went down the walkway toward the village. As Peter watched them thread their way among the merrymakers, a repentant tiger lady came to rub against his pant leg. He picked her up and tickled her behind her ears.

"Merry Christmas, Jane. If you mend your rowdy ways, maybe we'll ask Mrs. Santa Claus to bake you a nice fresh catnip cowpat."

We almost didn't get this story. Fortunately it was just after *Reginald Hill completed "The Running of the Deer" that he learned he'd won the British Crime Writers Association's Gold Dagger award for his novel* Bones and Silence. *Had the news arrived sooner, he says, he'd have been too excited to write.*

So far, the gentleman from Yorkshire has produced only one other short story starring the serendipitous West Indian detective, Joe Sixsmith. That one was selected for the Oxford Book of English Detective Stories . . . *not surprisingly, considering Reg Hill's international reputation for taut writing, wry humor, and wildly original plots.*

REGINALD HILL

THE RUNNING OF
THE DEER

Nettleton was a tall, tweedy man in late middle age
with a face like one of those snooty dogs that rich folk
crap up poor folk's parks with.

Joe Sixsmith was glad to see him, even though he
didn't like the look of him. Being glad to see people
you didn't like the look of was better than being guilty
about taking money from people you did like the look
of. How a good private eye *should* feel he didn't know,
mainly because he suspected he wasn't a good private
eye. Not that he didn't find things out, only they often
weren't the things he was being paid to find out.
There was a word for this.

Serendipity.

He thought it meant something like bad breath the
first time he heard it and might have been seriously
offended if the old girl who told him he'd got it hadn't
been writing a check at the time.

"What's that then?" he'd asked.

"The knack of making useful discoveries by
chance," said Miss Negus, handing him the check

which was the first installment of the money he got to feel guilty about taking. "That's why I have come to you. I have applied all my ratiocinative powers to my problem and come up empty-handed. So now I am willing to pay for a more oblique approach."

After a lifetime in education, Miss Negus was devoting her retirement to good works. Her name appeared on the committee list of most major charities in the area, but the apple of her charitable eye was a group she'd founded herself, SPADA, the Small Pet Animals' Defense Association. SPADA had been functioning for five years, and the "problem" was that its income had gone into a slight decline over the last two. Miss Negus had a "feeling" that something was wrong. As most of SPADA's income came from collecting boxes, Sixsmith had his own feeling there was sod all he could do about it, even if there were anything to be done about. But Miss Negus was not to be denied and he spent many chilly hours, catching cold and guilt together, lurking around drafty shopping centers in hope of spotting one of SPADA's elderly collectors attacking her box with a table knife.

So when he found a message on his answering machine saying that a Mr. Nettleton would call at five, both his health and his higher feelings rejoiced at the prospect of a new client.

There was a phone number with the message in case he couldn't keep the appointment. He used the directory to turn it into a very posh address, then, feeling like a real PI instead of a balding, middling-aged, West Indian lathe operator who'd spent his redundancy money most unwisely, he made for the library to check the man out.

He came back well-pleased. Nettleton was, among other things, an accountant. He could smell real money.

And now the man was sitting before him and about to speak.

"Tell me, Mr. Sixsmith," he drawled, "when you hear the phrase 'an English country Christmas,' what images spring to your mind?"

"Now that's an interesting question," said Sixsmith, followed by a pause. It was his experience that twits who asked interesting questions were usually bent on answering them as well.

"I hope not an unfair one, though of course different cultures have their different traditions . . ."

He thinks I'm just off a banana boat! Time for a bit of role-play.

Sixsmith fixed Nettleton with his steely PI's gaze and hit the desk with his fist. The dramatic effect was rather spoiled by a protesting howl from the bottom drawer where his cat Whitey slept, but ignoring this, he leaned forward and said, "Okay, let's cut the cackle and get down to cases. I guess you know who I am, else you wouldn't be here. Let me return the compliment. You're Antony Nettleton, age forty-three, married, four children, two at university, two at boarding school. You are senior partner in Nettleton and Jones, Chartered Accountants, you are an Independent member of South East Herts County Council, Chairman of Rotary, Captain-elect of the Golf Club, Coordinator of the United Appeal Fund, and Great Unicorn of the Worshipful Order of Stags. Right?"

He sat back with some complacency.

Nettleton was reduced to silence by his surprise.

Then he said, "No, I'm not."

"Eh?"

"You're confusing me with my more famous and much more active young brother, Antony, with whom I happen to be staying. I'm *Ambrose* Nettleton."

"Oh, shit," said Sixsmith.

"Not at all," smiled Nettleton. "A natural mistake. We were talking about a country Christmas . . ."

Such generosity of spirit deserved a reward. The least he could do was play the man's game.

He said, "Dickens, stagecoaches and such?"

"That's right," said Nettleton, taking over as Sixsmith had guessed he would. "Log fires, skating on the pond, mulled wine, blindman's buff, hunt the slipper, all the old games. Well, let me tell you, Mr. Sixsmith, Dickens got it wrong. I live and work in France, but earlier this year I acquired a small estate in Cumbria and my wife and I have been looking forward to spending Christmas there. But the closer it comes, the more we realize it's not like Dingley Dell. Oh, there are traditional games being played, but nothing like hunt the slipper and blindman's buff. These are much rougher games, like poaching the pheasant, and chopping the fir, and running the deer."

"Poaching the peasant, eh?" said Sixsmith. "Man, that sounds really heavy. And chopping the fur? That'd be rabbits maybe?"

"*Eff eye are,*" said Nettleton. "The tree. We have a plantation. Had. Someone chopped most of the young trees down the other night. They'll be on some market stall now, no doubt. Christmas trees, you see. You have Christmas trees back home, do you?"

"In Luton? Yeah, it's like a forest down Luton High

Street this time of year." Careful! Don't trade ironies with the punters, not till you've cashed their check. "Deer you mentioned too. *Rubbing* the deer, was it?"

"*Running.* Like in the carol . . . 'The rising of the sun and the running of the deer . . .' it means hunting. Crisp winter mornings, red-coated huntsmen, hounds running free, traditional Christmas-card stuff. Only this isn't like that. This is nasty, furtive, dead-of-night stuff. They call it 'lamping.' What they do is go out in the woods or up the fells where the deer are sleeping, then switch on a powerful light suddenly. The deer are dazzled and transfixed in the beam. Then the bastards send in their lurchers to pull them down. Or they finish off the job themselves with an ax or pick handle. Disgusting."

"What's a lurcher when it's at home?"

"Crossbreed, something between a sheepdog, say, and a greyhound."

He spoke with such contempt that Sixsmith, despite his resolution, couldn't help saying, "Purebred staghounds use humane killers, I suppose."

"What's that supposed to mean?" snapped Nettleton. "No one can object to properly organized field sports. They're part of our old country tradition. But I do object to mindless thugs coming onto my land to perform their monstrous slaughter. The other day in the woods just a few hundred yards above the Hall, I found a great pile of blood and guts, plus a deer's head and hooves. They'd actually drawn and dismembered the beast right there! Mary and I are by ourselves just now, but come Christmas we'll have a houseful of guests, and I don't care to think of them or their children experiencing that kind of shock, I tell you."

"You've told the police?"

"Of course. But it's the usual story, too little, too late. We're pretty remote, you see. Got to look after yourself up there, only the locals warn us not to investigate if we see a light. These bastards have as little respect for human life as for animals, and are quite capable of attacking you with a pick handle or even a shotgun."

Sixsmith was not liking the sound of this. He said, "Mr. Nettleton, what do you want from me? Take a good look before you answer. I'm not one of those martial-arts freaks you see in the movies. I don't suddenly uncoil and start parting the bad guys' hair with my feet. What you see is what you get."

"I'm not looking for a hard man," said Nettleton. "You've been recommended to me as a man who comes in at things subtly, from the side. You see, I believe these lampers live in our area. The evening of the day I found the guts, we went down to our local, the Hunnisage Arms. Naturally we got talking with friends about the lampers. My wife expressed her opinion of them in very forceful terms. Anyone could have heard, and the pub was crowded. When we left pretty late—they have very flexible hours up there—I found that some bastard had scratched the outline of a deer's antlers on my car bonnet."

"One of the lampers, you think? Any ideas?"

"There's a nasty piece of work called Eddie Stamp. I caught him in my woods once. He said there was a path, but I told him I'd kick him so hard he wouldn't need a path if I found him there again. Could be him, it'd be his style. But I've no proof. That's why I'd like to hire you, Mr. Sixsmith, to go up there and investigate. There's a converted barn on the estate, which is let out during the holiday season. You can stay there."

"A black man by himself in the middle of winter? I'd stick out like a live sheep in a Sainsbury's freezer."

"No you wouldn't. Lots of people holiday in the Lake District at Christmas. As for being by yourself, take your wife. Or a friend."

"I don't have a wife. And this is the only friend I'd take."

A black-and-white cat had stepped out of a drawer onto the desk and was yawning impolitely in Nettleton's face. "What do you think, Whitey? You fancy a trip to the country?"

"I'm sorry, no pets," said Nettleton. "It's a rule."

"No? Well, I'm sorry too. No Whitey, no darkie, that's the rule here, Mr. Nettleton."

The man frowned, then said grudgingly, "All right. Bring the cat. So it's settled?"

It still seemed crazy to Sixsmith, but he needed the job, not least because it gave him a good reason to stop spending Miss Negus's money.

When he rang her to tell her he was going away, she said, "No matter. At this time of year, SPADA comes under the aegis of the United Appeal Fund. So our collectors are well supervised anyway, but do keep on thinking about it, Mr. Sixsmith. I know what a trivial matter it must seem but during my teaching days I always had this nose for something not quite right the moment I entered a classroom."

Poor old cow, thought Sixsmith. Even noses had to grow old. He went home to pack all his thickest jumpers in preparation for the first journey he'd ever made north of Birmingham.

* * *

It was even worse than he expected. He passed
through three sub-Arctic storms, lost his way at least
five times, and saw the temperature gauge of his
ancient Morris Oxford dip into the red as he scaled
hills like the Eiger before he crawled up the winding
driveway to Skellbreak Hall. He couldn't see much of
the house in the gloom but it looked to be a long
rambling Hammer Films sort of place.

A woman answered the door, thirtyish, slightly
overblown though not yet ready for dead-heading,
with a cigarette dropping from an ill-natured mouth.

"Oh it's you," she said with the peremptory clarity
of the tennis-playing classes. "Wait there."

He waited there till she came back with a key.

"Back down the drive, there's an opening on the
left. Barn's straight ahead. What are you gawping at?"

Sixsmith said, "When you said, 'it's you . . .'"

"'Small, shabbily dressed black man,' that's what
my husband said. You are this detective thing, aren't
you?"

"Well yes. And you're Mrs. Nettleton?"

"Who the hell else would I be?" she demanded.

"I'm sorry. Your husband didn't give me quite so
detailed a description. Pleased to meet you, Mrs.
Nettleton. I look forward to helping sort out your little
problem."

That was pretty smooth, he thought. Show her she
was talking to class.

"What problem?" she said.

"These what-you-call-'em? These lampers."

"Oh, those bastards. No problem," she said dismiss-
ively. "Couple of blasts with a shotgun would see
them on their way."

"But if they're poaching game on your estate . . ."

"*Estate?* Jesus Christ, he's not been shooting that estate shit again? Listen, twenty acres of boggy fellside and a bit of woodland doesn't add up to an estate. As for game, there's a bit of rough shooting, but these deer aren't game, there's no official hunting of them. Scrubby little roe they are, come down and eat the flowers if you're not careful."

"So you wouldn't object to a proper hunt?"

"On horseback? Or course not. Fat chance of that round here, where they even chase foxes on foot."

"But you do object to lamping?" said Sixsmith, eager for clarity.

"Of course I do. That's not sport. Lot of nasty little erks come crawling out of their slums to make a bit of money. The Arabs have got it right. Chop off a few hands, that'd bring the crime wave down. What the hell Ambrose thinks you can do about it, I can't imagine. Well, it's his money. Just keep out from under my feet, okay?"

She began to close the door. Sixsmith said, "I take it Mr. Nettleton's not at home."

"You don't think I'd be freezing my tits off out here if he were, do you?" she snapped, slamming the door.

He found the Barn without difficulty. After his ungracious reception, he wouldn't have been surprised to find he was expected to sleep on a bale of straw surrounded by oxen. Instead it turned out to have been very effectively converted into a two-bedroomed cottage with all mod cons. Someone had even switched on the electric radiators and stocked the pantry and the fridge.

He opened a tin of tuna fish and put it in a saucer for

Whitey, who returned from a tour of his new domain purring.

"You like it, huh? That's fine, but I don't want you molesting the local wildlife, do you hear me now?"

He himself dined on scrambled eggs. About an hour after he'd arrived, he saw a headlight moving along the driveway and heard the growl of a supercharged engine. Probably Nettleton returning, he thought. But if it was, the man didn't think it necessary to call on him.

He went to bed about half past ten, with Whitey snuggled beside him on top of the duvet. He fell asleep instantly, but woke again sometime after midnight with a sense of how utterly dark it was with no comforting rectangle of dim light at the window from the refracted glow of a nocturnal city.

Whitey had managed to get his head under the duvet.

"Good thinking, man," said Sixsmith, pulling it over his head and going back to sleep.

He was woken once more by the same car engine. This time the window was visible as a pale square and he lay there till the pallor began to glow. Then he got up, pulled back the curtains and found himself looking at blue skies above trees made gold by the rising sun. Among the trees something moved. He pushed the window open, and to his delight away up the wood bounded a pair of deer.

Nettleton called to see him late in the morning.

"Settled in?" he said. "Sorry I couldn't be here, but business kept me in Manchester overnight."

"I'm very comfortable. What do you want me to do?"

"Start detecting, I suppose."

"Oh, yes. Any suggestion where? My Indian track-ing's a bit rusty."

"How about the pub? I'll give you directions."

According to Nettleton's directions, the Hunnisage Arms was only a mile up the road. Sixsmith clocked fifteen finding it. A battered pickup with carburetor trouble preceded him onto the car park. Three men got out, rustic types in cloth caps, gum boots, and shirt sleeves, despite the sub-zero temperature. Sixsmith let them go into the pub while he examined the car park. It was large with no sign of any lighting. Perfect for your bonnet artist.

The bar was empty apart from the three men, who didn't even glance his way as he entered. The land-lord, a small bearded man, compensated for this lack of interest with a warm welcome; probably, Sixsmith thought cynically, in the hope that this was a scouting expedition for a large and hungry family out in the car.

If so, to his credit his bonhomie survived the disappointment of being told Sixsmith was alone. "Till my kid brother and his family join me for Christmas," he added, this being the story he'd con-cocted to account for his unseasonal solitariness. "I volunteered to come up early, get the place aired out, suss out the nice pubs. Don't reckon I need go no further."

"We try to please."

"You're succeeding. Where's the name come from, by the way?"

"Hunnisages are the local gentry," explained the landlord. "They own half the land round here. Your landlady is a Hunnisage."

"Mrs. Nettleton?" said Sixsmith, surprised.

"That's right. She's some sort of second cousin to

young Sir Andrew. He came into the title when his uncle died last spring. The Manor and the main body of land were all entailed, of course, but Skellbreak Hall had come into the family late and never been included in the entail, so he left that to Mary Nettleton. He'd always had a soft spot for her mother, it seems."

"So it's hers, not Nettleton's?" said Sixsmith.

"That's right, though he'd like folk to think different. Not that I've anything against the man," he added with a publican's caution.

They parted on first-name terms.

"Cheers, Joe, see you again soon, I hope?"

"Tonight, Dave. I'm not a man who likes to cook for himself."

In the car park the three men, who'd left just ahead of him, were standing peering under the bonnet of the pickup.

"Looks knackered to me, Charley," opined one of them.

Charley, the oldest and clearly the owner, cursed savagely.

"I suppose I'd better ring that git at the garage," he said.

Sixsmith strolled over and said, "Having trouble?"

"You've noticed," growled Charley.

"Mind if I look?"

He peered in with the expert eye of one well-versed in keeping ancient engines going well beyond their expiry date. Then he went to the boot of his own car, came back with the cardboard box in which he carried tools and a huge assortment of spares, and set about the carburetor.

"Try her," he said.

Charley tried her. The engine started first time and his look of ill-tempered skepticism was replaced by one of amazed delight.

"By Christ, it sounds better than it's done in years!" he cried. "Thanks, mate. I owe you a drink. Can't stop now, we're late already. But if you're staying at Skellbreak Barn, you'll be in again, eh? See you!"

The pickup roared off.

So much for rustics paying no attention, thought Sixsmith. The sods had probably earwigged every word he'd said!

But it was all bread upon the waters.

When he entered the Arms that night (a journey he'd reduced from fifteen miles to three), he hadn't got a yard beyond the door when Charley rose from a crowded table by a roaring fire and cried, "Over here, Joe! Sit down. Your money's no good tonight."

Joe. He probably knows my National Insurance number too, thought Sixsmith. There's a lot I've got to learn about this detection business!

He sat down and was introduced as a visiting mechanical genius to the seven or eight men around the fire. He soon realized they were already in full possession of every scrap of disinformation he'd given Dave, the landlord, and they seemed genuinely friendly, with none of that suspicious reserve he'd been conditioned to expect from country folk. Only one of them, a small wiry man with a swarthy complexion, came over as less than wholehearted in his welcome. When he was identified as Eddie Stamp, for once Sixsmith found himself fully in sympathy with Nettleton.

Charley, after his fourth pint, became expansive.

"You ought to settle up here, Joe," he said. "Lad with your talents'd never be short of work."

There was a chorus of approval, but Eddie Stamp said, "A bit far north, I'd say. You lot aren't built for the cold, are you?"

Before Sixsmith could pick his response, Charley said, "Your mam's family managed all right and they came from Egypt originally, didn't they? Whose shout is it? Eddie, it must be you."

As the man rose reluctantly and went to the bar, Charley said, "Half Gyppo. Pay him no heed, he's harmless enough."

Sometime later there was one of those twenty-to-the-hour silences which often fall on noisy groups, and from the car park came the roar of a powerful sports-car engine.

"That sounds like Randy Andy. Better lock up your old lady, Dave," Stamp called out.

There was a general laugh which Dave didn't join in.

"Randy Andy? Who's he?" said Sixsmith.

"Sir Andrew Hunnisage of Hunnisage Manor," said Charley. "Half the buggers in here work on his estate or on farms rented from it. They might have a laugh behind his back but just watch them touch their caps when he comes in."

Sixsmith watched. In fact, there wasn't all that much touching of caps but nearly everyone returned the hearty "good evening!" with which the willowy young man in jeans and a tartan lumberjack shirt announced his entry to the bar. He had a bored-looking young woman with him who sat on a barstool, showing a great deal of rather chubby leg, while her escort

chatted to various individuals with apparently effort-
less ease.

"He seems to get on well with people," said Sixsmith.

"Bred to it," said Charley. "No use trying to put it on
like some buggers."

"I wouldn't mind breeding her to it," said someone
with a lascivious glance toward the bar.

And in the laughter Sixsmith heard Eddie say, "I
know someone who'll have her nose put out of joint."

In the days that followed, Sixsmith found to his
surprise that he was rather enjoying his stay in these
foreign parts. Charley had "adopted" him and missed
no chance of showing him (in every sense) round the
district.

As to his investigation, he made only negative
progress. It was easy after a while to get Charley
himself to bring up the subject of "lamping" deer. The
countryman expressed his own obviously genuine
revulsion for the practice. And while there might have
been some partiality in his assurances that no one
local would do such a thing, this seemed to be
supported by Sixsmith's own assessment of his nightly
drinking companions, with the possible exception of
Eddie Stamp. And even here, Sixsmith wondered
uneasily whether his distrust might not be a crypto-
racist response to the man's "half-Gyppo" origins.

After a while he began to feel as guilty about
wasting Nettleton's money as he had about Miss
Negus's, but during their brief daily encounters, he
got no sense of pressure from the man, so it was easy
to drift along with the slow current of country life. He
even began to enjoy his gentle strolls around the

"estate" in an over-large pair of gum boots he'd found in the Barn. To his relief he found no grisly evidence of lamping, but he saw plenty of live deer and got a great deal of pleasure out of watching these timid, graceful animals.

Then one day he bumped into Mary Nettleton and her reception more than compensated for the lack of pressure from her husband.

"You still here?" she snapped. "You earn your money easy, don't you?"

"You'll need to discuss that with your husband, ma'am," he replied.

"Yes, I will. Just keep out of my way, will you? I like a bit of privacy when I'm walking around my own land."

And she'd stood and glowered at him till he retreated out of sight.

He returned to the Barn, where Whitey was lying stretched out in front of the log fire. The cat had taken to the life even more thoroughly than Sixsmith.

"Whitey, my boy," said Sixsmith, "enjoy yourself while you can. I reckon our time here is going to be cut short when that angry lady talks to her man. I think she thinks we're here to chase after other things than deer, and maybe that's what her man thinks too. What do you think?"

Whitey yawned, licked a paw in a desultory fashion and turned over to singe his other side.

That night as he returned from the pub full of beer, he made up his mind that he'd see Nettleton in the morning and tell him he was cutting loose. But he still felt guilty at a job undone.

Guilt and beer are a dangerous combination, he realized later.

He was just about to turn off the main drive toward the Barn when he saw it, through the trees of the woodland behind the Hall, fragmented by their thick-crowding skeletal arms but unmistakably there: a distant bright light, probably halfway up the fellside.

It could only be lampers.

First off, he did the sensible thing and drove up to the Hall to get Nettleton to ring the police. But the building was in darkness and there was no response to his ringing. And now the beer/guilt stupidity began.

Instead of going to bed, he opened the boot of the car, pulled on the oversized gum boots, took his torch out of the glove compartment, and set out into the wood.

At first all went well. He was familiar enough with the paths, and there was sufficient light from his torch to keep him right. He glimpsed the light on the fell only intermittently, but that didn't matter. Onward and upward must bring him within striking distance of his goal.

It was as he clambered over the drystone wall which separated the wood from the bare fellside that the first doubts began to struggle through, but he thrust them back down. There was an animal in danger up there, and he'd been paid to prevent such slaughter.

He pressed on. The lampers' light had vanished completely now. In fact, just about everything had vanished. He realized why as the belt of solid rain rolling down the fell hit him. And as if that weren't enough, what had hitherto been a rather still night suddenly exploded in a raging gale which almost drove him off his feet and filled his ears with the roar of pounding surf.

Beer and guilt were instantly washed away. Time for bed and cocoa. So he was blind and deaf? It didn't matter. All he had to do was head downhill.

Which was what he started to do. Till he realized the ground was rising again.

Easy to deal with, just change direction till you're going down once more. Except that after a little while, he was climbing again!

Now he recalled that the apparent smooth rise of the fell was deceptive. It was full of hollows, not to mention steep and stony gills. One foot caught in a clump of heather and he nearly fell. The other foot stubbed against a solid rock and he did fall. He lay winded for a while, then rose, moved slowly forward once more, took one step, two steps, and added one more shriek to the shrieks in the wind as his left leg touched the ground and kept going till he felt an ooze of ice-cold bog over his gum-boot top. He eased his foot up. It came out minus the boot. It took all his strength to pull the gum boot free. How the hell could you have a bog like this on a slope like this? Surely the water should all drain away?

His geological musings were interrupted by the eruption of a huge shape right in front of him with a terrible roar. He fell back into the bog he'd just escaped from and lay completely open to attack. But all his staring eyes showed him was a white rump vanishing into the mist.

He'd disturbed a deer! Even his townie's mind was telling him now that this was no night for lamping. The only animal in danger on this fell was a half-wit called Joe Sixsmith . . .

He realized he'd lost his torch, probably sucked down into the bog. Simplest thing to do was sit fast and wait for dawn. Only, as he felt the cold seeping through to his bones, he knew he just didn't have the time.

So off he set once more, this time on all fours, crawling like an awkward injured animal, desperate for sanctuary.

And it was now that the lampers' light hit him.

Hit was no metaphor. Out of the dark it came like a solid bolt of whiteness that jerked his head back with the force of its impact, leaving him dizzy as well as blind. It held him pinned there, his mind desperate for flight, his limbs unable to move. He was totally at their mercy. They could send the dogs in to tear out his throat, or come strolling in themselves with ax and knife to rip the life out of him.

"Don't move!" yelled a voice above the wind. "Stay quite still."

He would have laughed if there had been any strength to laugh with. Why waste breath telling a rock not to move, a tree to stand still?

They were coming for him now. He couldn't see them but he could sense their approach, closer and closer, till they were alongside him and he felt their hands on his arm.

"Christ, lad," said an anxious voice. "You're a hard bugger to see in the dark! What the hell are you playing at, wandering around up here at this time of night?"

And the torch beam moved aside so that its refracted light showed him Charley's troubled face, and showed him also the steep and rocky gully which another yard of crawling would have plunged him into.

"You left your wallet in the pub," said Charley as

they sat in the cozy living room of the Barn, drinking
Scotch. "I thought I'd better drop it by on my way
home. I saw your car outside the Hall but no sign of
you. Then I thought I saw a torchlight high up in the
woods, so I went after you. What the hell were you
playing at, Joe?"

"Didn't you see the other light up on the fell? The
lampers' light?"

"Lampers? On a night like this? No way! All I saw
was . . ."

Charley began to laugh.

"What's up?" demanded Joe, piqued.

"Don't you buggers down south ever see the moon
then?"

"The moon? Don't muck about! Of course we see
the moon. Big round thing up in the sky. This was low
on the fell. And it wasn't round . . ."

"I saw it too! It were just rising over the fell and it
was all broken up by the branches of the trees and the
cloud blowing across it. You silly bugger. You've been
chasing the moon!"

Sixsmith took another pull at his drink. Whitey
strolled in to see what all the fuss was about and
rubbed against him with all the soothing sympathy of
one who fails to see anything so foolish in pursuing
the moon.

Still, thought Sixsmith, his luck had held. Perhaps
serendipity could mean having a knack for *losing*
things luckily too.

He said, "Just as well I left my wallet. I owe you,
Charley."

"Yes, aye. Your wallet," said the Cumbrian signifi-
cantly. "I took a look inside to see whose it was. I saw
that card thing. Why'd you not let on you were a 'tec?"

"I'm sorry, Charley, but at first I didn't know you, did I? And once we'd become friendly, I didn't want you to think I'd just been trying to pump you. I mean, I was to start with, but after that, well, I just started enjoying myself. You're not offended?"

"Offended with a man who goes chasing the moon? Don't be daft! But you *are* here on a case, are you?"

He's just fascinated, thought Sixsmith. It's all this television!

He said, "Yes. That's why I went up the fell."

After he'd explained, Charley shook his head and said, "Lamping? Doesn't sound like a job for a private eye to me."

"Nor me either. What I think is, Nettleton suspects his wife's having a fling with someone, and he wants me to check it out without actually asking me!"

"That's a bit round the houses. Mind you, he's right, isn't he?"

He looked at Sixsmith expectantly.

"So I gather. Randy Andy, isn't it? Keep it in the family."

"Hey, you really are a detective," said Charley, delighted. "How did you figure it out?"

"His car came up to the Hall the night I arrived, when Nettleton was stuck in Manchester. And it didn't leave till morning. Also, Mrs. Nettleton got very edgy about having me around the place. She obviously thought he was on to her. How about you? How did you find out?"

"Oh, nothing so clever as that," said Charley. "Eddie Stamp came across them up the fell this back end, her with her legs wrapped round his neck."

"It was Eddie scratched the antlers on Nettleton's

car that night, wasn't it? Only they weren't antlers, they were cuckold's horns."

"I expect so. A right gypsy trick. He'd not have done it if I'd been by, but to be fair to Eddie, Nettleton's been bloody high-handed with him in the past. So what do you do now, Joe? Tell him, or what?"

"I got hired to catch some lampers and I nearly got killed trying to do it," said Sixsmith. "I'd say I'd earned my fee."

The door opened. Nettleton stood there. His face was flushed with drink. Or something.

"Oh I'm sorry," he said. "It was just that we found your car up at the Hall when we got home and I wondered if there was anything wrong."

"No, everything's fine, Mr. Nettleton," said Sixsmith.

Charley got up and made for the door.

"Will I see you before you go back, Joe?" he asked.

"I'll make sure you do. Thanks again, mate."

Nettleton didn't say anything till the door closed behind Charley.

"Go?" he said. "You're planning to leave?"

"There's only a couple of days till Christmas," said Sixsmith. "You won't want me around when your guests start arriving. Anyway, I think I've done all I can here."

"You think so? Not been very much, has it?"

The man didn't speak on a particularly complaining note, but in a way his indifference was more biting than a sneer.

"Depends how you look at it, Mr. Nettleton," snapped Sixsmith. "Maybe if you'd told me the real reason why you wanted me up here, I could have done more."

He was regretting saying it even before he'd finished, but Nettleton's expression showed him the
shaft had struck home.

"What do you mean, the real reason?" he demanded
with unconvincing bluster.

"Look. I'm sorry. Forget it. Makes no difference. My
rates are the same for domestics."

"Domestics?" said Nettleton. "You mean servants?"

Funny bugger. Who the hell did he think he was?

"No. I mean husband-and-wife cases, keyhole-
camera stuff. Like I say, I'm sorry, but I do have a right
to know what I'm into . . ."

He saw that his concern was unnecessary. Nettleton
was smiling. It was a genuine, unforced smile. A
smug, self-satisfied smile. A totally incomprehensible
smile.

"You know, Mr. Sixsmith," he said. "I really think
you have been a waste of money, but you'll get paid,
never fear. Send me your bill. And in case I don't see
you again, a very merry Christmas."

He went out, laughing. He didn't sound like Santa
Claus.

Sixsmith took his whiskey to bed and lay there
looking up at the light and talking to Whitey, who was
in his usual position on the duvet.

"That's a very funny man, Whitey," he said. "Gets
me up here on pretense of catching some deer lampers, only he don't really give a damn about the deer, so
what he really wants maybe is I should check out his
cheating wife, only it seems he don't give a damn
about her either. In which case, Whitey, what the hell
is going on? Why does he really want me up here?
Why, Whitey? Why?"

The only answer was a gentle snore. Sighing, he

reached up and pulled on the cord that switched off the light.

It was as if his mind had been pinned helpless, running meaningless circles around its dazzling corona, for now, as the dark rushed in, he suddenly saw everything plain.

He'd been asking the wrong questions, not: Why does he really want me up here? but: Why *doesn't* he want me down there?

Antony Nettleton came out of his office, locking the door carefully behind him. He was the very last to leave and it wouldn't be opened again till the New Year. It was Christmas Eve. Tonight he would be driving up to Cumberland with his family to join his brother for a good old-fashioned English country Christmas. It was a prospect which filled him with genuine pleasure. He loved this time of year. "The holly and the ivy," he whistled as he walked down the dimly lit corridor . . . "The holly bears the crown . . . The rising of the sun, And the running of the deer . . ."

Suddenly the corridor light went off, plunging him in total darkness.

"What the hell . . . ?" he cried.

It only lasted a split second. Out of the dark came light, no dim strip this but a dazzling beam, blinding him more than the darkness.

He held his hand up before his face, but it was no use, he could see nothing. Then the whispering started.

"Hi there, Mr. Nettleton. Mr. Antony Nettleton. Tony. Got a message for you from brother Ambrose. Message is, it didn't work out. Your trouble was, you tried to fix something that was never really broken, all because Miss Negus told you that this guy she'd hired to look into her little bit of bother had a reputation for finding more than he was looking for."

"What the hell are you talking about? Who is this?" he demanded.

"Two years Miss Negus has been having her worries. Three years since you became a coordinator of the United Appeal Fund for those occasions like Christmas when all the charities pull together and share out proportionately. One year to check it was possible, then straight in. It was a great idea, Tony. Ten percent creamed off across the board, all receipts to you, all accounts through your firm. If only you'd stuck to the biggies, Tony, the ones whose computers talk to your computers. Computers don't get nosy. But you had to include Miss Negus's little outfit too, and she works with an abacus. She smelled something wrong and told you she smelled it, because she never dreamed it could have anything to do with the United Appeal Fund, specially not when it was run by little Tony Nettleton, who'd once been in her class. Now I'm sure SPADA's income would be right up to the mark from now on in, but this year you thought it best to get rid of this dumb private dick till the big Christmas haul was done. So when Ambrose comes visiting and tells you about his lampers, you say, 'Hey, brother, do me a favor, get this black boy out of my hair, hire him to look into it.' Mistake, man. All the black boy was doing was catching cold watching old ladies with collecting boxes."

"Is that you, Sixsmith? It is you, isn't it? What the hell do you think you're playing at?"

"They call it lamping, man. You're fixed there, can't move, can't think, can hardly breathe. There you stay till the lurchers come and finish you off. Can you hear the lurchers, Tony?"

"What do you want? Switch that thing off and let's talk!"

"Talk? What about, Tony? About charity? About Christmas? About the time of gifts? How generous are you feeling, Tony? Let's hear some figures."

Nettleton let out a sigh, almost of relief.

"I knew we could talk," he said. "What do you want? A thousand? A percentage? I've got the figures here. Let's sit down and look at them. Only, for God's sake, switch off the bloody light!"

"Okay, Tony, if that's what you want."

The beam died. The ceiling light came back on.

There were five figures standing there, not the one Nettleton expected. Two of them were in uniform. A third, in a gray suit, snapped his fingers and said, "Fetch him," as if sending in a pair of collies. The two constables advanced. One took his arm, the other removed his briefcase from his nerveless fingers. Then they led him away.

As he passed the two remaining figures, he said in a small child's voice, "Sorry, Miss Negus." He didn't even look at Joe Sixsmith.

"I was so wrong about him," said the woman as they went out into the street. "My nose must be failing."

Above the buildings a bright moon was shining. Sixsmith looked up at it and smiled.

"They say Scotch is good for a failing nose, Miss Negus. There's a nice pub round the corner."

"Why not?" she said. "I was, after all, right about you."

In the pub they were singing carols. "The Holly and the Ivy."

"But I couldn't help feeling sorry for him, he looked so utterly helpless in that light. Do they really catch deer that way? How vile."

"The rising of the sun, And the running of the deer . . ."

"Yes. Vile for a deer," agreed Joe Sixsmith.

But just about right for a rat.

Tough female detectives have been hitting the headlines lately, and they don't come any tougher than Liz Peters, PI. She's the spiciest Christmas cookie you'll meet this season: smart as Grey Poupon mustard, quick as a tigress, and twice as mean to tangle with . . . but maybe with a bit of pussycat underneath?

You may have previously met this versatile writer under one of her other personae: as Barbara Mertz, Ph.D., whose works on Egyptology have become standard classics; as Barbara Michaels, best-selling author of expertly crafted suspense novels; or as Elizabeth Peters, whose eruditely hilarious traditional mysteries have put more zing into history than Cleopatra ever dared to. Yes, she does love chocolate, cats, dogs, kids, and antique hatpins, not necessarily in that order. Yes, she's a feisty lady who's ready to fight for what she believes in. No, she's not taking on any private-eye work at this time . . . pity, but not even a Grand Master can do everything at once.

ELIZABETH PETERS

LIZ PETERS, PI

I did not have a hangover. Those rumors about me aren't true; they are spread by people who are jealous of my ability to handle the hard stuff. The truth is, I can polish off three giant-sized Hershey bars before bedtime and wake clear-eyed as a baby.

All the same, I wasn't at my best that morning. When I put my pants on, one leg at a time (I always do it that way), my heel caught in the hem, and then the zipper jammed and I broke a fingernail trying to free it. The weather was lousy—gray and bleak and dripping cold rain that didn't have the guts to turn into snow. On Christmas Eve, yet. You'd think that the Big Gal Up There would have the decency to provide a white Christmas. I didn't count on it. I don't count on much.

My office was pretty depressing too. The velvety bloom on the flat surfaces wasn't the winter light. It was dust. My cleaning woman hadn't shown up that week.

I work out of my house because it's more conve-

nient; I mean, hauling a word processor and printer
around with you gets to be a drag. I'm a mystery
writer. It's a dirty job, and nobody really has to do it.
I do it because it's preferable to jobs like embalming
and mucking out stables. They say a writer's life is a
lonely one. That's a crock of doo-doo. I've got enough
of a rep so that people come to me. Too darned many
of them, but then that's the way it goes in my business.
Too darned many people. You could say the same
thing about the world in general, if you were philo-
sophically inclined. Which I am.

You might ask why, if my profession is that of writer,
I call myself a PI. (You might ask, but you might not
get an answer. It's nobody's business what I call
myself.) The truth is, I don't know how I got myself
into this private-investigating sideline. It sure as heck
wasn't for the money. Everybody knows PIs can't
make a living; look at their clothes, their scrungy
living quarters, their beat-up cars. Some of the gals
can't even afford to buy a hat. So why did I do it?
Simple. Because it was there—the dirt, the filth, the
injustice, the pain. All of suffering humanity, bleeding
and hurting and crying for help. When one of them
bled on my rug, I had to do something. I mean, what
the heck, that rug set me back a bundle. It's an antique
Bokhara. I should let people bleed all over it?

I have to admit it wasn't a pretty sight that morning.
Dust, dog hairs, cigarette ashes, and a few other
disgusting objects (including the dogs themselves)
dulled its deep-crimson sheen. After a cup of the
brew, with all the trimmings—that's how I drink it,
and if people want to make something of it, let
them—my eyeballs felt a little less like hard-boiled
eggs. I lit a cigarette. What the heck, you only die

once. My desk squatted there like an archaeological mound, layers-deep in the accumulated garbage of living. I had to step over a couple of bodies to get to it. There was another limp carcass on my chair. When I moved it, it bit me. So what was one more scar? I'm covered with them. That's the way it goes in my business. Cats are only one of the hazards. The dogs are no picnic either. They don't bite, but I keep falling over them.

I sat down on the chair and lit a cigarette. The blank screen of the word processor stared at me like the eye of a dead Cyclops. My stomach twisted like a hanged man spinning on the end of a rope. Shucks, I thought. Here we go again. I forced my fingers onto the keyboard. It was like that every morning. It never got easier, it never would. There are no words. That was the trouble—no words. At least not in what passes for my brain. But somehow I had to come up with a few thousand of them, spell them right, put them into the guts of the machine and hope they came out making sense. That's my job. There are worse ones— performing autopsies and cleaning litter boxes, for example. But at 9 A.M. on a dreary winter morning on a mean street in Maryland, with dust and cat hairs clogging my sinuses and a couple of dogs scratching fleas, and my head as empty as Dan Quayle's, I couldn't think of one. I lit a cigarette.

The coffee cup was scummed with cold froth and the ashtray was a reeking heap of butts when I came out of my stupor to see that there were words on the screen in front of me. They seemed to be spelled right, too. I wondered, vaguely, what had interrupted the creative flow—and then I heard the footsteps. Heavy, halting steps, coming nearer and nearer, down the dim

hallways of the house, inexorably approaching. . . .
I looked at the dogs. They're supposed to bark when
somebody comes to the door. They never do. If I hadn't
heard them snoring I'd have thought they were dead.

Closer and closer came the footsteps. Slower and
slower. He was deliberately prolonging the suspense,
making me wait. I took one hand off the keyboard and
pushed the shining waves of thick bronze hair away
from my brow.

The lamp on the desk beside me cast a bright pool
of light across the keyboard, but the rest of the room
was dark with winter shadows. He was a darker
shadow, bulky and silent. I lit a cigarette.

"Hey, Jaz," I said. "Got time for some—"

He didn't. He was a big man. When he hit the floor
he raised a cloud of dust that fogged the lamplight and
my sinuses. Got to call that cleaning woman, I mused
between sneezes. She was Jaz's cousin, or grandmother, or something. He'd found her for me. He was
always doing things like that for me. He always had
time for some . . .

I got to my feet and looked over the desk. He lay
face down, unmoving. A film of gray covered his thick
black hair. I know what death looks like. I've dealt
with it . . . how many times? Forty, fifty times,
maybe more. I can handle it. But I found myself
thinking I was glad he'd fallen forward, so I couldn't
see his face—the strong white teeth bared, not in his
friendly grin but in a final grimace of pain, the soft
brown eyes fixed and staring and filmed with dog
hairs . . . Call me sentimental, if you want, but dusty
eyeballs still get to me.

As I stood there, fighting those softer feelings that
hide deep inside all us mystery writers who moon-

light as private investigators, despite our efforts to
build a tough shell so we can deal with the sick,
disgusting, hideous realities of life without losing our
integrity or our nerve and go on with our jobs of
removing an occasional small piece of filthy slime
from the world so it's a better place, if only infinites-
imally so . . . Anyhow, after I had wiped my eyes on
my sleeve, a little spark of light winked at me from the
center of his broad back.

I had to push the dogs away before I could kneel
beside him. They're so doggone stupid. They couldn't
even tell he was dead. They were nudging him,
wanting him to get up and play, as he always did.

It could have been a jeweled decoration or medal, if
it had been on his chest instead of his back. The
colorless stones glimmered palely in the dusky room.
They weren't diamonds or even rhinestones. They
were glass. I should know. I had only paid ten bucks
for the hatpin. I collect hatpins. Just one of my little
weaknesses. The last time I'd seen this particular
specimen . . . I couldn't remember when it was. Had it
been in the porcelain holder with the others, the last
time I looked? Trouble was, I hadn't really looked. You
don't look at familiar objects, things that have been in
their places for weeks or months or years. You just
assume they're there, the way they always have been. I
recognized it, though—the head of it, I mean—and I
knew only too well what the rest of it was like. Ten
inches of polished metal, rigid and deadly. In Victorian
days they passed laws limiting the length of the pins
women used to hold those enormous hats in place.
Ironic, I thought, lighting another cigarette. Men turn
purple with outrage when some legislator tries to keep

them from stockpiling Uzis, but a woman couldn't even own a lousy hatpin . . .

The mind plays funny tricks on you when a friend drops dead on your floor. I was wondering whether there were still laws on the books banning hatpins when I heard something that woke me up like a dash of icy water in the face. Mine is the last house on a dead-end road, out in the country, so when I hear a car I know it's heading for me. This one was coming too fast, tires screeching around the steep downhill curve. I got to the window in time to see it slow for the sharp turn into my driveway. Amazing. He'd had sense enough not to use the siren. He can never resist the flasher, though; it spun like a dying sun, sending red beams through the rain.

It was like a thick curtain had been yanked away, clearing my head; I saw it all, clear as a printed warrant. I'd been set up. But good. A dead man in my study, my hatpin through his heart, and the fuzz tipped off in time to catch me red-handed. (A figure of speech we PIs use; there wasn't much blood, and I hadn't been stupid enough to touch the body.) I was in deep doo-doo, though. That wasn't generalized fuzz, it was my nemesis, Sheriff Bludger. We had tangled before, on issues like gun control, and he wasn't awfully crazy about little me. A thickheaded red-necked male chauvinist, he would be drooling at the prospect of catching me with my hatpin in somebody's back.

The cruiser swung into the driveway and accelerated, sending the gravel flying. One of the cats growled. I looked at him. "Hold 'em off, Diesel," I snapped. He jumped off the windowsill and headed for the back door. The dogs were already there, stupid tails wagging. They could hardly wait to jump all over the nice cops and lick their hands and bring them balls to throw. The dogs were about as much use as fuzzy bunnies, but as I grabbed my purse I saw that Diesel had rallied the rest of the cats, six of them in all. They were all inside that day on account of the rain. Diesel himself weighs almost twenty pounds, and Bludger suffers from terminal ailurophobia. I figured I had maybe three minutes.

I went out the front door while Bludger and Company were trying to get in the back. Unfortunately the Caddy was also in the back. I circled carefully around the house, shivering as the cold rain stung my face, and crept through the shrubbery till I reached the garage. Peering around the corner, I saw the cruiser parked by the back steps. The back door was open, and from inside I could hear a lot of noise—dogs barking and men cursing. There was no sound from the cats. Unlike dogs and rattlesnakes, they don't warn you before they strike. They aren't gentlemen. That's one of the reasons why I like them.

The Caddy purrs like a kitten and turns on a dime. I was out of the garage and heading down the drive before Bludger got wind of what was happening. Darned fool—if he'd left the cruiser blocking the gate I'd have been in big trouble, but no, he had to come right up to the door. That big beer belly of his makes him reluctant to walk farther than he has to, I guess. It was wobbling like a bowl of custard when he came barreling out of the back door, waving his stupid little gun and yelling. I waved back as I sent the Caddy shooting through the gate.

I pushed a lock of shining bronze hair out of my eyes and shoved my foot down hard on the gas. The car roared up the hill like a rocket, taking the curves like the sweet lady she is. You can have your Porsches and Ferraris; I always say there's nothing like a Cadillac brougham for eluding the cops. Not that I was up for a high-speed chase across the county. Excessive speed is socially irresponsible, and besides, Bludger could cut me off at the pass; he knew the back roads as well as I did and he had plenty of manpower. I had to get out of sight, but fast—within the next thirty seconds—and I knew just how to do it.

I'm not given to praying, but I sent a passionate petition to the patron saint of private eyes as I thundered toward the stop sign at the top of the hill. She came through for me; the main road was clear. Instead of turning right or left, I hit the brake and sent the Caddy slithering across the road and up the bank on the opposite shoulder. A big green-and-white construction trailer stood there; the bridge across the creek had been finished three months earlier, but they hadn't got around to removing the trailer. Typical. And lucky for me. I barely made it, though. A couple of inches of my back fender were still visible when the cruiser appeared, but Bludger didn't notice. He was too busy trying to figure out which way I had turned. The decision was easy, even for his limited brain; a right turn would have taken me onto the bridge and a mile-long stretch of straight road. To the left the road rises and curves. He went left.

I waited till he was out of sight. Fastening my seat belt, which I hadn't had time to do before, I backed out of my hiding place and headed across the bridge. I have to admit my pulse was pretty fast; this was the tricky part, if Bludger got smart and turned back too soon, he'd see me. I couldn't stay where I was for the same reason, the Caddy would have been visible to a car coming down the hill.

Saint Kinsey was still with me. Across the bridge and over the hill, to Grandmother's house we go . . . The driveway was a rutted track, with only a few grains of gravel remaining, the house looked like an abandoned ruin. She came out on the sagging porch, her shotgun over her arm, squinting through the rain. When she recognized me, a toothless grin split the wrinkled face under the faded sunbonnet.

"Hey, Liz. Got time for—"

"No, Grannie." I slung my purse over my shoulder. "I need to borrow the pickup. If Bludger finds the Caddy, tell him I stole your truck, okay?"

Grannie spat neatly into the weeds beside the steps. "Keys are in the ignition. Leave yours; I'll pull the Caddy into the shed after you go."

Movement at the window caught my eye. Something fluttered against the pane, like a trapped moth. A hand—too small and thin, too pale . . . I swallowed hard and waved back. "How's Danny doing?"

"Okay. That wheelchair you got him was a big help. Don't s'pose you've got time to come in and say hello? He don't see many folks, and he's crazy about you . . ."

"That's 'cause he don't see many folks." I forced a smile, directed it at the window, where Danny's small pale face was pressed to the glass. The wheelchair might have been a help, but it was a heck of a Christmas present for a kid. I'd tied a big red bow across the seat and then ripped it off—too much of a contrast between holiday cheer and sad reality—one of those ironic contrasts we PIs keep seeing all around us . . .

I swallowed harder, stuck my cold hands in the pockets of my jeans. My fingers touched something soft. I pulled it out. It was a little squashed, but Danny and I had agreed we liked chocolate that way. "Give him this, Grannie. As a token of better things to come. Tell him—tell him I'll be back to spend Christmas Eve with him."

Grannie's rheumy eyes opened as wide as her wrinkled lids allowed—not much. "But, Liz, it's your spare. What'll you do without—"

"I'll manage," I said gruffly. "No big deal. See you later, Grannie—unless I'm in the slammer."

She offered me the shotgun, the sunbonnet, and the dirt-colored sweater she had thrown over her shoulders. I took the last two, winked at her, and headed for the truck.

Heading south on 75 I met two cruisers heading north. I smiled without humor. The county crooks would have a field day today, beating up their wives and dealing drugs and driving drunk unmolested; Bludger would have every available cop out looking for harmless little old me.

I'd had my eye on Bludger for months. I couldn't believe he was as stupid as he looked; but if he wasn't up to his thick neck in the drug traffic, why did he keep getting in my face very time I tried to nail a local dealer? Over the past years, drug traffic in the county had increased a hundredfold. It wasn't just kids and adult delinquents growing marijuana in woodland clearings, it was crack and coke brought in by big-city dealers who found lucrative markets and safer operations out in the boonies. Every now and then Bludger would round up some kids from the Projects, and there'd be a big hurrah in the local paper. But I knew, and Bludger should have known, that that wasn't going to solve the problem. The people who lived in the Projects weren't supporting a million-dollar industry. The buyers had to be people with money, and they weren't buying off the streets.

I had a personal interest in the drug biz. It lost me a darned good cleaning woman—Danny's mom. She was sixteen when she had Danny, after a hasty marriage to a scuzzball who beat her up with monotonous regularity before he got bored with the entertainment and walked out on her. Three kids (two of them died, don't ask how), no education, no skills—it's a wonder she stuck it out as long as she did. It was after the second baby died that she started doing drugs. Eventually, inevitably, they killed her. So now Grannie was trying to raise a seven-year-old on nothing a month and I was stuck with a lazy incompetent for a cleaning woman. You understand, it was the inconvenience that ticked me off. Not sentimentality. We tough female writer–PIs aren't sentimental.

Grannie's pickup made a noise like a tractor. I encouraged it onto the freeway ramp and headed east toward Baltimore. A couple of miles and I'd be over the county line. Not that that would do me much good; Bludger would certainly have alerted the state cops as well as his counterparts next door. I drove at about forty, not because I was trying to avoid traffic cops but because that was as fast as the pickup would go.

There had to be some connection between Jaz's murder and my recent investigations. Could it be Bludger himself who had set me up? I'd talked to Jaz about my suspicions, after he told me about a friend of his who'd been arrested for dealing dope down in D.C. (These days it's hard to find someone who doesn't know someone who's been arrested for dealing dope down in D.C.) Would Bludger commit murder just to get me off the trail? Not unless I was sniffing right at his heels. If I was, I sure as heck didn't know it.

The sleety rain was falling harder and the windshield wipers seemed to be suffering from mechanical arthritis. I decided I'd better get off the road. Pulling into a McDonald's, I ordered coffee and a Big Mac with everything (what the heck, you can only die once) and parked.

I always get my best ideas when I'm eating. Don't know why that is. Maybe cholesterol stimulates the brain cells. After finishing my Big Mac I lit a cigarette and drove on to the shopping center. It was all decorated for Christmas—had been since mid-October—and it was the most depressing darned sight I had ever seen. The plastic wreaths and garlands had faded to a sickly chartreuse; they hung like dead parrots from lampposts and storefronts. Rain dripped drearily off the shiny red plastic bows. Strategically spotted speakers blared out that lovely classic carol, "I Saw Mommy Kissing Santa Claus." Next on the agenda, no doubt, would be "All I Want for Christmas Is My Two Front Teeth," or "I Don't Care Who You Are, Fatty, Get Those Reindeer off My Roof." I swallowed the tide of sickness rising in my throat and reminded myself to replenish my supply of Di-Gel. We PIs buy a lot of antacids. Especially around Christmas.

I miss the old-fashioned telephone booths, with doors you can close, but Grannie's sunbonnet was a big help; it kept the rain off my face and kept passersby from hearing my end of the conversation.

First I called Jaz's office. Mary Jo was on that day. She wanted to talk, but I cut her short. I sure as heck didn't want to be the one to tell her about Jaz. I asked her where he was due to be that morning, before he came to me. Some of the names I knew, some I didn't. But they made a pattern. After I hung up I called Rick. He wanted to talk too. Everybody wants to talk. I told him what I wanted. He gasped. "G——d d——n it, Liz—"

"Watch your mouth, Rick. You know my readers don't like dirty words."

"Oh—oh, yeah. Sorry. But what—"

"Never mind what. Just be there. I've cracked the case. You can make the arrest. I don't want the credit. I never do."

"But—"

I hung up.

Rick already owed me a couple. This would make three—no, four. You could call our relationship a social one—at least you'd better call it that. We'd met at a party, one of those boring Washington affairs writers get sucked into; I was sulking in a corner, nursing my drink and wondering how soon I could cut out, when I saw him. And he saw me. Our eyes met, across the room . . . Later, we got to talking. He asked me what I did for a living, I politely reciprocated—and that's how it began. He'd been promoted a couple of times since I started helping him out and he was man enough to give me credit— privately, if not to his boss at the Agency—so I knew he'd respond this time.

It would take him an hour or more to get there, though. I dawdled in the drugstore, picked up a package of Di-Gel and a few other odds and ends I figured I would need, and then headed back to town at a leisurely thirty miles per hour. The rain slid like tears down the cracked facade of the windshield. Tears for a good man gone bad, for a sick world that teaches kids to get high and cop out. I felt sick myself. I chewed a Di-Gel and lit a cigarette.

I had to circle the block three times before I found the parking spot I wanted, right across from the sheriff's office. No hurry. Rick wouldn't be there for another half hour, and I sure as heck wasn't walking into the lion's den without him. I'm tough, and I'm smart, but I'm not stupid. I ate a couple of Hershey bars while I thumbed through the latest issue of *Victorian Homes*. Then I lit a cigarette. I had smoked three of them before Rick showed up. I watched him as he trotted up the stairs. He was a big man. (I like big men.) I waited till he'd gone in, then pulled my sunbonnet over my head and followed.

A fresh kid in a trooper's uniform tried to stop me when I headed for Bludger's office. I straight-armed him out of the way and went on in. Rick was sitting on the edge of the desk and Bludger was yelling at him. He hates having people sit on the edge of his desk. When he saw me, his face turned purple. "D——n it, Grannie, how'd you get past—"

"I don't allow talk like that," I told him, whipping off my sunbonnet. "And I'm not Grannie."

His eyes bulged till they looked like they'd roll out of the sockets. Rick was grinning, but he looked a little anxious. The third man started to stand up, and fell back into his chair with a groan. I sat down on the other corner of Bludger's desk.

"Hi, Jaz," I said. "Feeling better?"

Bludger got his voice back. "You're under arrest," he bellowed.

I raised one eyebrow. "What's the charge?"

"Attempted murder!"

"With this?" I picked up the plasticine envelope. The hatpin had been cut down from ten inches to about two. "Darn it," I said. "I paid ten bucks for this. It's ruined."

"You shoved that thing into him—" Bludger began.

"Is that what he says?" I looked at Jaz.

He ran his fingers through his thick dark hair. "I don't . . . I can't remember . . ."

I lit a cigarette. "Oh, yeah? Well, let me refresh your memory. You stuck that pin into your own back just before you walked into my house. It's three and a half miles from the previous stop on your schedule; you couldn't possibly have driven that far without noticing that you had a sharp object in your back. My cleaning woman is a friend of yours; she stole that hatpin for you, several days ago. I was getting too close, wasn't I, Jaz? And I made the mistake of discussing my ideas with you—my questions about how drugs were being delivered in the county. What better delivery system than good old reliable National Express? You're on the road every day, covering the same territory. You've got your own private delivery schedule, haven't you?"

His eyes narrowed. I wondered why I'd never noticed before how empty they were, like pale marbles in the head of a wax dummy. "You're bluffing," he snarled. "You can't prove—"

"I never bluff," I told him, brushing a lock of shining auburn hair away from my forehead. "The truck will be clean, but you had to package the garbage somewhere. Your own apartment probably.

I'd try the kitchen first, Bludger. There'll be traces left. Men don't know how to clean a kitchen properly. And, as I have reason to know, neither does Jaz's 'cousin.'"

I didn't expect him to break so fast. He got to his feet and started toward me. Rick moved to intercept him, but I shook my head. "Don't dirty your hands, Rick. Come any closer, Jaz, and you get this cigarette right in the face."

"You don't understand," he groaned. "It was her idea. She made me do it."

"Sure," I said bitterly. "Blame the dame. You and that MCP Adam."

"Adam?" He looked like a dead fish, eyes bulging, mouth ajar. "How many guys do you have dropping by for some—"

"Never mind." It was all clear to me now. I felt a little sick. Men, I thought bitterly. You try to be nice, offer a guy some milk and cookies, listen to his troubles, and he starts getting ideas.

I lit a cigarette. "He's all yours, boys. You'll have to figure out who has jurisdiction."

"I'm sheriff of this county," Bludger blustered.

"I wouldn't be surprised if a state line got crossed," Rick drawled. "And the DEA has jurisdiction—"

"Fight it out between yourselves," I told them. "Frankly, I don't give a darn."

Jaz dropped back onto his chair, face hidden in his hands. A lock of thick black hair curled over his fingers. I headed, fast, for the door.

Rick followed me out. "What say I drop by later for some—"

"You're all alike," I said bitterly. "Wave a chocolate-chip cookie in front of you and you'll do anything, say anything."

He captured my hand. "For one of your chocolate-chip cookies I would. They're special, Liz. Like you."

"Sorry, Rick." I freed my hand so I could light another cigarette. "I've got a chapter to finish. That's what it's all about, you know. The real world. Putting words on paper, spelling them right . . . All the rest of it is just fun and games. Just . . ."

The words stuck in my throat. Rick leaned over to look into my face. "You're not crying, are you?"

"Who, me? PIs don't cry." I tossed the cigarette away. It spun in a glowing arc through the curtain of softly falling snow. Snow. Big fat flakes like fragments of foam rubber. They clung to my long lashes. I blinked. "Rick. Isn't there a reward for breaking this case?"

Rick blinked. He has long thick lashes too. (I like long thick lashes in a man.) "Yeah. Some guy whose kid died of an overdose offered it. It's yours, I guess. Enough to buy a lot of cigarettes and chocolate chips."

I took his arm. "You'll get your chocolate chip cookies, Rick. But first we're going shopping. Toys 'R' Us, and then a breeder I know whose golden retriever has just had a litter. A tree, a great big one, with all the trimmings, the fattest turkey Safeway has left . . . Pick up your feet, Rick. We've got a lot to do. It's Christmas Eve—and it's snowing!"

I lit a cigarette. What the heck, you only live once.

Naturally we expect somebody who's specialized in Medieval Studies to be well-informed on the subject of Angels. But Medora Sale's not just another pretty Canadian M.A., Ph.D. How many aspiring writers have fathers who filled their infant ears with bedtime stories about the quiddities of criminal courts, and even, as a special treat, used to take them, on school holidays when court was sitting, to watch actual trials?

With this highly specialized background, is it any wonder that Medora, after having tried free-lance writing, social work, and advertising, took to a life of crime herself? She won the coveted Arthur Ellis Award for first novel with Murder on the Run *in 1986. Since then, she's published three more mysteries with Scribner's and has recently completed a term as president of the Crime Writers of Canada. When not engaged in criminous literary pursuits, Medora Sale lives quite angelically with her husband Harry Roe, a professor at the University of Toronto, and their daughter, Anne.*

MEDORA SALE

ANGELS

Annabel Cousins looked at her watch. "We're on in five minutes. Where is that wretched girl?" Her eyes fell on the last set of angel wings spread over the huge table in the vestry. Angels. She hated angels. They went on at the very beginning, and they had to be dressed at the very last minute or the stupid creatures would smash their wings—magnificent structures made from a clever mix of real and fake feathers, at least six feet wide and over three feet high.

"Ashley?" said a muffled voice. "She might be in the washroom."

"For the last twenty minutes, Heather?" said Annabel, trying very hard not to reveal her panic to her already highly nervous charges. "She hasn't even picked up her costume yet. Are you two sure you saw her downstairs? Stand still, Jennifer!" she snapped in exasperation. "And don't sit down. Or lie down, or lean against that wall or do any of the other things you were thinking of."

"I *thought* I saw her," said Jennifer. Her voice was also muffled behind her gold-and-white angel mask.

Annabel's heart sank. "Thought? You said you *had* seen her."

"Do you want me to go down and look?"

"No, I don't want you to move. Where's Mrs. Toomey? She's supposed to—damn it all. Erica," she said, grabbing a short, thin girl preposterously garbed as a shepherd, "run down to the washroom and get Ashley. Tell her she's dead meat if she isn't up here in thirty seconds."

Erica, current holder of the Independent Schools Track and Field Association record for the 1500 meters (sixteen and over), disappeared without a word in a blur of brown wool and greasepaint.

Two painful minutes ticked by. "I can't find her, Miss Cousins," said Erica, whose arrival was as silent and as swift as her departure. "She isn't in the washroom, the furnace room, or the other dressing room, and she isn't up in the choir loft either."

Annabel Cousins allowed herself half a second to appreciate Erica's speed and thoroughness before panicking. She sat down on the only available chair. "My God, what do we do now?"

"We get someone else." The speaker was a tall, dark-haired woman engaged in sewing up a ripped hem for another shepherd. This one was standing on the vicar's desk, barefooted, on top of a page from tonight's sermon. "No one will know the difference. As long as she's taller than Jennifer and Heather, relatively reliable, and has long hair. There certainly aren't any more tall redheads around, so blond, don't you think?" She turned to the already garbed angels. "You two—out into the corridor and stand where I put you on Friday. Sideways, remember!" She whipped the thread around a couple of times and broke it off. "You're done, Laura. Keep your feet out of your hem, please. Off you go."

The two teachers looked at each other. "I should have known those wretched girls were covering for Ashley," said Annabel gloomily. "Where do we find another angel? The entire senior school is in there singing."

"Who's closest?" The two teachers slipped out of the room and up the stone passage to peer in at the students crowded into the chancel. They were in the middle of a long, difficult carol in the modern mode, hanging desperately on the conductor's every movement, including those of his lips, as he mouthed the words for those who had not, in spite of threats and pleadings, managed to memorize them. Every girl within discreet grabbing range appeared to be short and dark. Or hopelessly unreliable.

Helen Armstrong, who had learned during fifteen years of working on the pageant just what could—and could not—be expected from the average senior at the school, shook her head at the selection available. "We'll go on with two," she whispered. Because as soon as the girls finished this interminable number, the entire school, from the babies in kindergarten up, would start a medley of traditional carols, and the pageant would begin its stately and gradual progression into the center of events.

Everyone loved the graduating-class pageant, except the drama coach and the English teacher who were responsible for producing it. Every year it was exactly the same; every year the kindergarten babies would ooh in astonishment and parents would sniffle sentimentally. And every year it was seen by at least twenty-five hundred people, crowded into the largest church in the city, for the Kingsmede Festival of Carols was justly famous.

"Is everything okay?" The high-pitched whisper came just as the modern carol was drawing to its pianissimo close, and earned a vicious glare from the conductor. It issued from a tall, thin, elegant woman with pale-red hair skewered into a bun—a beautiful woman with a voice of hideous timbre and formidable carrying power. "Sorry," she went on, "I got talking to Jeff and lost track of the time."

Annabel Cousins winced before pivoting her head in the direction of the whisperer. For a moment, she froze, fixing her with a glassy-eyed stare, and then turned in amazement to Helen Armstrong, who nodded. "No," said Annabel, "it isn't okay. But you're just in time."

"O Come, All Ye Faithful" saw Helen Armstrong in the narrow passageway behind the altar, herding Mary and Joseph ahead of her. Mary's name was Mary and she looked more like an Icelander than an Israelite, but she had bagged the job because she was head of the Drama Club. Joseph's name was Deborah, Deborah Levinson. She knew full well why she had suddenly been handed the part. It had been someone's notion of broad-minded equality to choose a Jewish girl, and the vision of herself in a Christmas pageant tickled her so immensely that she was having trouble maintaining the gravity of expression proper to an old man with a pregnant wife who was on his way to pay his taxes. She conjured up a vision of her father at tax time and settled her countenance appropriately.

The ending of "O Little Town of Bethlehem" brought on Mary and Joseph; with "Angels from the Realms of Glory," Annabel shoved the three angels toward the wooden dais on which they would spend ten agonizing minutes with their hands raised aloft. Three heads of golden-red hair and three sets of wings moved with great care until they reached their posts. As they raised their arms on Annabel Cousins's vigorous cue, Mary sank—a little too gracefully—into her chair and discovered, with much too much astonishment, the infant Jesus in the crib.

"That's the last time I let someone who thinks she's Sarah Bernhardt play Mary," muttered Annabel to Helen Armstrong, who had just finished creeping back from the other side of the altar. "Deborah makes a good Joseph, though."

Helen nodded. "Are the kings in position yet?"

"Omigod," said Annabel, "I haven't checked their makeup." And she tore downstairs.

"Shepherds in the Fields Abiding" brought two light-footed shepherd boy-girls frolicking joyously up the side aisles, carrying an improbable number of toy lambs. Erica appeared last, careening up the center aisle as if she had been entered in the Bethlehem Olympics. Helen Armstrong sighed; she knew it had been a mistake to tell Erica Henry to run, no matter how gladsomely. The side-aisle shepherds caught sight of their speedy companion and broke into a panicked race for the front. All three came skidding to a halt at the chancel steps, giving the unfortunate impression that they were escaping prisoners who had just been nabbed by a posse of their schoolmates. Erica finally remembered to point at the angels before she dashed through the narrow pathway between the second sopranos and the altos.

The organ ran through a graceful modulation in key and mode, and the senior school altos started "We Three Kings." From her strategic spot behind the latticework, Helen Armstrong saw with great relief that Annabel Cousins was standing at the back with three completely attired Orient kings. They looked impressive, she reflected complacently. Of course, the three tallest girls in the senior class swathed in black velvet and scarlet-and-gold brocade were bound to look impressive.

Melchior paced solemnly up the aisle, apparently unaware of the three thousand or so people watching her, and took her place slightly to the left of the narrow passage up the chancel steps. The junior-school treble voices took up Caspar's verse, sounding perilously frail and alone in a cruel and hostile world. The second king seemed to panic and hastened to take her place in the center, as if she could hear Herod's soldiers at the door. The richer voices of the senior sopranos picked up Balthazar's mournful wail and the third king paced ahead steadily, like one who had traveled at this same speed for years through the desert. They stood at last shoulder to shoulder, facing the altar. In a huge outpouring of sound, the organ screamed and every voice cried out the triumphant last verse; the three kings raised their offerings high above their heads.

It was at this rather noisy point that the Kingsmede School Annual Festival of Carols suffered its first alteration in procedure in seventy-five years. The center angel staggered slightly, dropped her arms, and collapsed on top of Joseph, before tumbling onto Mary's lap.

"Omigod," said Helen Armstrong, and hurried behind a line of senior second sopranos to rescue Mary from her angelic burden.

"She fainted," whispered Mary accusingly. "You said no one ever fainted." The school sang lustily, now onto "See Amid the Winter's Snow," covering the noise of two gym teachers and the school nurse swooping in on the trouble spot as rapidly as possible.

Helen ignored her, and bent to help Deborah turn the middle angel over to get the mask off her face and let her breathe.

It was then that the second departure from routine occurred. Mary was the first to notice the blood pouring out of the white-and-gold mask, soaking into her blue robe. Her screams brought down the house, drowning out all six hundred joyful voices.

"She was shot?"

"Looks that way."

"And nobody saw anybody firing at her. No one saw a weapon."

The larger man in the grey suit shook his head, with a what-did-you-expect shrug of his shoulders.

"What have they done with the body?" asked Inspector John Sanders. He was standing in the chancel looking down at the blood-soaked carpet.

"Apparently there were twenty doctors in the first two rows of the audience, all tripping over each other to make medical history by saving her life," said his partner, Sergeant Ed Dubinsky. "She got whisked away to the hospital. But she's dead all right. He got her right between the eyes. Couldn't have done it better myself."

"Who was she?"

"That's interesting," said Dubinsky, dragging out his notebook. "She was supposed to be a girl called Ashley Wallace. But Ashley didn't show up, and at the last minute they grabbed a teacher. They needed someone who could stand still, and had hair to match the other two."

"What in hell are you talking about?" Sanders stared at his partner in bafflement. "The other two what? Hair to match?"

"The other two angels. She was an angel, in the pageant—you know. The Christmas pageant. Like Sunday school and all that." Ed Dubinsky was moving into his mode of long-suffering patience. "And the angels all wear masks, so you can't tell who they are. Like this." He moved over to where the plastic-shrouded, bloodstained mask with its neat bullet hole in the center of the forehead lay waiting to be carried off to the lab. "But every year they have angels that match—"

"Angels that match?"

"Yes, Inspector," said a clear voice from behind Dubinsky. "The angels always have long hair, by tradition, and we have cycles—black, brown, red, blond. When I first got here, they were always blond, and that seemed to me to be discriminatory. The girls consider it a great honor to be an angel. My name is Helen Armstrong, by the way. I look after the angels, among other things. Not that I did a very good job today."

Sanders looked at her and then shook his head. "Beautiful. We have a maniac going around shooting

angels in Christmas pageants. That was all I needed.
It'll be Santas next. Let me get this straight. The angel
was supposed to be a girl named Ashley Wallace but
she didn't show—and?"

"It was at the very last minute, literally, before we
realized she wasn't here. We had wasted a lot of time
searching for her. She's like that, though. Totally
unreliable."

"Then why did you put her in it?"

Helen Armstrong smiled grimly. "You haven't heard
of Wilfred Wallace, the Minister of Justice? The Wal-
laces felt that little Ashley hadn't received the
recognition she deserved from the school over the
years." Mrs. Armstrong's voice was thick with sarcasm. "He spoke to his good friend the chairman of
the board, who begged us on bended knee to let
Ashley be an angel and get Wallace off his back. It's no
big thing—not like asking us to raise her marks or
make her Head Girl—so we cast Ashley. Wallace was
certainly rewarded for that piece of arm-twisting—he
thought that was his darling going face-forward into
the crèche. He almost had a heart attack." She grinned
wickedly and then shook her head. "Sorry. I didn't
mean to sound quite so callous. Anyway, we were
going to go on with just two angels, when—" Helen
Armstrong's eyes suddenly filled with tears. She
shook her head angrily and continued in a low voice.
"—when Cynthia Toomey finally turned up. She was
supposed to be a floater, helping us do the pageant,
going from one potential trouble spot to the next, but
she was hiding in the choir loft talking to Jeff. Anyway, we took one look at that gorgeous red hair and
bundled her into Ashley's costume. With the mask,
you couldn't tell the difference."

"Who knew about the switch?" .

"Just the two of us. Annabel Cousins—she's the drama teacher—and I. As far as as anyone else was concerned, it was Ashley in that costume."

"Did you see it happen?"

"My God," interrupted Dubinsky, "everybody saw it. There were about six hundred girls up here and down there," he said, pointing to the pews in front beyond the side aisles. "There were twenty-five hundred more spectators, and about forty teachers roaming around. Carstairs said he felt like he was in court—he recognized at least three judges, and about thirty lawyers. They all have kids here. Not only that, but the dead woman's husband was up there taking pictures of it." He pointed to the choir loft at the west end of the church.

"Where are they all?"

"We let the spectators go, except for the parents of kids still here. They're at the back. We kept the kids in the pageant, Ashley's friends, the teachers who were roaming around and the choir director. They're sitting up here. We haven't been able to get rid of the chairman of the board, two of his lawyer friends, the principal and the vice-principal. They're down in the first two pews." He peered down as he spoke. "With Miss Jeffries," he added, his voice heavy with disapproval.

"Don't be so damned righteous," muttered Sanders. "We were having lunch across the street when they tracked me down. She's brought a book and I'll take her home as soon as we've cleared up here."

Dubinsky paid no attention. "And the husband is in the vestry."

"The husband?"

"Yes, the husband. Jeff Toomey. The one who was photographing it all."

"I'll see him first."

"By the way, the rector wants us out before even-song, the Minister of Justice wants a province-wide search instituted for his daughter, and half the powers in the country are down there screaming for blood. So we're supposed to do something and be quick about it."

Jeff Toomey was a startlingly good-looking man, in the square-jawed, blue-eyed style, with the face of a twenty-year-old, except for a sprinkling of lines around his eyes and a slight thinning of his blond hair. He stumbled to his feet, looking blankly exhausted, when they walked in. "I'm Jeff Toomey," he said, holding out his hand. His voice was hoarse.

"You were up in the balcony all the time?"

"Yes, from about two-thirty until—until after Cynthia collapsed and someone came to tell me it was Cynthia, not one of the girls."

"Alone?"

He shook his head. "Not really. Some girl came looking for someone and Cynthia was . . ." He swallowed hard and stopped. "Every year I photograph the whole thing. You know, for fund-raising. They sell prints to the kids' parents. I've been doing it for ten years, ever since we got married. And I shot it," he cried suddenly, causing Sanders's wandering attention to snap back, "I shot someone killing Cynthia." He dropped his head in his hands. "Just as she fell. What in hell was she doing up there? No one seems to know."

"The student who was supposed to play the center angel didn't show."

"Why would someone want to shoot one of the students?" said Toomey, his face crumpled in bewilderment.

Sanders thought of the Minister of Justice, sitting grim-faced in the back of the church, and of the number of enemies he had acquired in the last four years. He shook his head. "Did you notice anything out of the ordinary, Mr. Toomey? While you were taking pictures?"

Toomey stared at him as if he hadn't understood. "Notice anything? I didn't have much chance. I had two cameras going—a wide-angle and a long lens—and a video camera. The video I left running, checking it now and again. Otherwise, I was setting up shots, going back and forth."

"And except for those two visitors, you were alone."

"Once the choir left. That was at the end of the first song." He paused, as if for thought. "There was a man standing just below me in the center aisle. He was carrying something—I assumed at the time it was a camera. Now—I'm not so sure. And I may have heard a bang when I was taking that last picture. The music was so damned loud, I couldn't tell." A knock on the vestry door interrupted his reflections.

A constable walked in, dragging behind him a tall, thin, redheaded girl dressed in wet jeans, running shoes, a sweatshirt and a jacket. She was shivering visibly and her cheeks were wet with tears. "The missing girl, Inspector. She just arrived. Her father would like to speak to her also."

Sanders could imagine the minister invoking the wrath of everyone from the Chief of Police to the

Prime Minister on the constable's stubborn head, without result. "So you're Ashley Wallace," said Sanders, looking closely at her. "And where have you been?"

Ashley looked Sanders woefully in the eye, and then her glance skewered sideways toward Jeff Toomey. "I'm sorry," she began in a voice choked with tears. "It's been the most awful day. I don't think I can . . ."

"Sit down, Miss Wallace," said Sanders. "Start from the beginning."

"Okay," she said, and he caught a glimpse of a wad of blue gum between her teeth. Jeff Toomey frowned. "I left home early because I had to get into my angel costume and everything and I didn't want to wait for my dad, because sometimes he can't get away, and he didn't want me to take the car because of the snow and everything. So I went to catch the bus and I realized that I'd forgotten my wallet. I didn't have any money and this guy was driving by and he offered me a lift right to the church."

"What kind of car was he driving?" asked Dubinsky, writing rapidly.

"Uh—" Her eyes slipped around the room, as if the answer might be engraved on a wall somewhere. "A black car. A big black car, I think it was—maybe a Mercedes or something."

"A big black Mercedes," said Dubinsky calmly, writing on still.

"Uh—yeah. And the driver was this big black guy, really scary-looking."

"And you got into the car with him?" asked Sanders, allowing amazement to flood his voice.

Red blotches sprang up on her pale cheeks. "Yeah—

well, he looked really nice at first, and then when he didn't drive me to the church, but went way out by the lake, I got scared, and I jumped out of the car when he had to slow down and I walked here. It was a long way, but I figured my dad would wait for me." A tear spilled onto her cheek.

"How old are you, Miss Wallace?" asked Sanders.

"Nineteen." There was suspicion in her voice. "What difference does it make how old I am?"

"No difference. You seem a bit old for high school, that's all," said Sanders mildly.

"I wanted more breadth in my education, so I took an extra year." Suspicion gave way to hostility. "Is there something wrong with that?"

The inspector smiled peaceably. "Why did you walk all the way up here instead of telephoning the police?"

"I didn't have any money. I told you that."

"You don't need money for emergency calls," he said. "You might want to remember that. We like to investigate incidents like abduction."

"Well—he never hurt me, just scared me. And anyway, if I'd caught my bus, I would have been shot. That's what they told me. I'm really sorry, Mr. Toomey. About your wife. She was a great teacher."

Jeff Toomey turned away, an expression of agony on his face.

"You can wait out in the church with your father, Miss Wallace," said Sanders. "But please don't leave just yet." With a jerk of his head, Sanders walked out of the room. Dubinsky rose hastily and followed.

"Lousy liar, isn't she?" said Sanders as he walked back into the chancel. "If she'd said it was a green car, she'd have been abducted by little green men, I suppose."

"Yeah. But ten to one it doesn't mean a thing—she was out with a boyfriend or something like that."

Sanders glanced speculatively at the girl as she walked toward the back of the church. "How old did you say Mrs. Toomey was?"

"I didn't," said Dubinsky, flipping back through his notebook. "Thirty-five."

"And her husband?"

"Thirty-two. Doesn't look it, does he?"

"Where do you have to be to shoot someone standing on this platform?" he asked, as he scrambled up to the position of the center angel.

Dubinsky backed away between the choir stalls in the chancel, looking up at the grey-suited figure of the inspector. Then he turned and surveyed the church. "Where's the edge of your line of sight?" he called up.

"Just past that constable over there," said Sanders, and jumped down. "It's what I thought—to get a clear shot at the angel you had to be in the balcony or right under it, unless you wanted to be observed by a couple of thousand witnesses. And Toomey was up in the balcony, taking a picture just as the shot was fired, right? They've taken his film off to check that?"

"And there were at least four teachers standing under the balcony," said Dubinsky. "The drama teacher and three more floaters."

"The balcony," said Sanders. "Could someone hide up there?"

"Naw," said Dubinsky. "It was the first thing we thought of. Nothing up there but camera equipment, chairs, and some old wooden—" He turned and moved with astonishing speed toward the back of the church.

They found the lightweight assault rifle in a large wooden box that looked as if it had once contained a speaker for the grandfather of all sound systems. It was standing upright, its open side pushed back against the wall, another small wooden box perched inside it. "A stool," said Dubinsky, giving the small box a kick. "All the time Toomey was fiddling with his equipment, this guy just sat here, waiting for the pageant to start. When Toomey was focusing on the pageant scene, he stood up, and picked her off. Only he got Toomey's wife, instead of Wallace's daughter."

"Why didn't Toomey hear the shot?"

"No one did. These things aren't that noisy and he waited until the music was loud before he fired. And then in the confusion, he slipped down the stairs and out the side door. He was pretty safe, really. Toomey was too busy to poke around."

"Wait there," said Sanders. "I'll be right back."

Dubinsky leaned on the railing of the balcony with a growing sense of irritation. So far, he had been the one to field the flak from the furious Minister of Justice, not to say the equally enraged minister of the church, the chairman of the board, the principal of the school, and everyone else in the building. And what was Sanders doing? Murmuring sweet nothings into the ear of the green-eyed woman sitting in the front pew. It wasn't that he had any objection to Harriet Jeffries as a human being; so far, she had passed his two tests: she drank beer and she was said to be an expert photographer. He admired expertise, in any field. It was his sense of the fitness of things that was offended. What would Sanders say if he turned up for work with his wife Sally draped over his arm? Not that she'd be fool enough to be here. Sally, thank God, had too much sense.

Now Miss Jeffries was putting down her book and walking back with Sanders. Dubinsky sighed and sat down. Shootings in churches made him very uncomfortable. Especially political ones.

"Hi, Ed," said Harriet Jeffries, looking slightly embarrassed. "Sorry to barge in, but John wanted me to check for something . . ." She was opening Jeff Toomey's camera case as she talked, carefully picking up pieces of equipment and putting them to one side. "Here it is," she said. She pulled out a long grey cord neatly rolled and fastened with a garbage-bag tie, undid it, and brought it over to the camera closest to the center line of the church. She snapped one end into place and began to unroll the cord. "That box?" she asked.

Sanders nodded.

She continued unrolling it until it reached the box with about five inches to spare. There was a grey bulb on the end, lying on the floor. "It's a cable release. You've seen them. Okay—you stand back here— you've already focused on the spot in front of the altar where the angels will be—and at the right moment you fire your gun and then just step on the bulb. *Voilà*—you have a picture of the woman collapsing, apparently taken while you were standing behind your camera. I'm surprised that you two didn't think of it earlier. It's the most obvious thing in the world."

"So why does Toomey want to shoot Wallace's daughter?" said Dubinsky, his mind still firmly fixed on politics.

"He doesn't. He wants to shoot his wife, of course," said Harriet. "Who else do men shoot? You know that. And since the girl must have been in on it, I would guess you don't have to look very far for a reason."

"And the lying little bitch was sitting somewhere drinking coffee until it was time to show up. He knew she wouldn't be there. But how could they be sure that Cynthia Toomey would take her place?"

Harriet shrugged. "I don't know, but you might ask how many people there are in the school with long red hair who are over five foot nine. It seemed awfully important to everyone that all the angels look the same."

"So Toomey keeps her in the balcony chatting until he knows they'll be panicking, and then reminds her she's supposed to be helping with the pageant. Down she goes, red hair and all. Ninety percent chance they'll use her," said Sanders reflectively. "And if a third redheaded angel turns up onstage, he knows it has to be his wife and he has ten minutes to set up his stunt. Looks good to me. Let's get him."

"Do you think they'll let us cancel the pageant next year, Helen?"

Helen Armstrong shook her head as she finished packing the last of the costumes into their boxes. "No. But I think this is the last year they're going to expect us to find three girls in the graduating class with long hair all the same colour."

"How about three angels with short curly hair, all different colours? Dear Lord," Annabel muttered suddenly. "They're trickling in for evensong and the police are still in the vestry talking to ghastly Mr.

Wallace. Do you suppose they've arrested Ashley as well?"

"I hope so," said Helen with an enormous yawn. "Then I won't have to mark her essay on George Eliot over the holidays." She stuck a long piece of masking tape across the last box to keep it closed during its short trip back to the school. "There. We're finished. Why don't you and Rob come back to our place for a drink? We'll send out for a pizza and start celebrating Christmas. For real, this time."

What a wonderful surprise this was for a Gilbert and Sullivan fan to find in her Christmas stalking! John Malcolm, whom I'd met at a convention in Philadelphia, was ready to oblige when I asked him to write us a story. He says this one's been waiting to come forth for a long time. He hopes we like it. How could anyone not?

John Malcolm has written eight crime novels featuring Tim Simpson, an art-investment specialist with a London merchant bank, whose work involves him in the desperate dealings and acquisitive violence of the art and antiques underworld in Europe and North America.

He has also written short stories for Collins Crime Club's Diamond Jubilee Collection and Macmillan's Winter's Tales 22 *and is the author of books and articles on antique furniture. He lives in Sussex, England.*

JOHN MALCOLM

THE ONLY TRUE UNRAVELLER

Submit to Fate without unseemly wrangle
Such complications frequently occur
Life is one complicated tangle
Death is the only true unraveller

> The Grand Inquisitor
> *The Gondoliers*
> by Gilbert and Sullivan

It does not often snow on Christmas Eve in London. Winters have been mild for two or three years, and London has never been a snowy spot. It was very cold that day, however, and as we strolled down the tree-lined central avenue in the Brompton Cemetery I was more than a little mystified, when the first flakes began to fall, at why my friend Quentin Cranbrook should have been so insistent on this excursion. After all, as afternoon darkness fell, it would have been much more sensible to have remained in the Cranbrooks' comfortable flat just round the corner in Earls

Court Square, where his charming wife, Jill, was preparing a succulent turkey and suitable embellishments for our traditional meal the following day.

But Cranbrook had insisted, and it had been so kind of him to invite me, knowing that since the death of my dear wife two years previously I had faced my Christmases alone. I had not wished to demur. Cranbrook was an old acquaintance and in years past we had often made up a foursome. The death of my wife in childbirth changed all that; I had worked very hard at my small export business to overcome my loss and Cranbrook had been much engrossed in his biographies. For once the literary tide seemed to be flowing his way and, with the increasing popularity of biography, he was expecting at last to support his lovely wife fully, without needing the financial resources with which she had loyally sustained their life in London.

"You enjoyed the Gilbert and Sullivan last night, I think?" he queried heavily, rhetorically, as we strolled along the wide path flanked by those plane trees which, in the summer, make the Brompton Cemetery a shady place for workers to relax in at lunchtime.

"Indeed I did." We had gone, the three of us, to a performance of *The Gondoliers* by a company part revived D'Oyly Carte and part new. It is the Americans who have re-energized our taste for Gilbert and Sullivan with their wonderful version of *The Pirates of Penzance*, performed in London by Pamela Stephenson and George Cole, showing how radical, how fresh the original version must have seemed to Victorian eyes. This, however, had also been a fine performance; the melodies still rang in my ears.

"That is why I have brought you here." Cranbrook

flashed me a significant glance. "I have something to show you which will interest and, perhaps, amuse."

I looked at him in some surprise. He was getting to be a bit of an odd fellow, I thought, so immured in the research which the production of biographies demands. The details of past relationships and actions fascinated him; to him the long hours in libraries and archives, the poring over books, documents and letters were no hardship, no task, but physically the occupation had taken its toll. Looking now at his big frame, wrapped up in a bulky overcoat and muffler against the freezing cold, I saw how it was becoming hunched from hours of study, bent, as it were, into an attitude of seated literary attention. His hair too, always a little wild, had receded from the brow and bore the occasional trace of grey not just temporarily induced there by a melting flake of snow but, alas, more permanently inscribed among his locks.

At that hour, on Christmas Eve, the cemetery was emptying of those souls who had come to place an occasional memorial wreath or flower to lost ones. The lights and roar of traffic along the Old Brompton Road were dimmed behind us by the high entrance wall as we progressed farther toward the colonnaded mausoleum at the center. The Brompton Cemetery has not suffered quite the neglect and vandalism that Highgate has endured but, beyond the well-kept central avenue, I could discern areas of uncultivated growth in which the tombstones fought to maintain their dark, formal dominance among the trees. Here and there a memorial had fallen, toppled by weather or time or, perhaps, the sacrilegious antagonism of youth. It is sad that such attacks should occur, especially in so distinguished a cemetery, with so many notables among its residents, recumbent amid some two hundred years of history.

We had just passed, for instance, the marble tomb of one Colonel Byrne, a doubtless courageous officer whose inscription recorded his gallantry whilst serving with Garibaldi in Italy, the Sixty-fourth Regiment of Foot in the American Civil War, and our own Yeomanry in the Boer War. A man, I mused, who showed an enthusiasm for the cannon's mouth which might not be approved of in our own, less military times. There is a fascination about the inscriptions on tombstones which has always held me; it was instructive, in the fast-gathering, chilly gloom, to read those letters close at hand, still visible on the vertical planes where the thinly falling flakes of snow had not yet settled.

"Here we are." Cranbrook stopped and produced a flashlight. "I think you will agree that it will have been well worth it." He stepped off the gravel path and bade me to follow him into the second row of tombs lining the route. He did not hesitate but I followed a little more gingerly; the gap between the rows of stone in the first line was narrow and my shoes, leather-soled, would not keep out much of the half-inch surface covering of snow.

He pointed to a pair of vertical monuments set on a gravel panel with a molded stone surround. Separating them was another memorial, almost lying flat, in the shape of a small stone cross. Cranbrook gesticulated at the brown stone of the left-hand monument with an air of triumph and flashed his torch upon it, standing back so that I could see.

"Joseph Ballard Carter," I read aloud, feeling that it was expected of me. "Of Brimfield, Massachusetts.

Born August 21st 1813. Died May 22nd 1889. Also his wife, Mary Chamberlain Carter."

"No, no," Cranbrook interrupted. "Not them. They're the parents. Here."

He concentrated his torch upon a scrap of white stone, a scroll added like an afterthought to the base of the memorial. It was in the shape of a piece of paper or curled sheet, held at an angle against the heavy, pedimented base. The inscription was becoming faint and I had to concentrate to read it as the occasional snowflake drifted across my vision.

"Mary Frances Ronalds," I read aloud. "Née Carter. Born August 29th 1839. Died July 28th 1916. 'Ever Near.'" Beneath the faded inscription there were some other engravings and faint straight lines almost like hieroglyphs which, on peering closer, I could just faintly discern. "Good heavens," I said. "I do believe that's a bar of music."

"Correct. Sullivan's music." Cranbrook's voice was eager, full of satisfaction. "That is the grave of Fanny Ronalds."

"Fanny Ronalds?"

"Mrs. Fanny Ronalds. The Belle of New York. The woman who captivated the two finance kings, Augustus Belmont and Leonard Jerome, simultaneously. She sang, of course. Not professionally, that would not do for one of New York's top four hundred. But very well. That's why Jerome was after her; he had a thing about opera singers. Jenny Lind—he named his daughter after her."

"Jennie Jerome?"

"The same. Winston Churchill's mother. She knew Fanny Ronalds well, of course."

"Good heavens."

Cranbrook's voice thickened. "Fanny Ronalds was a celebrated beauty. Her husband is said to have left her after they had three children." He gesticulated vaguely at the other memorials. "Two of them here. But Belmont and Jerome vied for her affections. She gave a huge ball in New York—this was in the 1860s—at which she wore an extraordinary harp-shaped crown lit by gas jets. She tricked both Jerome and Belmont each into paying for the ball."

"Tut, tut." The idea of a harp-shaped crown lit by gas jets stirred a memory in my head, but I was becoming uncomfortable. The snow seemed to be settling a little more. It was incredible to think of a white Christmas in London, but the chance was becoming very strong. I had not brought my gloves, and my overcoat could have been thicker. "The music?" I let the question hang.

"Ah, yes! The music!" Cranbrook waved his torch excitedly. "Mrs. Ronalds went to Paris, like the Jeromes, to star at the court of Louis Napoleon. She improved her lungs as the guest of the Bey of Algeria. But the Franco-Prussian War brought them all over to London where, as a musical enthusiast, she soon met Arthur Sullivan. She was the love of his life. His diary records his meetings with her, almost daily, over thirty years. They give no doubt as to the nature of their relationship; Sullivan always noted the number of times he had engaged with her sexually on his visits. He was, like many creative artists, very active in that direction."

"Oh, dear." My hands were becoming numb. To keep a diary is a dubious enough pastime; to record such events in it is not only ungallant but certainly not the action of a gentleman.

"They were treated virtually as man and wife in the upper London crust." There was, now, a feverish quality to Cranbrook's voice. "They could not marry, of course, because a divorced woman was excluded from society. But everyone knew. Everyone. She sang, accompanied by Sir Arthur at the piano, divinely. Everyone celebrated her performances of his 'Lost Chord.' Royalty particularly. Sullivan was not always faithful to her, but he maintained her and her family— parents included—in a separate house at 7 Cadogan Place. He was certainly deeply attached to her. And she to him. She outlived him by sixteen years." He flashed his torch at the small stone scroll. "She left no doubt of that. The bar of music engraved thereon is said to provide the clue for music lovers. I believe it is from 'The Lost Chord.' The particular association signifies the words 'Forever Thine.' As I say, she left no doubt as to whom her heart belonged."

"That's extraordinarily romantic." I peered at the faint lines. "This was a very kind thought of yours, Quentin. What a splendid idea, especially after last night. London is a city with many fascinating sights, but I would never have come across anything like this." I looked up at him. "How on earth did you come across it?"

He paused a moment before answering. In the gloom his big figure loomed back behind the torch, which he still pointed downward at the tomb. As I straightened from my crouch upon the gravel I became aware of how isolated we were. The center of Brompton Cemetery is cut off from the surrounding city like a great walled park, and the street lighting glowed only faintly in the distance. The sound of a jet airplane passing overhead was muffled by the falling snow which, if anything, seemed to be increasing.

"The Duke of Edinburgh," Cranbrook replied cryptically. "Not the present one, of course. Alfred, the younger brother of Edward the Seventh, who would have been Prince of Wales when Fanny Ronalds came to London. Edinburgh was a rather gruff, reserved man. Married off to a Russian grand duchess. Was elected King of Greece but had to decline. Naval officer. Eventually became Prince of Saxe-Coburg-Gotha, poor fellow, and had to lose his English title, home, and succession. Typical of Victoria's younger children, really. Rough deal. There's never been a biography of him. I'm working on one."

I wondered when the cemetery would officially be closed. We were far from the entrance gates. Surely, on Christmas Eve, the guardians would push off early? A glance back toward the tree-lined avenue told me nothing; the flakes were thickening and darkness was now becoming intense. Behind Cranbrook only a jumble of tombstones, crosses, bending angels and sarcophagus shapes could darkly be discerned. It really was time for us to leave. What a strange fellow he was, his mind occupied with these late-nineteenth-century biographical details, culled from dusty tomes, memoirs, and letters in dry libraries. How unlike my own life, with its commerce abroad, travel, and business contracts. And yet, and yet; the story of Fanny Ronalds was surely an unexpectedly romantic bonus from so moribund a quarter. What days those must have been; what a glittering, lavish life the fortunate few had led before the Great War ended all that. I glanced down at the now dim scrap of stone upon the monument; what little residue

it was for so passionate and sought-after a beauty, one
who had mingled with and loved the cream.

"A biography?" I queried, moving away slightly in
hope of drawing Cranbrook away too, of breaking his
concentration. "Of the Duke of Edinburgh? I can't say
I know anything about him."

Obstinately, his bulk did not shift. "He was musical
as well. A violinist; quite good, apparently. A great
patron of music, too. He and Sullivan played together
frequently."

"Really? Where?" Surely, I thought, this could be
discussed in the warm?

"At Sullivan's house, sometimes. I had theory that
Sullivan might have met Fanny Ronalds through him
originally. You see, when she first came to London she
was undoubtedly Edinburgh's protégée. She headed
for royalty like a homing pigeon. Anita Leslie implies
that she obliged Edinburgh with more than just piano
and vocal accompaniment to his violin."

"Tut, tut."

"It's quite possible. My idea was that they might
have met—Sullivan and Fanny, I mean—at one of
Edinburgh's musical weekends at his country estate,
Eastwell Park."

"I beg your pardon?" It was now intensely cold.
Suddenly my coat seemed insubstantial, papery. A
chill took hold of my ribs and spine. The idea of
returning to the Cranbrooks' flat in Wetherby Man-
sions was becoming desperately attractive. I was
going to catch my death of cold here.

"Eastwell Park, in Kent. It was Edinburgh's country
estate. Sullivan went there often in the 1870s."

"Eastwell?" My throat had become very dry. An icy
dampness was seeping through my leather shoes.

Cranbrook's little cultural outing had gone on far too long in this paralyzing weather.

"Yes. Eastwell. It's now an expensive country hotel. Eastwell Manor, near Ashford. You know it, don't you, my dear, Jones?"

The emphasis he gave my surname made his question vaguely menacing. I stared at him. "Know it?"

"Yes, know it. You know it. I know it, too. I went there to do my research two weeks ago. I couldn't afford to stay there myself, of course. I put up at a bed-and-breakfast place in Ashford. But you, you could afford it, as a businessman. And you were there. I saw you. I even checked the register. What a common name Jones is. How very easy for you."

"Easy?" My throat was arid. The word came out as a croak.

"Easy! To register. As Mr. and Mrs. Jones. You and my wife! Jill! You thought I was away doing my research. Ironic, wasn't it? The research was on the very place you chose to take my wife for your luxurious, debauched weekend!"

"Oh, no. No, no. It wasn't—look, Quentin—I—"

"Don't deny it!" he shouted. "Don't dare to deny it!" The torch flashed in a wave as he tugged at his clothes. "I saw you! And Jill! Faithless bitch!" A dreadful gleam caught the torchlight.

"Jesus! That's the turkey knife!"

"It is! It is! I shall have the pleasure, when I carve the bird tomorrow, of knowing what it will have done to you!"

"Quentin! For heaven's sake!"

"Submit to Fate!" he shouted. "Submit to Fate without unseemly wrangle!" Then he lunged.

I had a second's lead on him and leapt backward

before turning to plunge across the farther path into the deeper jungle of tombs and vegetation. A single apposite inscription caught my eye.

Nearer, My God, to Thee.

The man was mad. Raving mad.

"'Death,'" he shouted, jumping after me, "'is the only true unraveller!' I'll unravel you!"

Never had a line from *The Gondoliers* been so sinister. Gilbert had a nasty sense of humor. If only Jill had listened to my plea to go to Paris for the weekend! But she was too cautious; she feared we would bump into someone who knew us at the airport. A quiet drive off somewhere in the country, with a fire and oak beams, would be more discreet. God, how I'd wanted her! The hotel had been superb. And her enthusiasm—she had clung to me so passionately. How could this situation be resolved?

"For God's sake, Quentin! Listen!" He was almost on me; only a solemn angel with one broken wing and a sad expression separated us. Reproach was written on its every lineament: *O death, where is thy sting? O grave, where is thy victory?*

Right here, might have been the answer; fortunately he stumbled on a stone edging and, clutching wildly to balance himself, grabbed a marble obelisk that teetered dangerously under the impact. He tumbled sideways, knocking his head on a projecting molding impressed with Gothic lettering:

The very hairs of your head are all numbered.

He blinked owlishly, half-stunned, as I took the opportunity to beat a retreat behind a more substantial monument embodying a huge sarcophagus that would have accommodated Henry the Eighth and all his wives.

"Adulterer!" Recovering, he advanced round the huge rectangular stone casket, knife gleaming, a flash of teeth matching the falling flakes of snow in that sepulchral gloom. "Traitor!"

"Wait! Quentin! For God's sake, man! Can't we discuss this sensibly?"

"You bastard! Wait till I get you! 'He who lives more lives than one, more deaths than one must die'!"

Wilde! Oscar Wilde! The man was completely demented! Biographical research of his type must, obviously, corrode the brain.

"Wilde?" I shouted, dodging behind what looked like an enormous stone mushroom. "Really! We are in Brompton, not Père Lachaise! Please! Listen to me! Surely we can talk?"

"Talk? To a swine like you? I'll slit your guts first! I've worked like a dog! Only to be betrayed!" His bulk rushed at me, weaving around a marble bust of a bald worthy strongly resembling Gladstone. Was there no one left in the place? I glanced around feverishly. We were working away from the central avenue, he was herding me like a sheepdog, forestalling me, blocking any move toward the now far-distant entrance. Indeed, we were much farther away.

"You can't get away with this!"

His answering cackle, as I dodged a fearful swipe with the huge carving knife, struck an all-too-confident note. "Oh, yes, I can! I can! I've planned this for a fortnight!" He pulled up, panting, his face close, much too close, behind a simple but heavy urn, inscribed across the base with, I fancy, an item from the Book of Common Prayer.

In the midst of life we are in death.

He grinned savagely. "Jones! So appropriate. I've

found the place for you. There's an area behind you where vandals have been at work. A sarcophagus at ground level, moved aside. Aaron Jones, 1843. In you'll go! Eh? Remember G. K. Chesterton? The safest place to hide a body? In a grave!"

At this, great prickles of fear paralyzed me. To know that such deliberate preparations had been made drained my legs of strength. For a moment I was unable to speak. His eyes, suddenly visible clearly in that petrifying air, fastened hypnotically on to mine. He smiled a horrible smile. I said the first thing that came into my head, to break the spell. My voice, strange to my own ears, was shrill.

"But what on earth will you tell Jill?"

He leered at me. "That under the pressure of my accusations and remorse you confessed to me, begged my forgiveness, and promised to leave immediately. And never to contact her again. I shall then exact a pleasurable atonement from her for her infidelity. In at least six ways that I can think of."

"My God! That's disgusting! You couldn't!"

"Oh, yes, I could! Just as I shall—" He jumped, but I had anticipated him, springing backward. It was a dreadful error. My thin leather shoes slipped on the snowy stony surface behind me, my whirling hands found no support, and in a moment I was dazed upon my back in the wet vegetation, staring, horrified, upward at him and the outstretched arms of yet another stone angel and its inscription.

Peace to him that is far off, and to him that is near. Isaiah 57:19.

Never would I enjoy cemetery inscriptions again! My voice pitched to a scream; he was above me, knife raised.

"Oh, God! Were you right?"

"Eh?" He paused, arm uplifted.

"Was it where they met? Fanny and Sullivan? At Eastwell Park?" It would be too horrible an irony if, after all that, he was wrong.

He blinked. The knife lowered a little. "No, actually, it wasn't. I found that Sullivan had met her first in Paris, perhaps as far back as 1867."

"1867? But the Franco-Prussian War wasn't until 1870."

A look of intense irritation replaced the savage anger of his countenance. "I know that! Don't patronize me! He told his nephew that everyone from the Emperor downward was at her feet. It was almost certainly Juliette Conneau, a patroness of Sullivan's and a lady-in-waiting to the Empress, who introduced him to Fanny in Paris."

"So how did Edinburgh get to her?"

He waved the knife impatiently, "I haven't had time to establish that yet. For God's sake! I've only been working on the bloody biography for six months. Give me a chance! Through music, it must have been. Obviously."

Mad, as I've said. Obsessed. I had wondered, at Eastwell, why he and Jill had never had children. Was that the reason for her enthusiasm with me? Or was it the prospect of traveling, eventually, abroad, with a man whose occupation was not to be contained within libraries, archives, places of dusty study?

"Fond of women, was he? Edinburgh, I mean."

Cranbrook seemed uncertain of himself for a moment. Perhaps no one, apart from his publisher, had expressed any interest in his subject to date. Then his face twisted again; I had made a mistake.

"Like his brother Bertie? Or like you? Fond of other men's wives, you mean? Yes, I think he was." The knife raised, the arm tensed. "It's right by you, Jones! Your final resting place!" His left finger stabbed sideways. "Look!"

A desperate glance to my right revealed the full horror of his grisly plan. A jumble of stone surrounded a geometric granite lid swiveled to one side. Most of a vile black space beneath was exposed. Across the lid, quite clearly, I could see the name, "Aaron Jones, RIP 1843," and an inscription:

Be thou faithful unto death, and I will give thee a crown of life. Revelation 2:10.

Cranbrook cackled loudly. Useless to protest that my Christian name is not Aaron; he was quite clearly deranged. Just then, however, the inscription inspired my memory.

"It was electrified," I shouted, flat on my back. "The gas jets were electrified!"

"Eh?" Cranbrook halted again, puzzled.

"The harp-shaped crown! Fanny Ronalds's crown! The one she wore in New York! Years later! She wore it to the Duchess of Devonshire's famous fancy-dress ball in London. She'd had it electrified! 1897? Your man must have been in Germany by then."

How strange the human memory can be! It was a quirk of those amazing grey cells that had invoked an article I'd read, a year earlier, in a fashion magazine, about the great balls of history.

Cranbrook stopped again and blinked. The poor fellow's mind was clogged, of course, internally encrusted by barnacle-facts from the history and biography he studied and imbibed so much. Every detail is important to the biographer; he leaned a little forward, the better to absorb what I'd just said. It was enough. I swept my legs around in a last, desperate kicking arc to catch his ankles. He staggered, with a roar of fury, reaching out to steady himself in that dark, monumental setting.

Cranbrook grasped the angel. It held for a moment, taking his bulk, and then, my eyes starting in concentration and hope, I saw its square base lift, separating moss, weeds, and detritus from its pediment. He gave out a hoarse cry as the extra movement took him farther off balance. He threw out his arm, the right arm clutching the great carving knife, to reach the angel's waist. He was now totally dependent on the upright stone figure for support. There was a moment of breathless poise, of silence, as the two engrappled figures held together. Then the angel tilted over and toppled, its great stone wings sweeping through the air as it fell and crushed him, drawing a hideous grunt from him as it broke on his head and smashed to pieces. The murmuring silence of the vast cemetery returned, except for the blessed wail, far off, of a siren in the city.

I drew myself to my feet, gasping with shock, wet, cold, and dirtied. My frozen legs were trembling. Cranbrook lay quite still as I approached him. A feel of his pulse confirmed that indeed the angel had brought him peace; the inscription was still intact across its base. My mind raced; I reflected that Cranbrook was given to travel when researching his biographies but usually only in England and never with Jill. This time his research on Edinburgh of Saxe-Coburg-Gotha should quite legitimately have taken him to Saxony, a place easily reached by ferry across the Channel, that splendid, unrecorded way of leaving the country. Why should he not leave indefinitely? Who would know what had befallen him? How long before inquiries were made?

I dragged him carefully to Aaron Jones's dark sarcophagus-space and tumbled him in. To close the lid required enormous effort but, my legs shaking, I managed to brace myself against it and got the necessary leverage. Slowly I edged the lid closed. Snow began to patter onto the neatened tomb.

"Aaron Jones. RIP 1843." Who would disturb so quiet a grave?

As I moved away, a gleam in the grass caught my eye. It was the turkey knife, lying where he'd dropped it. I picked it up and put it carefully under my coat. It was a happy thought that, in addition to her enthusiasm for reproduction, another of Jill's attractions was her ability as a cook. We'd need the knife to carve our celebration turkey tomorrow, when the unusual snow would have covered London with a white Christmas blanket. Then we could raise our glasses to the memory of Mrs. Fanny Ronalds of New York, and her harp-shaped crown.

The only true unraveller of Quentin Cranbrook.

The final entangler of Jill and me.

Dorothy Cannell didn't mean to be a writer. What drove her to it, she maintains, was her young son's complaint that she didn't DO anything. Unlike his friends' mothers, she didn't go out to a job, she just stayed home and kept house. To help him save face around the neighborhood, she protested that she did, too, have a job, she was writing a book. Then, to save her own face, she had to write one. The Thin Woman *was an immediate success, so she kept on writing. Aren't you glad?*

British-born Dorothy now lives in the quaint little village of Peoria, Illinois, with her husband, her children, a dog named Charlie who claims to be half pony, and three cats named respectively Lovey, Mocha, and Witches.

DOROTHY CANNELL

THE JANUARY SALE STOWAWAY

Who would have guessed that Cousin Hilda had a dark secret? She was tall and thin, with legs like celery stalks in their ribbed stockings. Her braided hair had faded to match the beige cardigans she wore. And once when I asked if she had been pretty when young, Cousin Hilda said she had forgotten.

"Girly dear, I was fifty before I was thirty. You'd think being an only daughter with five brothers, I'd have had my chances. But I never had a young man hold my hand. There wasn't time. I was too busy being a second mother; and by the time my parents were gone, I was married to this house."

Cousin Hilda lived in the small town of Oxham, some thirty miles northeast of London. As a child I spent quite a lot of weekends with her. She made the best shortbread in the world and kept an inexhaustible tin of lovely twisty sticks of barley sugar. One October afternoon I sat with her in the back parlor, watching the wind flatten the faces of the chrysanthemums against the window. Was this a good moment to put in my request for a Christmas present?

"Cousin Hilda, I really don't want to live if I can't have that roller-top pencil box we saw in the antique shop this afternoon—the one with its own little ink-well and dip pen inside."

"Giselle dear, thou shalt not covet."

Pooh! Her use of my hated Christian name was a rebuff in itself.

"Once upon a time I put great stock in worldly treasures and may be said to have paid a high price for my sin." Cousin Hilda stirred in her fireside chair and ferried the conversation into duller waters. "Where is that curmudgeon Albert with the tea tray?"

A reference, as I understood it, to her lodger's army rank—a curmudgeon being several stripes above a sergeant, and necessitating a snappy mustache as part of the uniform.

"Cousin Hilda," I said, "while we're waiting, why not tell me about your Dark Secret?"

"Is nothing sacred, Miss Elephant Ears?"

"Mother was talking to Aunt Lulu and I distinctly heard the words 'teapot' and 'Bossam's Departmental Store.'"

"Any day now I'll be reading about myself in the peephole press; but I suppose it is best you hear the whole story from the horse's mouth."

While we talked the room had darkened, throwing into ghostly refliefthe lace chair backs and Cousin Hilda's face. A chill tippy-toed down my back. Was I ready to rub shoulders with the truth? Did I want to know that my relation was the Jesse James of the China Department?

Hands clasped in her tweed lap, Cousin Hilda

said—in the same voice she would have used to offer me a stick of barley sugar, "No two ways about it, what I did was criminal. A real turnup for the book, because beforehand I'd never done anything worse than cough in church. But there I was, Miss Hilda Finnely, hiding out in the storeroom at Bossam's, on the eve of the January Sale."

To understand, girly dear, you must know about the teapot. On Sunday afternoons, right back to the days when my brothers and I were youngsters in this house, Mother would bring out the best china. I can still see her, sitting where you are, that teapot with its pink-and-yellow roses in her hands. Then one day—as though someone had spun the stage around, the boys had left home and my parents were gone. Father had died in March and Mother early in December. That year, all of my own choosing, I spent Christmas alone—feeling sorry for myself, you understand. For the first time in years I didn't take my nephews and nieces to see Father Christmas at Bossam's. But by Boxing Day the dyed-in-the-wool spinster suspected she had cut off her nose to spite her face. Ah, if wishes were reindeer! After a good cry and ending up with a nose like Rudolph's, I decided to jolly myself up having tea by the fire. Just like the old days. I was getting the teapot out of the cupboard when a mouse ran over my foot. Usually they don't bother me, but I was still a bit shaky—thinking that the last time I used the best china was at Mother's funeral. My hands slipped and . . . the teapot went smashing to the floor.

I was distraught. But always a silver lining. My life had purpose once more. Didn't I owe it to Mother's

memory and future generations to make good the
breakage? The next day I telephoned Bossam's and
was told the Meadow Rose pattern had been discon-
tinued. A blow. But not the moment to collapse. One
teapot remained among the back stock. I asked that it
be held for me and promised to be in on the first bus.

"I'm ever so sorry, madam, really I am. But that
particular piece of china is in a batch reserved for the
January Sale. And rules is rules."

"Surely they can be bent."

"What if word leaked out? We'd have a riot on our
hands. You know how it is with The Sale. The mob
can turn very nasty."

Regrettably true. On the one occasion when I had
attended the first day of the sale, with Mrs. McClusky,
my best bargain was escaping with my life. Those
scenes shown on television—of customers camping
outside the West End shops and fighting for their
places in the queue with pitchforks—we have the
same thing at Bossam's. The merchandise may not be
as ritzy. But then, the Bossam's customer is not looking for an original Leonardo to hang over the radiator
in the bathroom, or a sari to wear at one's next garden
party. When the bargain hunter's blood is up—
whether for mink coats or tea towels, the results are
the same. Oh, that dreadful morning with Mrs. Mc-
Clusky! Four hours of shuddering in the wind and
rain, before the doors were opened by brave Bossam
personnel taking their lives in their hands. Trapped in
the human avalanche, half suffocated and completely
blind, I was cast up in one of the aisles. Fighting my
way out, I saw once respectable women coshing each
other with handbags, or throttling people as they tried
to hitchhike piggyback rides. Before I could draw

breath, my coat was snatched off my back, by Mrs. McClusky, of all people.

"Doesn't suit you, ducky!"

The next moment she was waving it overhead like a matador's cape, shouting, "How much?"

The dear woman is still wearing my coat to church, but back to the matter at hand. For Mother's teapot I would have braved worse terrors than the January stampede but, hanging up the telephone, I took a good look at myself in the hall mirror. To be first at the china counter on the fateful morning I needed to do better than be Hilda Jane. I'd have to be Tarzan. Impossible. But, strange to say, the face that looked back at me wasn't downcast. An idea had begun to grow and was soon as securely in place as the bun on my head.

The afternoon before The Sale I packed my handbag with the essentials of an overnight stay. In went my sponge bag, my well-worn copy of *Murder at the Vicarage*, a package of tomato sandwiches, a slice of Christmas cake, a small bottle of milk, a piece of cardboard, and a roll of adhesive tape. And mustn't forget my torch. All during the bus ride into town, I wondered whether the other passengers suspected— from the way I held my handbag—that I was up to something. Was that big woman across the aisle, in the duck-feather hat, staring? No . . . yes, there she went elbowing her companion . . . now they were both whispering. So were the people in front. And now the ones behind. I heard the words "Father Christmas" and was put in my place to realize I wasn't the subject of all the buzzing on the bus. That distinction belonged to the stocky gentleman with the mustache, now rising to get off at my stop.

He was vaguely familiar.

"Dreadfully sorry," I said as we collided in the aisle. His Bossam's carrier bag dropped with a thump as we rocked away from each other to clutch at the seat rails. My word, if looks could kill! His whole face turned into a growl.

Behind us someone muttered. "No wonder he got the sack! Imagine him and a bunch of kiddies? Enough to put the little dears off Christmas for life."

Silence came down like a butterfly net, trapping me inside along with the ex–Father Christmas. For a moment I didn't realize the bus had stopped; I was thinking that I was now in no position to throw stones and that I liked the feeling. We "Black Hats" must stick together. Stepping onto the pavement, it came to me why his face was familiar. That day last year, when I left my wallet on the counter at the fishmonger's, he had come hurrying after me . . .

His footsteps followed me now as I went in through Bossam's Market Street entrance.

Now was the moment for an attack of remorse, but I am ashamed to say I didn't feel a twinge. Familiarity cushioned me from the reality of my undertaking. The entire floor looked like a tableau from one of the display windows. The customers could have been life-size doll folk already jerkily winding down.

Directly ahead was the Cosmetics Department, where bright-haired young women presided over glass coffins filled with a treasure trove of beauty enhancers sufficient to see Cleopatra safely into the next world.

"Can I help you, madam?"

"I don't think so, dear, unless you have any rejuvenating cream."

"You might try Softie-Boss, our double-action moisture balm."

"Another time. I really must get to the China Department."

"Straight ahead, madam; across from the Men's Department. You do know our sale starts tomorrow?"

"I keep abreast of world events."

Well done, Hilda. Cool as a cucumber.

The ex–Father Christmas headed past and I mentally wished him luck returning whatever was in his carrier bag. Probably a ho-hum present or, worse, one of the ho-ho sort . . .

Perhaps not the best time to remember the year I received my fourth umbrella and how accommodating Bossam's had been about an exchange. Rounding the perfume display, I reminded myself that no bridges had been burned or boats cast out to sea. I had a full half hour before closing time to change my mind.

Courage, Hilda.

There is a cozyness to Bossam's that ridicules the melodramatic—other than at the January Sale. It is a family-owned firm, founded after the First World War and securely anchored in a tradition of affordability and personal service. The present owner, Mr. Leslie Bossam, had kept a restraining hand on progress. Nymphs and shepherds still cavort on the plastered ceilings. The original lift, with its brass gate, still cranks its way from the basement to the first floor. No tills are located on the varnished counters of the Haberdashery Department, which comprised the first store. When you make a purchase, the salesperson reaches overhead, untwists the drum of a small container attached to a trolley wire, inserts the payment, reattaches the drum and sends it zinging down the wire to the Accounts window, where some unseen person extracts the payment and sends a receipt and possible change, zinging back. A little bit of nostalgia, which appears to operate with surprising efficiency. Perhaps if I had presented my case, in person, to Mr. Bossam . . . ?

"In need of assistance, madam?" A black moth of a saleswoman came fluttering up to me as I reached the China Department.

"Thank you, I'm just looking."

The absolute truth. I was looking to see where best to hide the next morning, so as not to be spotted by the staff before the shop doors opened, at which moment I trusted all eyes would be riveted to the in-rushing mob, permitting me to step from the shadows—in order to be first at the counter. The Ladies' Room was handy, but fraught with risk. Ditto the Stock Room; which left the stairwell, with its landing conveniently screened by glass doors. Yes, I felt confident I could manage nicely; if I didn't land in the soup before getting properly started.

Parading toward me was Mr. Leslie Bossam. His spectacles glinting, his smile as polished as his bald head under the white lights.

"Madam, may I be of service?"

One last chance to operate within the system. While the black moths fluttered around the carousel of Royal Doulton figures, I pressed my case.

"My sympathy, madam. A dreadful blow when one loses a treasured family friend. My wife and I went through much the same thing with a Willow Pattern soup tureen earlier this year. I wish I could make an exception regarding the Meadow Rose teapot, but the question then becomes, Where does one draw the

line? At Bossam's every customer is a valued customer."

Standing there, wrapped in his voice, I found myself neither surprised nor bitterly disappointed. The
game was afoot and I felt like a girl for the first time
since I used to watch the other children playing
hopscotch and hide-and-seek. My eyes escaped from
Mr. Bossam across the aisle to Gentlemen's Apparel,
where the ex–Father Christmas hovered among sports
jackets. He still had his carrier bag and it seemed to
me he held it gingerly. Did it contain something
fragile . . . like a teapot? The thought brought a
smile to my face; but it didn't linger.

"Rest assured, madam, we are always at your service." Mr. Bossam interrupted himself to glance at the
clock mounted above the lift. Almost five-thirty. Oh,
dear! Was he about to do the chivalrous thing and
escort me to the exit?

"Good heavens!"

"I beg your pardon, madam?"

"I see someone I know, over in Gentlemen's Apparel. Excuse me, if I hurry over for a word with him."

"Certainly, madam!" Mr. Bossam exhaled gracious-
ness until he followed my gaze, whereupon he turned
into a veritable teakettle, sputtering and steaming to
the boil.

"Do my spectacles deceive me? That man . . . that
embezzler on the premises! I warned him I would
have him arrested if he set one foot . . ."

Mr. Bossam rushed across the aisle, leaving me
feeling I had saved my own neck by handing a fellow
human being over to the gestapo. No, it didn't help to
tell myself the man was a criminal. What I was doing
was certainly illegal. Slipping through the glass doors

onto the stairwell, I fully expected to be stopped dead by a voice hurled hatchet-fashion, *That's not the exit, madam.* But nothing was said; no footsteps came racing after me as I opened the door marked "Staff Only" and hurried down the flight of steps to "Storage."

Electric light spattered a room sectioned off by racks of clothing and stacks of boxes into a maze. "Better than the one at Hampton Court," my nephew Willie had enthused one afternoon when he ended up down here while looking for the Gentlemen's. When I caught up with him he was exiting the staff facility. And, if memory served, the Ladies' was right next door, to my left, on the other side of that rack of coats. No time to dawdle. As far as I could tell, I had the area to myself, but at any moment activity was bound to errupt. The staff would be working late on behalf of The Sale, and no doubt crates of merchandise would be hauled upstairs before I was able to settle down in peace with *Murder at the Vicarage.*

These old legs of mine weren't built for speed. I was within inches of the Ladies' Room door, when I heard footsteps out there . . . somewhere in that acre of storage. Footsteps that might have belonged to the Loch Ness Monster climbing out onto land for the first time. Furtive footsteps that fear magnified to giant proportions.

"Anyone there?" came a booming whisper.

Huddled among the wool folds of the coat rack, I waited. But the voice didn't speak again. And when my heart steadied, I pictured some nervous soul tiptoeing into the bowels of the store to search through the maze for some carton required double-quick by an irritable section manager. Silence. Which might mean Whoever had located what was needed and beaten a hasty retreat? But it wouldn't do to count my chickens. Stepping out from the coats, my foot skidded on something. Jolted, I looked down to see a handbag. For a flash I thought it was mine, that I had dropped it blindly in my panic. But, no; my black hold-all was safely strung over my arm.

Stealthily entering the Ladies' Room, I supposed the bag belonged to the attendant who took care of the lavatory. I remembered her from visits to spend a penny; a bustling woman with snapping black eyes who kept you waiting forever while she polished off the toilet seat and straightened the roll of paper, then stood over you like a hawk while you washed and dried your hands—just daring you to drop coppers into the dish. Even a sixpence seemed stingy as you watched her deposit the damp towel, slow-motion, into the bin.

Fortune smiled. The Hawk wasn't inside the La- dies', buffing up the brass taps; for the moment the pink-tiled room was empty. Opening my handbag, I withdrew the piece of cardboard and roll of adhesive tape. Moments later one of the three lavatory stalls read "Out Of Order."

Installed on my porcelain throne—the door bolted and my handbag placed on the tank, I opened my book; but the words wouldn't sit still on the page. With every creak and every gurgle in the pipes I was braced to draw my knees up so that my shoes would not show under the gap. Every time I looked at my watch I could have sworn the hands had gone back- ward. Only six-thirty?

I had no idea how late people would stay working before The Sale. But one thing I did know—my feet

were going to sleep. Surely it wasn't that much of a
risk to let myself out of my cell and walk around—just
in here, in the Ladies'. After I had warmed my hands
on the radiator, I felt reckless. The sort of feeling, I
suppose, that makes you itch to stick your finger
through the bars of the lion's cage. Hovering over to
the door, I pushed it open—just a crack.

Standing at the rack of coats was the Ladies' Room
attendant—yes, the one I mentioned. The Hawk.
Unable to move, even to squeeze the door shut, I saw
her button her coat and bend to pick up a handbag and
a Bossam's carrier bag. Now she was the one who
stiffened; I could see it in the set of her broad
shoulders and the tilt of her head. I could almost hear
her thinking . . . Is someone here? Someone watching?

Shrugging, she headed around a stack of boxes taller
than she.

Gone.

I was savoring the moment, when the lights went
out. The dark was blacker than the Yorkshire moors on
a moonless night. Believe me, I'm not usually a
nervous Nellie, but there are exceptions—as when the
mouse ran over my foot. Instead of celebrating the
likelihood of now having the store to myself by
breaking open my bottle of milk, I was suddenly
intensely aware of how mousy I was in relationship to
three floors of mercantile space. To my foolish fancy
every cash register, every bolt of fabric, every saucepan in Housewares . . . was aware of my unlawful
presence. All of them watching, waiting for me to
make a move. I couldn't just stand here, I slipped out
the door, then hadn't the courage to go any farther in
the dark.

"Lord, forgive us our trespasses."

Opening my handbag, I dug around for my torch and felt my hand atrophy. A light beam pierced the dark and came inchworming toward me.

I grabbed for cover among the coats in the rack, felt it sway and braced myself as it thundered to the floor.

"Ruddy hell."

The light had a voice . . . a man's voice. It was closing in on me fast. Intolerable—the thought of facing what was to be, defenseless. Somehow I got out my torch and pressed the button.

"On guard!" came the growly voice as the golden blades of light began to fence; first a parry, then a thrust until . . . there was Retribution—impaled on the end of my blade.

"What brings you here, madam?"

"I got locked in at closing."

"Herrumph! If I believe that, I'm . . ."

"Father Christmas?"

"If you know what I am," he grumped, "you can guess why I'm here."

He was prickly as a porcupine with that mustache, but my torch moved up to his eyes and they were sad. Here was a man who had done a good deal more wintering than summering during his life. How, I wondered, had he escaped the clutches of Mr. Bossam?

"So, why are you here?" My voice was the one I had used for Mother when she was failing. It came echoing back to me from the blackness beyond our golden circle, but I wasn't afraid. "You won't remember me, Mr. ——?

"Hoskins."

"Well, Mr. Hoskins, I remember you. About a year

ago I left my purse on the counter at the fishmonger's and you came after me with it. So you see—whatever your reasons for being here, I cannot believe they are wholeheartedly wicked. Foolish and sentimental like mine, perhaps. I'm jumping the queue on The Sale, so to speak. I'm after a teapot in the Meadow Flower pattern . . ."

A ho-hoing laugh that would have done credit to Saint Nicholas himself.

"Don't tell me you're after it too?"

"No fears on that score, dear madam." He played his torch over my face in a way I might have taken to be flirtation if we weren't a pair of old fogies. "I came here to blow the place up."

Alone with the Mad Bomber! I admit to being taken aback by Mr. Hoskins's confession. But, having survived life with five brothers and their escapades, I managed to keep a grip on myself . . . and my torch.

"I've frightened you."

"Don't give it a thought."

He opened the door to the Ladies', and I jumped to the idea that he was about to barricade me inside, but I misjudged him. He switched on the light and propped the door open.

"All the better to see me?" I switched off my torch but kept it at the ready.

Looking as defiantly sheepish as one of my brothers after he had kicked a ball through a window, Mr. Hoskins said, "The least I can do is explain, Mrs. ——"

"Miss . . . Finnely."

Dragging forward a carton, he dusted it off with his gloves and offered me a seat.

"Thank you. Now you pull up a chair, and tell me all about it."

"Very kind." A smile appeared on his face—looking a little lost. He sat down, and with the rack of coats as a backdrop, began his story.

"Thirty-five years I gave B. & L. Shipping, then one day there it is—I'm turned out to pasture. Half kills me, but I'll get another job—part-time, temporary—anything. When I read that Bossam's was looking for a Father Christmas, I thought, why not? Wouldn't do this crusty old bachelor any harm to meet up with today's youth. Educational. But funny thing was I enjoyed myself. Felt I was doing a bit of good, especially knowing the entrance fees to the North Pole were donated by Bossam's to buy toys for needy kiddies.

"The person bringing the child would deposit two shillings in Frosty the Snowman's top hat. Each evening I took the hat to Mr. Bossam and he emptied it. A few days before Christmas I entered his office to find him foaming at the mouth. He told me he had suspected for some time that the money was coming up short and had set the store detective to count the number of visitors to the North Pole. The day's money did not tally. No reason for you to believe me, Miss Finnely, but I did not embezzle that money."

"I do believe you. Which means someone else helped themselves."

"Impossible."

"Think, Mr. Hoskins." I patted his shoulder as he sat hunched over on the carton. Dear me, he did remind me of my brother Will. "When did you leave the money unattended?"

"I didn't."

"Come now, what about your breaks?"

"Ah, there I had a system. When I left the Pole, I took the top hat with me and came down here to the Gents'. Before going off for a bite to eat, I'd hide it in the fresh towel hamper, about halfway down."

"Someone must have seen you."

"Miss Finnely"—he was pounding his fists on his knees—"I'm neither a thief nor a complete dolt. I made sure I had the place to myself."

"Hmmmm . . ."

"My good name lost! I tell you, Miss Finnely, the injustice burned a hole in my gut. Went off my rocker. As a young chap I was in the army for a while and learned a bit about explosives. I made my bomb, put it in a Bossam's carrier bag, so it would look like I was making a return, and . . ."

Mr. Hoskins stood up. Calmly at first, then with growing agitation, he shifted aside coats on the rack, setting it rocking as he stared at the floor.

"Miss Finnely, upon my word: I put it here and . . . it's gone. Some rotter has pinched my bomb!"

"Cousin Hilda." I was bouncing about on my chair. "I know who took the deadly carrier bag."

"Who, girly dear?"

"The Ladies' Room attendant. You saw her pick one up when she put on her coat. She didn't mistake that bag for her own. Remember how she stiffened and looked all around? Crafty old thing! I'll bet you twenty chocolate biscuits she was one of those . . . what's the word?"

"Kleptomaniacs."

"She stole the Father Christmas money!"

"So Mr. Hoskins and I concluded. She must have

seen him going into the Gentlemen's with the top hat and coming out empty-handed." Cousin Hilda rose to draw the curtains.

"What did you do?"

"Nothing."

"What?" I flew from my chair as though it were a trampoline.

"We agreed the woman had brought about her own punishment. A real growth experience, I would say—opening up that carrier bag to find the bomb. What she wouldn't know was that some specialized tinkering was required to set it off. And she was in no position to ring up the police."

Before I could ask the big question, the door opened and in came Albert the lodger with the tea tray. We weren't presently speaking because I had beaten him that afternoon playing Snap.

"Cousin Hilda," I whispered—not wishing to betray her Dark Secret, "do you know what happened to Mr. Hoskins?"

"Certainly." She took the tray from the curmudgeon. "Albert, I was just telling Giselle how you and I met."

"Oh!" I sat down with a thump. That was what she had meant about the high price of sin.

"One lump or two, girly dear?"

The teapot had pink and yellow roses.

Bill Crider's wife, Judy, says he's fun to live with. He's certainly fun to read, as mystery fans have been discovering in increasing numbers ever since his first Sheriff Rhodes story appeared in 1986, and as you're about to discover right now.

Bill's a mystery fan himself. He started writing articles and reviews for fanzines (publications intended specifically for aficionados, in case the word is unfamiliar to you) and gradually worked his way up to books. Now he's averaging two a year. As if this weren't enough to keep him busy, he's also chairman of the English Department at Alvin Community College in Alvin, Texas, where he lives. Daughter Angela and son Allen are both students at the University of Texas. Oh, and Bill has published a children's book called A Vampire Named Fred.

BILL CRIDER

THE SANTA CLAUS CAPER

P um-pum-pum-pum-*puuum*-pum—pum-pum-pum-pum-pum."

R. M. "Boss" Napier, Chief of the Pecan City, Texas, police, puffed his cheeks and pummed the words to the theme from his favorite TV show, "Hawaii Five-O." Still available every evening, thanks to cable. He accompanied himself by patting his hands on the edge of his battered wooden desk.

Thinking of white sand beaches, blue skies and bluer waves, he resolutely resisted turning to look out the window at his back. Had he done so, he would have seen that the dark sky in the north was getting darker still, turning a deep blue that was almost black as the norther that was sweeping down on Pecan City got closer and closer.

It wasn't so much that Napier disliked the wind and the cold that he knew were coming. After all, you expected that kind of weather in west Texas in December.

What he disliked was that it was almost Christmas,

133

a time of year that did not generally make him a more kindly and benevolent person.

As far as he was concerned, it didn't make anybody more kindly and benevolent. What it did was bring out the shoplifters and the burglars, increase the number of assaults and accidents involving drunken drivers, and generally wreak havoc with the community.

And worse even than those things, Napier had somehow let himself be talked into taking part in a community activity. He didn't like community activities, but he'd let himself be persuaded by Carl Burns, that wimpy English teacher out at the college, to be part of something Burns called a "readers' theater" version of *A Christmas Carol*.

"You'll love it," Burns told him. "And even if you don't, think of all the people who'll come and bring their kids. Think of all those potential voters."

It was something to think about, all right. In Pecan City, the office of Chief was elective rather than appointed.

"Besides," Burns said, "the Mayor will be reading a part. So will I. It's sort of like your civic duty."

Napier thought he was doing his civic duty by serving as police chief. He didn't see why he had to be in some ridiculous play.

"It's not ridiculous," Burns said. "Just think of it as a favor to me. I've helped you out a time or two."

Napier didn't like to admit it, but Burns had a point. The English teacher wasn't really such a wimp, and he'd been in on two murder cases that might not have gotten solved without him, or at least not solved as quickly as they had been.

"I don't like to read," Napier said. "Not out loud, anyway."

"It's easy," Burns said. "Miss Tanner will be reading, too."

Well, that was different. Elaine Tanner was the librarian at the college, and Napier liked her a lot. Her blond hair, her green eyes . . .

"So how about it?" Burns said.

"Okay, I'll do it. What part do I get?"

"Well, we might all be reading more than one, but you'll have at least one major role."

"Okay. What major role?"

"It'll be a good one. Don't worry."

"Yeah, I'm sure. But you better tell me what it is."

Burns smiled. "Tiny Tim," he said.

Napier had not killed Burns on the spot, though he'd thought about it. No jury in the world would have convicted him. After all, he was the Chief, and he could tell everyone that Burns had been killed while attempting to escape. It might have worked, as long as no one pointed out that Burns hadn't been a prisoner and therefore had no reason to attempt escape.

Anyway, much to Napier's surprise, things had worked out all right. Tiny Tim really was a good part, and Napier had a reading voice that carried well, even if it was a little deep and resonant for a kid like Tiny Tim. Napier refused to do the part in falsetto, though Burns had asked him to give it a try.

The best part about the whole thing was that Elaine Tanner was impressed by Napier's abilities, a fact that irritated Burns no end.

"You really are good at this, R.M.," she said after the first rehearsal. She was standing close to him, with her hand resting lightly on his arm. "Are you sure you've never been on the stage before?"

Napier had to admit that he hadn't. His only stage experience had been in the first grade, when he'd portrayed a woodpecker in some stupid play about where birds go in the winter. He'd had to stand on a chair behind a fake cedar tree.

"He's a natural," Burns said, walking over to join them. "I think he practices by intimidating criminals."

"Well, he's really very good," Elaine said. "No matter how he got that way."

Napier smiled at her, and he smiled even more when he saw how much Elaine's comment rankled Burns. The two men had been dating the librarian since the beginning of the school year in September, but neither one of them had gained an advantage to this point. Napier thought maybe he was gaining now.

So Napier really didn't mind leaving his office at the city jail for the rehearsal to be held in the college auditorium. He'd be seeing Elaine again, and he'd get yet another chance to provoke Burns. He didn't want to provoke him too much, though. He had something he wanted Burns to do for him, something that had to do with the reasons Napier didn't enjoy Christmas.

The norther struck just as Napier left the jail. It kicked up white dust in the parking lot and blew grit in Napier's mouth and eyes. Although it was not quite four o'clock in the afternoon, it was nearly as dark as night. The wind was whipping along at around thirty-five miles an hour, straight from the North Pole, and Napier was sure that the temperature dropped fifteen degrees between the time he left the jail and the time he reached his car. He pulled his leather coat tighter around a waist that seemed a little thicker than he remembered it and thought about surfers flashing across the tops of the blue waves in the opening scenes of "Five-O." He wondered if they needed any more cops in Honolulu.

"God bless us, every one," Napier said.

Don Elliott, the director, applauded. "Very well done. Very well done, indeed. I especially liked the way you read the part of Scrooge this time, Mayor Riley. Just the right amount of menace." Elliott was short, hardly more than five feet, but his voice was even more impressive than Napier's. It could be heard all over the auditorium.

Mayor Riley smirked at Elliott's compliment. Riley was a lawyer, and he fancied that he knew a thing or two about menace.

"Professor Burns, you need to do a bit more cringing as Cratchit, at least at first. You can't let the audience off the hook too easily," Elliott said.

This time it was Napier who smirked, but not for long. He didn't want to alienate Burns just now. After Elliott was through with his comments, Napier walked over to where Burns was talking to Elaine Tanner. Napier thought again how much he liked the way Elaine's glasses magnified her green eyes.

"Sorry," Burns said when Napier reached them. "No time to talk this evening. Elaine and I are going out for a bite to eat."

"Why don't you come with us, R.M.?" Elaine said. "Unless you have some important police business to attend to?"

Napier smiled, not so much at the invitation as at a noise he was sure must be Burns's teeth grinding.

"Thanks," he said. "I need to talk to Burns anyhow. This'll give me a chance."

"Talk to me?" Burns said. "What about?"

"I'll tell you while we eat," Napier said. "Why don't we go to the Taco Bell?"

There weren't many good restaurants in Pecan City, but Burns plainly had somewhere a little fancier in mind. He started to say something, but Napier beat him to it. "My treat."

"Well," Burns said, "since you put it that way, how can I refuse?"

"You can't. Why don't I take Elaine with me? She can ride in the squad car."

"Oh, can I?" Elaine's eyes sparkled. She loved police talk, and she loved to ride in official vehicles.

"Sure," Napier said. "Meet you there, Burns?"

"Fine," Burns said, his teeth grinding as he watched them walk away.

The wind lashed the green plastic wreaths attached to the utility poles and tore at the red, green, and white Christmas lights strung in the trees. It shook Carl Burns's old green Plymouth as he drove toward the Taco Bell. He looked out at the decorations and tried to relax his jaws, though what he saw didn't help much.

Lawns and rooftops were covered with the usual floodlit Santas and reindeer, shepherds, Wise Men, and babes in mangers. The wind had bowled over some of the figures, and they lay face down on stiff brown grass. On one lawn there was a parade of the characters from the "Peanuts" comic strip, except for Snoopy. Where the dancing beagle should have been, there was a black-and-white sign that said: SNOOPY STOLEN FROM THIS SPOT 12/24/89.

And where was the Pecan City Police Force when that crime was being committed? Burns wondered. Probably scarfing fajitas at the Taco Bell.

When Burns pulled into the parking lot, the squad car was already there. Elaine and Napier were inside, sitting at a table, and Elaine was laughing at something that Napier had said. Burns punished his dental work some more. Who would ever have guessed that Boss Napier could be so smooth?

Napier got up when Burns entered, asked what he was having, and ordered for everyone. The food was ready quickly, and while they ate Napier entertained by telling them why he liked "Hawaii Five-O" and why he hated Christmas.

"As a matter of fact," he said to Burns, "that's what I wanted to talk to you about."

"You want me to make a list for you?" Burns said. He was fond of making lists, and he had one of his own about the Christmas season.

"Nope," Napier said. "I've got a job for you."

"A job?" Burns said. "I've already got a job."

"Sure you do, but not during Christmas. You teachers relax and get this long holiday while the rest of us have to work. So I know you're free. And besides, the way you get paid, you probably need the money."

Burns's first impulse was to tell Napier that Hartley Gorman College paid a very satisfactory wage, but he restrained himself. He didn't want to lie. Besides, he was curious.

"What's the job?" he said.

"I want you to go undercover," Napier said.

"Oh, Carl," Elaine said. "A police job!"

Napier suddenly had the sinking feeling that he'd made a big mistake, but he went on. "That's right. A police job. We're shorthanded, and I think you can handle this."

"I don't know," Burns said, keeping his eyes on Elaine.

"Of course you can," she said. "You've been a big help to R.M. in the past."

"True," Burns said. "I do seem to have a flair for investigative work."

"I wouldn't call it a flair," Napier said.

"He's done very well," Elaine said. She was sitting on Napier's side of the table, but she looked as if she might move over to join Burns at any minute.

"Tell me about the job," Burns said.

"'Investigative work' may not be the right phrase either," Napier said.

"Just tell me," Burns said.

"Well, you know how I said I'd be Tiny Tim for you?"

"Of course."

"This is sort of the same thing."

Burns looked skeptical. "You want me to be in a play?"

Napier grinned at him. "You might say that. I want you to play Santa Claus."

The beard itched, the red suit was hot, and the boots were too big. The red fur-trimmed cap kept slipping down over his forehead. The stomach padding made him feel like a whale in a red coat, and the wire-rimmed glasses made everything look blurry.

Carl Burns felt like a complete fool.

He was sitting in the big black chair in the middle

of Cameron's Department Store. In front of him, the line of little kiddies was forming. In moments, they would be taking their turns sitting in his lap as they confided to him their secret Christmas wishes.

If he'd had any sense at all, he would have choked Boss Napier with a taco shell, but Elaine had been there and she had looked awed at the idea of Burns's actually taking part in a police case, so what could he do? He'd agreed, of course.

The problem was a common one. Cameron's was experiencing high losses to shoplifters, higher than usual even for the season, and the management was at a loss. Their own trained plainclothes shoppers had been unable to detect what was going on. A few minor offenders had been nabbed, but not enough to stem the flow of merchandise that was leaving the store.

Burns's first thought was that the store owner should invest in a security system like the ones in the big cities, where an alarm went off if you tried to smuggle something past the sensors.

"They're not making enough money to do that," Napier said, which Burns knew was probably true. The store was old and old-fashioned, and most of the locals preferred to shop in Dallas or Fort Worth or at the Wal-Mart that had recently been built on the edge of town. Once the store had been the pride of the city, but now it was probably losing money eleven months of the year, and for most of the twelfth. It was only around Christmas that Cameron's had crowds inside, and even then the crowds were not as large as they had been only a few years before.

Burns got a short course in shoplifting from a bored young woman who'd seen it all: the false-bottomed-package gambit, the "I-was-wearing-that-watch-when-

I-came-in-here" gambit, the one-garment-over-the-limit-in-the-changing-room gambit, the oversized-handbag gambit, the shove-it-in-the-pants-and/or-coat gambit, and several more.

Then the owner himself, Jay Cameron, briefed Burns in the Santa routine. "My father used to play Santa himself, every year," Cameron said. "He seemed to enjoy it." He shook his head. "Not me, thank you."

He was dressed in an expensive suit that Burns suspected was not bought off his own racks, highly polished leather shoes, a blindingly white shirt, and an earth-tone tie that had probably cost about what Burns made in a week. Maybe the store was doing better than Napier thought.

"You've got to know the names of all the reindeer," Cameron said. "And don't forget Rudolph."

"I won't," Burns said. It wasn't Rudolph that worried him. It was the other six. Or was it seven? Eight?

"You can make up elf names," Cameron said. "But I don't think anybody'll ask."

Burns said that he was relieved to know it.

"Lots of kids are scared of Santa," Cameron said. "If they start screaming, just let 'em scream. Calming them's not your job. That's for the parents."

Burns didn't like hearing that. He hadn't thought about screaming.

"The suit's waterproof," Cameron said. "So that's one less worry."

"Waterproof?"

"Yeah. In case some kid gets excited and wets his pants."

Great, Burns thought.

"And don't forget to be jolly," Cameron said, dismissing him.

Burns was thinking about being jolly while kids wet their pants and screamed at the same time when the first one climbed in his lap and started explaining why he had to have a complete set of Teenage Mutant Ninja Turtles action figures. He didn't even ask about the reindeer.

By the time the third kid had finished, Burns had more or less relaxed. By the time the fifth had demanded a home computer—"IBM compatible, with a VGA monitor"—Burns was beginning to watch the goings-on around the store, paying special attention to the jewelry counter, but not neglecting the electronics section. He was positioned so that he had a good view of both, those being the areas from which a great deal of merchandise seemed to be vanishing.

Over the course of the next few hours, Burns didn't notice a thing out of the ordinary. He assured any number of bright-eyed boys and girls that they would be receiving all the outrageously priced gifts they asked for, explained at least seven times how he was able to cover the whole world in a single night ("Those reindeer are *really* fast. Trust me."), and explained to one very upset little girl that the Grinch was purely a literary conceit, whereas Santa was perfectly real, as the evidence of her own eyes should convince her. He wasn't quite sure she got the idea of the conceit, but he thought she got the point. At least she seemed happier when she got down, but that may have been because he had promised her three Madame Alexander dolls under her tree.

During that time, Burns had seen Jay Cameron visit the jewelry department three times, his eagle eyes seeming to X-ray every handbag and purse. The owner also toured Electronics and stared down several grungy teenagers who looked as if their only purpose in life was to steal personal CD players for their girlfriends. But as far as Burns could tell, none of them took a thing.

The best part of the day for Burns was when Elaine Tanner came in and asked if she could sit on Santa's lap. It really pained Burns to have to turn her down.

Napier turned up later in the afternoon, but Burns had nothing to report.

"Keep watching," Napier said. "We know they're here."

"What about the employees?" Burns said. "I think I read somewhere that employees do most of the shoplifting."

"Not here," Napier said. "Cameron practically undresses them before they leave."

Burns was allowed an hour's break for lunch and dinner. He needed the time. After several hours of balancing chubby kids on his knees, he could hardly stand, much less walk. He ate alone in the storeroom in the back of the store, surrounded by cartons and boxes. He didn't mind. The quiet was a relief.

It was after his dinner break, just past eight o'clock, that he spotted his first shoplifter. He was sure of her almost from the minute he saw her. She had a shifty look when she walked by him, tugging her little boy by the hand, and she didn't let the kid talk to Santa. He didn't even ask to do so. Very suspicious.

She spent quite a long time at the jewelry counter, looking at watches, and the clerk had to turn away several times to help other customers. Again, very suspicious.

Then she left without buying a thing.

Burns was convinced that she had taken something, though he hadn't seen what. Now she had to leave the store with it. That was what Napier had told him, anyhow. "Let 'em get out of the store. That constitutes theft. Just notify the security officer, and he'll do the rest."

Of course the security officer was nowhere to be seen. He was probably somewhere with a doughnut and cup of coffee.

When the woman started for the front door, Burns shoved a tow-headed boy off his lap and stood up.

"But, Santa," the boy said. "I haven't finished yet."

"Don't worry, Son," Burns said, trying to be jolly. "You'll get everything you want. Trust me."

"But how do you *know* what I want? I didn't have time—"

"Write me a letter," Burns said, jostling past the other kids in the line. The woman was already out the door, and he was afraid she would be in her car and gone before he got there.

She was only half in the car, however, with one foot still planted on the ground, when Burns tapped her on the shoulder.

"Ma'am?" he said. "Excuse me, ma'am." He had no idea what to say next. What did you say to a shoplifter?

"It's Santa, Mom!" the little boy on the other side of her screamed. "It's Santa!"

The woman looked at Burns. "Whatcha want?" she said.

She was big, Burns realized, almost as big as he was, and he was wearing padding.

"I, ah, I think you might have taken something in there."

The woman stared at Burns, then got slowly out of the car. The boy followed her out. He was very excited to see Santa. "I wanted to talk to you," he said, "but Mom said we didn't have time. I want a pony for Christmas."

"Be quiet, Larry," the woman said. She stared at Burns. "Whaddya mean about me taking something?"

"I, ah, well, if you'd just let me look in your purse, I'm sure we could clear this up," Burns said. He'd decided that she'd slipped whatever she'd taken into her oversized purse. It had to be there.

"You some kinda creep?" the woman said.

The little boy was shocked. "Don't say that, Mom! It's Santa!"

"Santa's ass," the woman said. "It's some kinda creep." She hugged her purse to her ample bosom as if it contained something precious. "He's one o' them creeps that steals a woman's purse from her at Christmastime."

"No, no," Burns said. "You've got the wrong idea. It's just that I've been—"

"Help!" the woman screamed. "Police! Fire! Rape!"

Burns hadn't noticed until then that there were other people in the parking lot. Now it seemed as if the entire population of Pecan City had arrived at just that moment to do a bit of shopping. Curious faces turned to see what was going on, and two people started walking rapidly in Burns's direction. Burns started to sweat, though the temperature couldn't have been much above freezing.

The little boy didn't know what was going on, but he didn't like it. He looked as if he might cry at any second.

"Help!" the woman screamed. "Police!"

Burns looked around, wishing that he had never seen Napier or Elaine Tanner. It was their fault that he was in this mess, though he knew he had been stupid to follow the woman out of the store. He had no idea how to handle the situation, and he should simply have allowed her to leave.

He turned back to the woman, intending to apologize and forget the whole incident.

She swung her purse and hit him in the side of the head. The purse was so heavy Burns thought it might have a compact car inside it.

He shook his head, trying to clear it, and the little boy kicked him in the shin. "You leave my mom alone!" he yelled.

Burns bent to look at his shin, and the woman hit him with her purse again, in the back of the head this time. The fur-rimmed cap protected him to some extent, but Burns went down to his knees on the parking lot.

He heard the horrified voice of a little girl. "That woman's killing Santa!"

The voice did not deter the woman. She hit Burns again.

"What's going on here?" Boss Napier said.

Burns had never thought the Chief's voice could sound so good. He stood up, his right hand pushing the cap out of his eyes.

"This creep was trying to take my purse," the woman said.

"He's a bad Santa," her boy said.

"I was just trying to do what you told me," Burns said.

"I didn't tell you to go picking on solid citizens like Mrs. Branton," Napier said. He looked around at the crowd of curious onlookers. "Everything's all right here now, folks. Just a little Christmas misunderstanding."

"That woman tried to kill Santa," the horrified little girl said.

"Santa's fine. Isn't that right, Santa?"

Burns rubbed the back of his head. "Yeah," he said. He didn't even try to be jolly. "Santa's just fine."

As the crowd drifted on into the store, many of them pausing to look back over their shoulders, Burns said to Napier, "You know Mrs. Branton?"

"Right. Mrs. Roy Branton and her fine son Larry." He smiled at the boy, who was watching Burns suspiciously. "This has all been a big misunderstanding, Larry. Santa wasn't trying to take your mother's purse."

"Yes he was," Mrs. Branton said.

"No, no," Napier said, must jollier than Burns had ever seen him. "He's working for me. It was just a mistake. Really. It won't happen again."

Mrs. Branton didn't look convinced. "He looks like a creep to me."

Napier got even jollier. "Well, he's not. You can take my word for it. Right, Santa?"

"Right," Burns said, grinding his teeth.

As Napier explained to Burns later in the storeroom while Burns was getting out of the Santa suit, Mrs. Branton was the ex-wife of one of Napier's best officers. She had quite a reputation around town for her fierce temper and for one other thing—her honesty.

"She's the kind of woman who wouldn't tell a lie even when it would be better than the truth," Napier said. "The kid, Larry, found a ten-dollar bill on the street one day, and she made him give it to Harve—

Harve's her ex—so Harve could turn it in at the station. We kept it for three weeks, and when no one claimed it, she let Larry have it. She wouldn't steal anything, Burns. She wouldn't even let the kid keep the ten dollars, not at first."

Burns stripped off the itchy beard. "I don't see how you can be so sure about her. I've read that shoplifting is like a disease. You never know who might have it. And since we're doing *A Christmas Carol*, I've been thinking about Dickens. She's probably a Fagin."

"What's a Fagin?"

"Who. Who's a Fagin. He's a character in *Oliver Twist*. He has a bunch of kids who do his thieving for him."

"You think *Larry* is doing the lifting?"

Burns shook his head. "Not really. To be honest, she's the only one I saw today who even looked the least bit suspicious. There's just no way anyone could be stealing stuff from this store."

"Sure there is," Napier said. "You just haven't given it enough time."

"Yes I have," Burns said. He threw the red cap on top of the pile he had made of the Santa outfit. "I've found out I don't have a flair for investigative work after all. I quit."

The first performance of *A Christmas Carol* was very well received. Many of the prominent members of the community were in attendance, including Franklin Miller, the president of Hartley Gorman College, who took the time to congratulate Burns on his reading.

"Excellent, Burns, excellent," Miller said, shaking Burns's hand. "This has been just wonderful for college-and-community relations."

His remarks didn't make Burns feel any better. Elaine had been ignoring him ever since the episode at Cameron's, though Burns had tried to put the best face possible on things when he explained to her why he had given up the job. He could tell that she was disappointed in him, however, and there was no telling what Napier might have said to her about why Burns was off the job.

Burns looked over the departing audience and saw several other people he knew. There was Marion Everson, editor of Pecan City's almost-daily newspaper; Gene Vale, president of the Chamber of Commerce; and several HGC faculty members, including Mal Tomlin and Earl Fox.

Even Jay Cameron was there. It was eight-thirty, and the store owner would just have time to get to his place of business before closing time for one last check of the premises. The shoplifters still had not been caught. Cameron, however, had not been sorry to see Burns resign as Santa. It was as if he was more willing to suffer his losses than to have Burns make another scene. Burns didn't blame him for feeling that way.

Then Burns had a thought. He walked over to where Napier was graciously accepting the congratulations of an admiring Elaine Tanner and several others for his sensitive interpretation of Tiny Tim.

Burns waited until Napier looked his way and indicated that he would like a word with the Chief. Napier shook a few more hands, laughed, and made his way to Burns, looking back to smile at Elaine over his shoulder.

Burns tried not to grind his teeth. "I think I've cracked the case," he said when Napier reached him.

"What case?" Napier said.

"You know what case."

"Oh, *that* case. I thought you quit."

"I did, but I've been thinking about it."

"Thinking about it. You cracked it by thinking about it? Like Sherlock Holmes?"

Burns smiled. "More like C. Auguste Dupin."

Napier thought about that. "Who?" he said.

"Never mind," Burns said. "Just meet me at Cameron's at nine o'clock."

"Tonight?" Napier said, looking at his watch.

"Right. In fact, why don't we go in your car?"

"You're not going to make more trouble, are you?"

"Who, me?" Burns said. "Of course not."

"You better not," Napier said. "If you do, I'll sic Mrs. Branton on you."

"Ha ha," Burns said. But he wasn't being jolly.

Burns and Napier sat in the squad car. Not wanting to alert anyone to their presence, Napier refused to leave the motor on and run the heater. He even rolled his window down a half inch and made Burns do the same so the windows wouldn't fog over.

Burns was freezing. He rubbed his hands together and stuck them between his thighs to warm them.

Napier hummed the theme from "Hawaii Five-O," tapping on the steering wheel to keep time.

"I wish you wouldn't hum that song," Burns said. "It bothers me."

"Those Five-O guys are my heroes," Napier said, thinking of warm surf and swaying palm trees. "You better be right about this, Burns. You know that?"

"I'm right. How much did you say the store lost the day I was there?"

"Four thousand. Little more. You stretch that out over three or four weeks, it mounts up."

The last customers left the store. Mrs. Branton and Larry. This time Mrs. Branton was carrying a bulging shopping bag. A salesclerk locked the door behind her.

"There she is," Burns said. "She sure does have a heavy purse."

"But she's not a thief," Napier said.

"I know that now," Burns said.

They waited in the car while balances were checked against the stock, Cameron no doubt moaning over his latest losses. The clerks began to trickle out.

Finally Cameron himself came out. The store was dark now, and Cameron carefully checked the door before he started across the parking lot to his car. He was wearing a bulky topcoat over his expensive suit.

"Now?" Napier said.

"Now or never," Burns said, opening his door and getting out.

They met Cameron just as he reached his car.

"Good evening, Chief, Dr. Burns," Cameron said. "I enjoyed your performance this evening."

Napier thanked him.

"And what brings you my way?" Cameron said.

"Well," Napier said, "Burns has this crazy idea that he knows who's been stealing from your store."

"He does?" Cameron said. "That's good news."

"Not so good," Napier said. "He thinks it's you."

Cameron seemed to pale under the glow of the lamps that lighted the parking lot. "Me?" he said.

"You," Burns said. "Chief Napier said it couldn't be your employees. You were too careful for that. And I sat there all day and never saw anyone take a thing. I thought I did, but I didn't. And neither did any of your professionals. So if no one was taking anything, that left only one person, one person who visited every department and had every opportunity to take whatever he wanted. You."

"I don't see how you could think such a thing," Cameron said, tucking his coat around him.

"Why don't you show us what's under the coat?" Napier said. "If there's nothing, then Burns was just wrong. Again."

"Of course he's wrong. I never heard of anything so outrageous. Why would I steal from my own store?"

"Money," Burns said. "The store's in trouble, but if you stole from yourself, you could collect twice. Once from the insurance company and once from the fence you sold the merchandise to. It makes sense to me."

"Me too," Napier said. "Open the coat." He reached out as if to pull open the front of the topcoat, and Cameron jerked away. A small bag dropped on the asphalt of the parking lot.

Burns grabbed it before Cameron could bend down. He opened it and looked inside. "Watches," he said. "Did you remember to pay for these, Mr. Cameron?"

Napier didn't appear interested in the watches. "Got anything else under that coat, Cameron?" he said.

Cameron looked at Burns, then at Napier. His face set itself for a second, then collapsed. He opened the coat to reveal several other sacks of merchandise tucked here and there.

Napier shook his head. "Looks like you were right, Burns. I hate to admit it, but maybe you do have a flair for this kind of thing, after all."

Burns smiled. "Book him, Tim-o," he said.

It started when she broke her leg. There she was in the Italian Dolomites with nothing to read while her companions were out skiing. So she thought up a mystery to entertain herself and wrote it down.

That was the start of something beautiful. Since then, Patricia Moyes has written enough excellent mysteries (seventeen at last count) to set her among the greats in traditional mystery fiction. Not bad for someone who never set out to be a serious writer.

Born in County Wicklow, Ireland, Patricia Moyes has been a flight officer in the WAAF, company secretary to Peter Ustinov Productions, has written movie scripts and an adaption of Jean Anouilh's Time Remembered, *which was successfully produced in London and New York. She has lived in Britain, Switzerland, Holland, Washington, D.C., and now lives in the British Virgin Islands. Perhaps it's not too surprising that, after such an eventful life, she's written us a story about a housewife who just sits quietly at home and does needlepoint.*

PATRICIA MOYES

FAMILY CHRISTMAS

Good King Wenceslas looked out
On the feast of Stephen . . .

The young voices were ragged and precariously off-key, but all the same Mrs. Runfold found them touching. She laid down her needlepoint embroidery and said, "Poor little things. They must be perishing with cold out there at this hour of night. I shall ring for Parker and tell him to give them five pounds and some hot soup."

"You'll do no such thing," replied her husband. He rustled his newspaper angrily. "They're nothing but a confounded nuisance, and it's not even Christmas Eve yet." He got up from his chair by the fire and pressed a bell. This produced, before the end of the carol, an extremely correct and unhurried butler.

"You rang, sir?"

"Yes, Parker, I did. Give those damned children fifty pence, and tell them to go away and not dare come back."

"Very good, sir."

Parker bowed slightly and withdrew. The voices straggled into silence as the big front door closed. Mary Runfold sighed and resumed her embroidery. She had learned, after thirty years of marriage, not to argue with her husband. Besides, Dr. Carlton had warned Robert against getting upset or angry, because of his heart condition. Mrs. Runfold changed the subject.

"How nice," she said, as her needle flicked deftly in and out of the canvas, "to think that all the family will be home for Christmas."

"You think so?"

"Well, of course, dear. It will be lovely to see the girls and their husbands."

Robert Runfold snorted. "I suppose you realize, Mary, that either one of those young men would cheerfully kill me if he thought he could get away with it?"

The needle stopped in midair. "Robert! What a terrible thing to say! How can you even think such a—?"

"Don't be silly, Mary. You know I'm right."

Timidly, Mrs. Runfold said, "Well, dear, perhaps if you were to advance them just a little money . . ."

"You know perfectly well that on principle I don't believe in giving young people money. Let them stand on their own feet."

"Yes, dear." The needle resumed its activity.

Defensively, Robert Runfold said, "They've both had expensive training and should be able to support themselves and their wives. All right, so Derek wants to buy his own pharmacy and have Anne give up her job and start a family. Let him, by all means. It's no concern of mine."

"But—"

"And as for Philip, it's absolutely disgraceful the way he's allowed himself to get into debt. Veterinary surgeons are very well paid these days."

"He's been giving free treatment to pets of people who can't afford his regular fees, Robert."

"More fool he. Alison should have stopped him. Shown a little common sense."

In the silence that followed, the grandfather clock in the big drawing room struck nine, and a glowing log tumbled slowly down into the fire basket.

Runfold went on. "Which reminds me, Mary. I've been meaning to say this. I want you personally to supervise everything I eat and drink over Christmas."

"Well, naturally, dear, I discuss all the menus with Mrs. Benson—"

"That's not what I mean. Derek and Philip both have access to prohibited drugs. They both know about my shaky heart. It would be perfectly easy for either of them to slip something into my food—or my glass."

Mary Runfold gave a little nervous laugh. "Oh, come now, Robert. You don't seriously believe that either of them would do such a thing."

"I'm taking no chances."

Gently, Mrs. Runfold said, "If you're really so suspicious, why did you invite them for Christmas?"

Runfold grunted. "I wanted to see the girls. And I knew you'd enjoy a family Christmas."

"Thank you, dear." There was no irony in his wife's voice. "That was very thoughtful."

"In any case," Robert went on, "I am asking you to

serve personally anything that I eat or drink. And tell Mrs. Benson that nobody but you may go into the kitchen over Christmas—particularly the four young people."

"Of course I'll do that, if it's what you want, Robert."

"Thank you, Mary." Robert Runfold smiled at his wife over his newspaper—that warm, sweet smile which transformed his face, and which had won her heart so many years ago. She gave a little sigh, knowing that she would always love, honor, and obey him, even though he might not be perfect. Charm is every bit as potent in a man as in a woman. She just wished that he would smile more often.

Then, of course, he had to go and spoil it. He said, "I've been worried lately, Mary. About you."

"Me?"

"Well, I know how soft-hearted you are. Either of those two young rascals could persuade you to part with my money once I'm dead and you've inherited."

"My dear, I assure you—"

"So I may as well tell you, I've changed my will. You will get a handsome income for life, so you needn't worry. But the capital is well and truly tied up until the youngest girl is forty." Runfold sat back in his chair with a little grunt of satisfaction. "Yes, they'll have to wait until they're forty, or until we're both dead. That's why I can have so much confidence in you, Mary."

"Couldn't you have trusted me anyway, Robert?"

Robert laughed. "Oh, I know you wouldn't try to kill me. It wouldn't be in your interest. But the thought of you being in control of all that money, without me around to advise you . . ."

"I'm sure you did the right thing, my dear," said Mary Runfold.

Two days later, on Christmas Eve, the daughters and their husbands arrived, and preparations went ahead for a jolly family Christmas. Everybody took turns at stirring the pudding—Robert could hardly object to this, since the mixture had been made months ago by Mrs. Benson, but he kept an extremely sharp eye on his sons-in-law all the same. Mary put in the little silver charms carefully wrapped in grease-proof paper—the spinster's thimble, the bachelor's button, the lucky wishbone, the Christmas bell, and the threepenny bit and the sixpence—two silver coins saved from Christmases long past.

That afternoon, Anne Walters (née Runfold) managed to corner her father on his own in the library, where he had taken refuge to escape helping with the holly-and-paper streamers which were being festooned over the drawing room.

Anne, a gravely dark beauty of twenty-eight, turned on all her charm. "You see, Daddy, Derek could make a whole lot of money with a pharmacy of his own. As it is, he's working for a rotten salary, and I can't possibly give up my job, and . . . you do want grand-children, don't you?" Anne smiled and put a persuasive arm around her father's shoulders.

Robert shook it off. "Whether or not you have babies is nothing to do with me, Anne. You and Derek are grown-up people. You must make your own decisions."

"But decisions often depend on money, Daddy."

"Not on mine." Robert shut the book he was reading with a snap. "If you want to talk about babies, go and have a word with your mother."

Anne looked at him reflectively. "Maybe I will," she said.

A little later, Alison Watts (née Runfold) came into the library. She was twenty-four, with her mother's dark-golden hair and a pert, pretty face which was currently marred by the fact that she was crying.

"What on earth is the matter, Ally?" In Robert's view, people had no right to spoil Christmas by displays of emotion.

"Oh, Daddy, it's about Philip. I'm so terribly unhappy."

"Then leave him," said Runfold bluntly.

"No, Daddy, you don't understand . . . I love Philip and I'll stand by him through anything— absolutely anything. But things are much worse than you know. If he can't pay his debts he'll have to go bankrupt, and his career will be finished! It's really not his fault—he's been too generous . . ."

"Which is a mistake I'm not about to make," remarked her father. "It's no good coming in here and weeping all over the place. You and Philip have got yourselves into this mess, and you can get out of it."

"But how?"

"Bankruptcy isn't the end of the world. Plenty of people have climbed out of it and made a success of their lives. In fact, it might be the making of that shiftless husband of yours."

Still in tears, Alison ran out of the room and went in search of her mother. She found her in the drawing room with Anne. Derek and Philip had been packed off on a long country walk to keep them out of the way.

One look at her sister's face was enough for Anne. "No luck?" she said.

Alison shook her head mutely. Mary Runfold said, "I'm so sorry, darling. I did think your father might help when it actually came to bankruptcy—but you know what he's like."

Alison blew her nose, stopped crying, and said, "I wish he was dead. I honestly do."

"You mustn't say such things, Ally. He's been a wonderful father to you."

"He's been no such thing!" Anne was vehement. "Ally's right. If he'd only drop dead, you'd have his money, and we know you'd help us!"

Mrs. Runfold shook her head sadly. "I'm afraid he's thought of that. You know his heart is weak—he can't live forever. So he's made a new will, giving me an income for life and putting all the capital in trust for you two girls—until Ally is forty."

"Forty!" Anne was outraged. "That means I'll be forty-four! It's wicked. Can't you break the trust, Mummy?"

"I very much doubt it. You know how thorough your father is. Anyway, please don't talk as though he were dead already. He may live for many years yet, please God."

"Well, we're in for a really merry Christmas, aren't we?" Alison was bitter. "When he actually invited us, we thought that he'd changed his mind."

"He never changes his mind," said Mary Runfold quietly. "That's one of the reasons why he's so rich."

Later that evening, Anne went to the kitchen. She and the cook were old friends.

"Hello, Bensy," she said.

"Why, good evening, Miss Anne! Merry Christmas! How well and pretty you're looking! And no wonder, with that handsome husband to look after you." Mrs. Benson, stout and good-humored, went on rolling pastry.

"Thank you, Bensy. Yes, I'm very happy." A little pause. "What's that you're making?"

"Pastry for this evening's apple pie, dear. Your father's favorite."

"Can I help?"

"Oh, my goodness!" Mrs. Benson looked up, red-faced and flustered. "Why, I'd quite forgotten! The mistress said none of you young people were to come in the kitchen. You'd better go, or I'll be in trouble."

"Not come into the kitchen?" Anne was puzzled. "Why ever not?"

"Don't ask me, Miss Anne. I expect your mother wants everything to be a surprise for you. Anyhow, off you go. And tell Miss Ally, will you? And your young men—husbands, I should say. I somehow can't get used to the idea of you two being married ladies. It seems no time at all since . . ." Mrs. Benson wiped away a furtive tear on the edge of her apron. "Well, run along now, dear."

Anne left, far from pleased.

Dinner that evening was a glum meal, although Robert Runfold gave no sign of noticing anything untoward. He tucked with relish into the apple pie and regaled his family with stories about his early struggles in the business world, and how he had pulled himself up by his own bootstraps, with no help from anybody. This information was received in bleak silence, broken only by Mary Runfold's urging of second helpings on everybody. After dinner, there was another visit from carol singers, which put Robert into a thoroughly bad temper. Parker was sent to get rid of them, and soon afterward the family went gloomily to bed.

Gloomily, that is, apart from Robert, who remarked cheerfully to his wife, "Well, I think they got the

message, eh, Mary? Nothing like being firm and
making oneself clearly understood." The look on Mary's
face must have caught his attention, because he patted
her hand and gave her his charmer's smile. "Now, stop
worrying, dear. They're young and they'll pull out of
these little difficulties. It'll do them good. You'll see."

On Christmas morning, the whole family went to
Matins in the village church. The vicar, the local doctor,
and other worthies thought how pleasant it was to see a
really united family praying together, in these days.

The vicar preached a short, hearty sermon on the
meaning of Christmas, emphasizing how the festival
united families and spread goodwill. Then the con-
gregation streamed out into the crisp winter air. A fine
sprinkling of snow was beginning to fall, and the
phrase "A white Christmas after all!" was repeated on
all sides. Then everybody scurried for their cars, and
home to the turkeys and plum puddings which had
been cooking all the morning.

Christmas lunch at the Runfolds' went as well as
could be expected. Mrs. Benson had excelled herself.
The turkey was succulent, the bread sauce creamy
and with just the right hint of onion and nutmeg, the
cranberries-and-chestnut stuffing made delicious contrasts of taste. However, the main course was not so
heavy as to leave appetites blunted when the Christmas
pudding was carried in by Parker, aflame with brandy
and accompanied by a positively alcoholic hard sauce.

Mrs. Runfold served the pudding herself, making
sure that everybody got one of the wrapped favors.
Derek got the sixpenny piece and Philip the threepenny, which caused Robert to remark that it was a
lucky omen for their future finances. Alison drew the
lucky silver wishbone and Anne the Christmas bell,

and there was laughter when Mary and Robert found, respectively, the spinster's thimble and the bachelor's button in their portions.

The meal over, everybody agreed that a short siesta would put them into good shape to tackle Mrs. Benson's royally iced Christmas cake. Only Mary Runfold decided to go first to the kitchen to confer with Mrs. Benson about the cold supper which was to be served before the young people departed for home.

Consequently, it was not until about half past three that she went upstairs, to find her husband slumped across their big double bed, not sleeping but dead.

Dr. Carlton arrived within a few minutes of Mrs. Runfold's anguished telephone call. He was not particularly surprised at what had happened. He knew only too well of Runfold's potentially dangerous heart condition.

"But *why? Why*, Dr. Carlton? Why should he die now? What happened?" Mary was obviously not far from the breaking point.

The doctor, who was engaged in writing out the death certificate, looked up. "Who can tell, Mrs. Runfold? Perhaps you know better than I do?"

"What do you mean by that?"

"Just that heart failure, in his condition, can be brought on by hypertension. Has he been worked up or overexcited lately? Has he been eating too much rich food?"

"I suppose he has," Mary admitted. "What with Christmas—and then, we have the girls and their husbands here, and . . . well, yes, he has been worried. Family matters, you understand."

"Of course. Please accept all my sympathy, Mrs. Runfold." Dr. Carlton signed the certificate and handed her a copy. "There. This will enable the

undertakers to arrange everything without any bother."
He cleared his throat. "I'm very glad, Mrs. Runfold, that
you have your family with you. They will be a greater
comfort to you than anybody else."

Hesitantly, Mary said, "You don't think . . . I
mean, could he have been given something . . .
something in his food or drink that could have brought
on the attack?"

The doctor smiled sadly. "What a bizarre idea, Mrs.
Runfold. In theory, of course—yes. Somebody could
have administered something. But there was nobody
here but the family, was there?"

"What sort of thing?"

"Oh, there are several substances—an overdose of
digitalis, for instance."

Mary Runfold had gone very pale. "Digitalis? I
thought that was a *cure* for heart disease."

"Given in very careful doses—yes, it can be helpful.
But an overdose, coupled with high blood pressure—
however, don't even think about it. You husband died
from natural causes—heart failure, which had been
threatening for some time. You must put anything else
out of your mind."

"Yes, Doctor."

Derek, the pharmacist, took control of the situation
with easy expertise. The undertakers arrived, muted
and unruffled, and removed Robert's body to their
chapel of rest. By common consent, Mary's daughters
and their husbands agreed to stay on until after the
funeral. Derek was on a week's holiday, and Philip
had left his veterinary practice in the hands of a young
locum, who was blithely unaware of the fact that he
would probably never be paid.

The next morning, Mary Runfold assembled her family in the drawing room. She was very calm.

She said, "There is something I have to ask all four of you, and I want truthful answers."

They looked at her, silent and surprised. She went on, "Did any of you tamper in any way with Robert's food or drink yesterday?"

There was a chorus of indignant denials. Mary rang the bell, and when Parker appeared, said, "Ah, Parker. Please ask Mrs. Benson to come here."

Parker's eyebrows went up a fraction of an inch, but all he said was, "Yes, madam."

As soon as the door had closed behind him, a babble of voices broke out.

"What on earth is all this, Mother?" This from Anne.

"I do assure you, Mother-in-law—"

"Just because I said yesterday . . . of course I didn't mean it . . ."

"What sort of fools do you think we are?" Philip sounded very grim. "You think Ally and I would poison her father just to . . . ?"

The voices fell abruptly silent as Mrs. Benson came in. She was red-eyed but composed.

"You wanted to see me, madam?"

"Yes, Mrs. Benson. You remember that I gave orders that nobody but myself was to go into the kitchen?"

"Yes, madam."

"Well, did anybody go in? Or try to go in?"

Mrs. Benson flushed deeply. "I don't really like—"

"What you like or not is immaterial, Mrs. Benson. Please answer my question."

"Well, madam, Miss Anne . . . beg pardon, Mrs. Walters . . . she did come in to wish me a merry Christmas, while I was making the pastry for the apple pie. But I told her to go away, because of what you said, madam."

"Did she say anything else, except 'Merry Christmas'?"

Mrs. Benson went an even deeper red and snuffled.

"She asked me if she could help with the apple pie. Miss Anne's always been so—"

"But you didn't let her?"

"Oh, no, madam."

"Anybody else?"

"No, madam."

"Thank you, Mrs. Benson. You may go now."

Before the door had closed behind the cook, Anne burst out, "Are you accusing me of . . . ?"

"I'm not accusing anybody," said Mary evenly. "How can I? Even though I'm convinced that Robert's death wasn't natural."

"Excuse me, Mother-in-law," said Derek. "You're accusing all of us, most explicitly. And it's ridiculous. As you told us yourself, under the new will we wouldn't get any money."

Mary Runfold looked at him steadily. "You didn't know that when you arrived here, did you?"

"Well—no. But—"

"There's no point in talking about it." Mary's voice was suddenly very weary. "Mrs. Benson seems to have cleared you all." She sighed. "I think I shall go and lie down now. I'm really very tired."

When her mother had gone, Alison said, "I honestly believe she suspects one of us."

"Or all of us," said Philip.

Anne said, "It's almost as though—oh, I don't know—as thought she *wanted* one of us to be guilty."

"That's crazy," remarked her husband.

"It may be crazy, but I think it's true," said Anne stubbornly.

It was when Mrs. Runfold did not appear for lunch that Alison went up to her room to wake her. She found her mother in a coma, with an empty bottle of sleeping pills beside her and a note propped up on the dressing table. The note read, "Forgive me. I couldn't face life without Robert, so I am going to join him."

Mrs. Runfold was rushed to hospital, but it was too late. She died that afternoon, without regaining consciousness. The inquest was brief, the coroner very sympathetic. The verdict: Suicide while the balance of her mind was disturbed.

When Alison and Philip arrived home after the double funeral, Alison was surprised and shocked to see a letter on the mat, addressed to her in Mary's unmistakable handwriting. While Philip carried in the suitcases, she slipped it unopened into her handbag. It was only the next day, after her husband had gone to work, that she read the letter.

It was postmarked on the day of her mother's death.

Dearest Ally,

I am giving this to Parker to post. It is for your eyes only. I am sure I can trust you to keep it secret. I feel I must tell somebody the truth.

I hardly know how to say this. You see, Robert was convinced that either Philip or Derek would try to poison him over Christmas—that is to say, give him some substance which would not be lethal to a healthy person, but would cause a heart attack to someone in Robert's condition. I am ashamed to say that, although I pooh-poohed the idea, I secretly agreed with him.

I knew that digitalis was a heart stimulant, and I had a foolish notion that if I managed to give him some, it would help him to withstand whatever drug he might be fed. In any case, I reckoned it couldn't do him any harm. You'll understand that I couldn't ask Dr. Carlton for advice without voicing my suspicions to him. And digitalis was something that I could get hold of.

I made my concoction late in the evening before you arrived, after Robert and Mrs. Benson had gone to bed. Then I soaked the paper wrapping of the bachelor's button in it, so that it would seep into the surrounding pudding—and of course I made sure that Robert would get it.

It was only after his death that the doctor told me that the wrong dose could have killed him.

I confess I hoped against hope that one of you might have tried to poison him, which is why I questioned you all so closely just now; but I can no longer escape the fact that I killed Robert myself.

At least, you and Anne will now get your father's money. There is nothing else I can do for you.

Whether or not you decide to sell the house, please destroy the clump of foxgloves near the gate. And tell Mrs. Benson to throw away the small copper saucepan.

With all my love,
Mother.

Evelyn Smith claims a rare distinction. She's one of those exotic few who were actually born and have lived their whole lives in New York City. And so, moreover, is her cat Christopher.

Unvaried as her physical surroundings have been, Evelyn's writing career has taken her all over the galaxy. It's said that her early science fiction and fantasy stories earned rave reviews on Alpha Centauri. Coming down to earth, she began working on and writing for women's magazines, winding up as Features Editor on Family Circle. *During that period, she was also writing Gothic novels, plus books and articles on witchcraft and mail order under the pen name Delphine C. Lyons.*

Then, out of the everywhere into the here, came Miss Susan Melville, another New Yorker with a unique approach to community service, and Evelyn Smith was again relaunched as a mystery novelist. This is Miss Melville's first appearance in a short story; we rejoice to have her.

EVELYN E. SMITH

MISS MELVILLE REJOICES

Darkness had fallen and a light snow was beginning to come down as a dim figure swathed in a voluminous raincoat crept furtively down the short flight of steps that led into the sunken yard of a white limestone-fronted building on a quiet, expensive street on New York City's quiet, expensive East Side. The dim figure disconnected the alarm system attached to the grille beneath the front stoop, unlocked the grille and swung it open, passed through, relocked the grille and swung it shut, reconnected the alarm, disconnected the alarm attached to the inner door, unlocked the three locks with which the inner door was fastened, opened the door, entered the basement, closed the door, relocked the three locks, and reconnected the alarm.

On the upper floors of the building there were lights and movement. Later there would be feasting and merriment, for it was Christmas Eve and the Melville Foundation for Anthropological Research was giving a party in honor of the deposed dictator of

Mazigaziland, the infamous Matthew Zimwi, the man
for whom *Time* magazine had established the category
of Monster of the Year.

Inside the basement all was dark and had been
quiet until the furtive figure entered and, stumbling
into a sawhorse—on which, for some unaccountable
reason, a bucket of small metallic objects had been
balanced—knocked down a group of boards propped
against it. There was a crash, followed by a ladylike
oath, for the furtive figure was a lady and not only a
lady but Susan Melville, world-renowned artist, en-
dower of the Melville Foundation, and owner of the
building she had so surreptitiously entered.

And why had Susan Melville entered her own
building so surreptitiously, over four hours before a
party which, she had informed Dr. Peter Franklin,
director of the Melville Foundation, not even wild
horses would compel her to attend? She had arrived
this early because in half an hour the catering staff,
and then the security guards without whom no New
York social occasion would be complete, were due to
arrive, considerably diminishing her chances of getting inside the building without being seen. The
reason she did not wish to be seen was that she was
planning to kill the guest of honor and wanted to be as
unobtrusive about it as she could.

Matthew Zimwi would not be the first person Susan
Melville had sent to his last reward, nor would he,
unless she was unlucky, be the last. Like so many of
the other old New York families, the Melvilles had a
long tradition of public service. They had founded
some institutions, served on the boards of others,
contributed to charity, and lent their names to causes

they deemed worthy. A few of the most zealous had even performed hands-on community service, though none quite so hands-on as Susan's.

Her line of good works consisted of executing individuals of bad character who were beyond the reach of the local law. Over the last few years, in her own quiet way, Susan had been very successful at this; and one of the secrets of her success had been that she prepared very thoroughly for each sortie. Never before, however, had she been forced to make such elaborate preparations as she had for this one, but never before had she been required to strike so close to home.

Susan didn't dare turn on a light in the basement, for, although the windows were covered with ornamental ironwork, this was designed to protect the interior from unauthorized entry, not to shield it from public view. The feeble beam of the pencil flashlight she had brought along was of little help in lighting her way through the shadowy masses that loomed up ahead of her. It had been a mistake, she thought, to give the workmen carte blanche to store their effects down here over the holidays. She had not realized there would be so much, or that the individual pieces would be so large and have so many painful protuberances. Each time she kicked something or tripped over something, she halted, fearful that someone on the floor above would hear the noises below and come down to investigate.

But no footsteps clattered down the narrow winding stairs; no creak came from the elevator. Not that it could creak, she recalled, because it was not there. Some days before, the elevator had been condemned by the building inspector and one of the last things the workmen had been supposed to do before they knocked off for the holidays was to eviscerate it. She had hoped that this mischance would put a stop to Peter's party plans; however, he pointed out, as the Foundation officially occupied only the first two floors of the building, the elevator was seldom used and did not enter into those plans.

Probably it was the elevator's innards that were taking up so much room, she thought. She noted with approval as she passed the elevator door that a notice saying "Out of Order" had been affixed to it. She had issued instructions that such notices were to be placed on all elevator doors—indeed, she believed that safety-code regulations required them—but workmen didn't always follow instructions (or safety-code regulations, either).

Just beyond the elevator door was the door to the back stairs, and beyond that, another door. Susan unlocked the third door, went inside, and relocked it behind her. An earlier tenant who went in for orgies had had this room soundproofed and the windows blocked, so she could safely turn on the light and breathe freely. She did both; then sat down on an old couch and relaxed. If she wished, she could read, listen to the radio, even have a bite to eat, for she had previously stocked her retreat with the wherewithal for all these activities. Now all she had to do was wait.

At this point in her life, Matthew Zimwi was not a person she would normally have chosen to kill. Once she might have considered an ousted tyrant an appropriate subject for her gun, but time and economic independence had mellowed her. Why bother with fallen tyrants who were unlikely to be in a position to commit any more atrocities when there were so many miscreants in power committing one atrocity after another? Furthermore, it was a long-standing custom of hers not to kill anyone over the Christmas holidays. Susan was not a conventionally religious woman, but she did feel there were certain things that should be kept sacred, even if you didn't believe in them.

However, Peter had forced her to put Zimwi at the top of her hit list. She and Peter had been together in the apartment they shared, preparing for quite another kind of party—the Fitzhorn Foundation's Winter Gala to benefit something or other; she went to so many affairs of that kind, she lost track of what they were for—when, casually, as if it were the most natural thing in the world, Peter told her he was planning to give a Christmas Eve party for Matthew Zimwi at the Melville Foundation Building.

Susan could not believe her ears. "You want to give a Christmas party for Matthew Zimwi—the Monster of Mazigaziland? Peter, either you're joking or you're crazy."

"I fail to see that either term applies, Susan. He was very hospitable to me when I went on that expedition to Mazigaziland back in '85. That's when he presented me with that beautiful tapestry that's hanging temporarily on the third floor until I can find a suitable place for it downstairs. It seems to me only fitting that I should try to repay his kindness."

"He's a sadist, a murderer, a cannibal. And that tapestry, as you call it, is an eyesore."

"Different cultures have different norms. You mustn't judge either the Mazigazians or their art by our standards."

"Apparently he was judged unworthy even by Mazi-gaziland standards. They threw him out, didn't they?"

"That was just politics," Peter scoffed.

"Politics or not, I'm sure, when you think it over, you'll see for yourself that it would be most inappropriate for you to give a party for him," Susan insisted. And when he opened his mouth, she added, "We'll talk about this after we come back from the gala. We're late already."

The subject of Matthew Zimwi inevitably came up at dinner, as subjects one is trying to avoid so often do. No one had a kind word for him. Tony Tuttle, the fashion designer, told the other guests at the table that he'd wanted to visit Mazigaziland some years back to study native dress. ". . . But the State Department strongly advised against it. They said, off the record, because Mazigaziland is one of our country's good friends and allies, that I stood a good chance of being eaten if I went."

"Well, you are a succulent little thing," said Mimi von Schwabe, who had been born a Fitzhorn, hence was hostess not only of the table but of the whole event. "I could eat you myself."

Everyone laughed dutifully, except Susan, who felt that she had done enough by paying two thousand dollars for the tickets, and Peter, who stuck up for all cultures except his own. "I don't see why everyone keeps harping on the Mazigazians' alleged cannibalism," he said testily. "Yes, they were cannibals once—as most peoples were if you go back far enough—but they gave it up generations ago. I know there's talk that Zimwi still went in for it, but nobody was ever able to prove a thing."

"How could they?" said a pudgy man whose name Susan hadn't caught but whom she'd seen on television either being let out of prison for insider trading or being put in prison for outsider trading. "The evidence was eaten."

"Whatever became of this Zimwi person?" Mimi asked. "Did they put him in the pot or did he get away?"

"He got away just in the nick of time," someone obscured from view by the floral centerpiece said. "He's said to be hiding now. Anyhow, nobody knows where he is."

"Hard for someone who's—what did *Time* say?—six feet, six inches tall and weighs three hundred pounds to hide," Tony Tuttle observed.

"I understand there's quite a substantial price on his head," the financier added wistfully. Financiers were always in need of capital. Besides, everyone could use a little extra cash at Christmas.

"I gather you know where Mr. Zimwi is," Susan said to Peter after they'd gotten back to the apartment; "otherwise you wouldn't have thought of giving him a party. Don't you see, though, that if you give him a party, everybody will know his whereabouts. There will be curiosity seekers, reporters, bounty hunters."

"I haven't told—I mean, I'm not going to tell—the guests whom the party is for. Afterward Zimwi's going directly to Washington—he's come here to seek asylum, you know—so let the reporters and curiosity seekers and bounty hunters bay at the Foundation's door; he won't be here for them to harass."

But you will be, she thought, and I will be. Not here, of course; I'll be sure to stay away for the next couple of weeks or months, but there's nothing to keep the reporters—she didn't worry about curiosity seekers and bounty hunters—from baying outside my apartment house. Over the years she had grown used to publicity, which was the natural concomitant of a successful artistic career; but, even if she was no longer able to keep her low profile, she had at least been able to keep her elevated image. The presence of Matthew Zimwi in the Melville Building would not enhance that image. Of course she could say she had nothing to do with inviting Zimwi, but people would either think she was lying, or that she was repudiating Peter.

She sighed. "Is Mr. Zimwi in New York at the moment?"

"Well, I don't suppose there's any harm in telling you—yes, he is."

"Where is he staying? I can't believe any hotel would have him, especially after what happened at the Mazigazi Hilton the year before he was thrown out."

"He's staying at a friend's apartment."

"I didn't know he had friends in New York. Or anywhere, for that matter. Anyone I know?"

Peter avoided her eye. "If you must know, he's staying in that old apartment of Roland's on the third floor of this building. I told the workmen to keep away from that floor until after the holidays. They have enough to do on the other floors. You've never objected to my letting guests stay there before, so I was sure you wouldn't mind now."

She'd never objected to his having guests there; she'd never objected—at least verbally—when he stayed there the night himself on occasions when he said he had to work late. The truth was, Susan had always suspected that he was dallying with his assistant, Dr. Katherine Froehlich, celebrated ethnologist and bimbo. She was furious but naturally she did not show it. "This is just a little different, Peter. Matthew Zimwi is not an ordinary guest."

Peter assumed his martyred look. "Of course it's your building and your Foundation. As director, I'm merely your employee, so to speak. If you're absolutely set against my letting him stay, there's nothing I can do. In the morning—I assume you won't mind if I wait until morning—I'll tell him he has to go."

That effectively stopped her, as he had known it would. He was an anthropologist; he knew the customs of her tribe. If she had been married to him, she could have put her foot down, but he was her lover— had been her lover for more years than most marriages endured in her circle—and so she had an obligation to him that would not have devolved upon a wife. "No, Peter, you're the director of the Foundation. Yours is the final authority. Although, strictly speaking, the apartment is not part of the Foundation. Remember, that's why we're renovating the place, so we can put the upper floors to use. And, speaking of renovations, I don't see how you can possibly think of giving a party with the place in such a mess."

"It isn't in nearly as much of a mess as it looks. All they've really done downstairs is dump that stuff in the foyer, and I've told them to put it down in the basement when they knock off for the holidays. That is, if I have your permission to tell them to put the stuff in the basement; that isn't part of the Foundation either, strictly speaking."

"Don't be silly, Peter. You know you've always been free to use the basement."

All except the back room. From the start Susan had reserved the back room as hers. In it she'd stored some bits and pieces that no longer fitted in her apartment but that she was reluctant to throw away. Mostly she'd wanted it as a place where she could keep her guns. The locked suitcases on the closet shelf in the apartment had become inadequate, not only for security reasons, but because one suitcase, or even two, would no longer be enough to contain them. Once she had discovered how easy it was to get guns in the South, she had found herself picking them up whenever she traveled, the way other people picked up antique napkin rings. In order to explain the maximum-security lock she'd had installed on the door, she'd let it be known that she kept some of her paintings there. Since Susan Melville's paintings sold well into the six figures, that was explanation enough.

She kept on trying to dissuade Peter from his ill-advised project. "How can you possibly expect to get a party organized at such short notice?"

He smiled in a superior sort of way. "This will be a quiet little private party, not one of those elaborate affairs you're always going to. I haven't even—I'm not going to send out invitations. I've—I'm just going to call up a few friends and colleagues—no more than thirty or forty or so—and ask them informally."

"Won't people already have made plans for Christmas Eve?"

"Not people like these—scholars, academics, intellectuals—simple folk, not your jet-setters and social butterflies, who make their plans weeks, even months, in advance. And most of the people I'm asking would jump at the chance to attend a party at the Foundation." Peter seemed very confident. But of course he was. He had already made sure of his guests before he sprang the party on Susan.

She sighed. "I can't stop you from giving your party," she said, which was not quite true, but she was reluctant to have a showdown with Peter, especially at Christmas. "But don't expect me to act as hostess."

"That will be a great disappointment, but I wouldn't want you to do anything that goes against your conscience. I'm sure Dr. Froehlich would be happy to act as hostess."

Susan went to bed and dreamed that she was chopping Dr. Froehlich into very small pieces with one of the primitive weapons with which the Foundation's offices abounded. When she awoke she found that Peter had already gotten up and was in one of the guest rooms contemplating his Oupi warrior outfit, which he had laid out on the bed. "It's getting to look a bit grungy," he mused. "I wonder whether I dare send it to the dry cleaner's."

"It has always looked grungy. Don't tell me you're planning to wear it again somewhere?" A dreadful suspicion hit her. "This party of yours—it isn't going to be a costume party, is it?"

"Oh, didn't I mention that it was going to be a costume party? I always think costume parties are so much more festive than—er—non-costume parties. And I'd like to know what happened to my spear!" He rummaged in the closet. "Oh, there it is. It looks as if somebody had been sticking things with it. If that housekeeper of yours—"

"Don't you dare say anything about the spear to

Michelle. She's going to be upset enough about those feathers you've gotten all over the bed."

The costume was ridiculous. Peter was ridiculous. He had looked a fool in it when he'd been young—well, younger—and still had his waistline and most of his hair. Now . . . Susan didn't like to think of how he would appear in it. But what did she care? He probably wouldn't look any more ridiculous than many of the others.

"I've asked all the guests to dress up in the costumes of their specialties," Peter went on. "For instance, Dr. Nestor will be an Ojibway chief and Dr. Rappaport a Mongolian tribesman. Dr. Kimmelman says she's coming as an Egyptian of the Middle Period. I don't know what Dr. Pastore will do—he's a bone man, you know—but I expect he'll think of something."

"He could come as a fossil," Susan suggested. "Which means he can just come as he is. What is Mr. Zimwi going to come as? Some sort of native garb? Which wouldn't exactly be a costume, would it?"

There was a pause. "He's coming as Santa Claus," Peter said.

She thought she must have heard wrong. "You mean he's going as some mythological Mazigazian figure with a similar name? Or a similar function?"

Peter shook his head.

"You don't mean he's coming as our Santa Claus, old Saint Nick, red suit, bag of gifts, ho, ho, ho? You don't mean that."

Peter said he did mean it. "Ever since his days at missionary school, Matthew told me, he's dreamed of being Santa Claus at a Christmas party but he never had the chance before. You'll have to admit he's the right shape for it. Strange, isn't it, that obesity, which is otherwise regarded by Americans as equivalent to, say, leprosy or pediculosis, is considered not only acceptable but endearing when it comes to Santa Claus? Now among the Magugu of Lower Gambogia—"

"Forget the Magugu. You're not going to stand there and tell me that Mr. Zimwi is going to be Santa Claus at this party of yours?"

"Why not?"

Susan was shocked. How dared the Monster of Mazigaziland dream of impersonating one of this culture's most cherished icons? And how dared Peter abet him in this act of sacrilege? She had been wrong to think that once Matthew Zimwi was deposed, he was powerless to commit any more significant atrocities. It would be the greatest atrocity of all if he were allowed to go through with this. That was when she decided that, holidays or no holidays, it was her moral duty to put an end to Matthew Zimwi.

Ever since the renovations on the building had begun, Susan had dropped in from time to time to keep an eye on things, more to establish her authority than in the mistaken belief that this would expedite the proceedings. Now she'd started coming in almost every day. "I am not going to let Mr. Zimwi's presence affect the work on the building," she told Peter. "I'm anxious that as much as possible gets done before the holidays, and, if it incommodes Mr. Zimwi—or the Foundation—that's too bad."

"It won't incommode him. In fact, I'm sure he'd be delighted to see you if you stopped by for a chat. He has to stay shut up in the apartment while the work-men are around, and it's pretty lonely now that his bodyguards have quit. He has nothing to do but sit and watch television."

Almost, Susan thought, Zimwi was paying for his sins.

"Dr. Froehlich and I both drop in whenever we can," Peter added, "but we're very busy with the preparations for the party, and, of course, with the Foundation's work."

"Oh, his bodyguards have quit, have they?" She could have coped with bodyguards, but this would make things much easier.

"I told him that in this country you're not allowed to kick your employees, but I couldn't get the concept across. I've been trying to get replacements, but it's very difficult this time of the year, when bodyguards are so much in demand, what with all the parties and meetings and demonstrations. If worst comes to worst, we'll just have to make do with the regular security guards we've always laid on for the occasion. They'll stay downstairs, so he won't have a chance to—"

"Impress them with his cultural differences?" Susan suggested.

"If you like to put it that way. Now, if you'll excuse me, there's Foundation work to be done."

Peter went off in the direction of his office, which was on the second floor. As soon as the door had closed behind him, Susan nipped up to the third floor. The apartment did not occupy the whole of that floor. On the other side of the hallway that bisected it was a large room which the previous owner had planned to use for the overflow of exhibits from his art gallery, a project cut short by his untimely death. Susan had not made it available to the Foundation because she felt that two floors were quite sufficient for the Foundation's purposes. In fact, two floors were more than enough for its purposes, which, as far as she could see, were to keep Peter happy and occupied. Sometimes she wondered why it was necessary to keep Peter happy and occupied. She was beginning to wonder why it was necessary to keep Peter at all.

Although Peter had never gone to the extent of formally taking possession of the room, little by little he had moved in some pottery here, some shrunken heads there, until most of his collections were stacked in heaps against the wall. "Just temporary," he kept assuring her, "until I've arranged suitably secure display cabinets for them. They're much too valuable to put down in the basement. Not as valuable as those paintings of yours, of course, at least not in monetary terms, but to an anthropologist they're priceless."

Susan hadn't really objected to his commandeering the room, but she had spoken out on the subject of the Zimwi tapestry. Actually it wasn't a tapestry but a loosely woven hanging made of a variety of native materials and depicting a variety of natives engaged in gross activities. It offended her from both an aesthetic and a moral standpoint. Also, even after all this time, it smelled. "Why did you have to put it up there? Why not in your offices?"

"It's the only wall space large enough to accommodate it."

"The wall isn't large enough to accommodate it. You've had to hang it over the door."

"That was deliberate," said Peter. "By concealing

the fact that there is a door, I've put temptation out of the way of my colleagues. There are archaeologists wandering about the place all the time and, although I am sorry to have to say this, some of them are very light-fingered. Once you start robbing tombs, you're capable of anything. I know the door is always kept locked, but some of those fellows are adept lock-pickers."

The lock presented no obstacle to Susan because, as owner of the building, she possessed keys to all the doors, including the little one in the rear that opened onto the back stairs. Her idea was to come into the room via the back door, open the front door, shoot Zimwi through his own hanging—a bit of poetic justice there—then depart via the back stairs.

First she examined the hanging from the back to see whether its interstices would be large enough for her to both see and shoot through. She didn't think they would suffice, so she came around to the front to see if it would be possible to enlarge some of the openings into out-and-out holes without making the alterations too noticeable.

Suddenly the floor behind her seemed to shake and she heard a rumbling sound. She turned. There stood Matthew Zimwi in the considerable flesh. He had, Susan thought, gained weight; she would judge him now to be at least four hundred pounds on the hoof. He also seemed to have grown; he looked more like ten feet tall rather than a simple six feet six, but that could be her imagination. In his bright-yellow silk robe, which she took at first to be some sort of ceremonial attire, then recognized as a dressing gown, he was an awesome sight.

"Dr. Froehlich," he said, "I am most displeased."

"Dr. Froehlich!" she repeated angrily. "I am not—" Susan bit off the disclaimer she was about to make. No doubt to him all white women looked alike. Let him take her for Dr. Froehlich. Then Peter need never know she'd been snooping around up here.

"Why are you displeased, Mr. Zimwi?" she asked, trying to make her voice dulcet and Froehlich-like. "Isn't everything to your satisfaction?"

"Nothing is to my satisfaction. There is no one to attend to my needs. I am forced to draw my own bath and dress myself. The food is bad. There is no more whiskey. And I was promised women." He looked at Susan appraisingly. "Young women. I am very disappointed in Dr. Franklin. Very disappointed, indeed."

"Dr. Franklin will be sorry to hear that. I'm sure he has done his best."

"I am sure he has not. He thinks that because I am no longer in power, I am of no account, but Matthew Zimwi will always be of account. Tell him that."

"I'll give Dr. Franklin your message," she said, showing all her teeth in an approximation of the Froehlich simper.

He turned and waddled away without so much as a thank-you. Pig, she thought.

That evening when she and Peter were having a simple dinner for two at the Quilted Giraffe, he told her about the arrangements he had made for the party. He was very proud of them. "The guests will be arriving at eight and there will be food and music and general jollification."

"Music?" Music was always good for drowning out the sound of a shot. "Will there be dancing?"

"Yes, anthropologists are particularly fond of dancing. They spend so much of their time observing, they welcome a chance to participate in their own tribal steps. Just records, of course. Nothing extravagant."

"Just records!" Susan was outraged. "I don't want to encourage you into extravagance, but you don't want to go too far in the other direction. How would it look for a party at the Melville Foundation to have canned music? Chintzy! No, you must have an orchestra, Peter—a good loud one with plenty of percussion. And how many guests did you say you were having?"

"Fifty, well, maybe sixty. Since there's going to be a buffet rather than a sit-down dinner, I figured I could keep the guest list flexible."

It would be impractical, she had realized, for her to retreat to her basement lair after she had polished off Zimwi, because the police were likely to search the whole place; they were always so officious after a murder. She would have to wear a costume and disappear into the crowd of guests, in which case the bigger the crowd, the better. "Have a hundred," she said. "A hundred's such a nice round number."

"It is, isn't it?" he said. "Well, a hundred it shall be."

"Will Mr. Zimwi be dressed as Santa Claus on the receiving line?"

"No, as I've said, this will be quite informal. Besides, I don't want to spoil the surprise. There isn't going to be a receiving line. In fact, he won't make his appearance until it's time for Santa Claus to arrive— around nine or so. I'll come down first, make a short speech, and tell the guests of the treat they have in store, after which Dr. Froehlich has planned to play a few bars of stirring music on the piano. However, if there's to be an orchestra, then the orchestra will give him a fanfare and play a march, possibly the national anthem of Mazigaziland, provided they can learn it at such short notice. Matthew will make his entrance and make another speech, which I hope will be equally short. Like most dictators, he does tend to be rather long-winded, since he's used to a captive audience. After that, he will join in the festivities. What do you think?"

"It sounds very . . . well-planned."

"You seem to be taking quite an interest. Are you sure you don't want to act as hostess after all? It's always been a woman's prerogative to change her mind, you know."

After which they had their short exchange on the subject of wild horses and he returned to the Foundation while she went to the apartment to ponder on her choice of costume.

Susan decided to go as Annie Oakley. That way she could carry her gun openly in the holster; otherwise she'd need to wear a costume that included a handbag, and the only one she could think of was a suffragette, which she didn't much care for. She had a happy thought. She would provide herself with a water pistol. On her way back from the shoot she would substitute it for the real gun, just in case the police got snoopy. It was these little details, she thought, that really counted.

Now it was Christmas Eve, and so far everything had gone smoothly. At half past eight, Susan started putting on her costume. At a quarter to nine, she unlocked the door of her retreat and emerged into the main body of the basement. Above her she could hear the strains of music and what sounded like a herd of cattle stampeding. No need for her to move quietly; she could have fired off a cannon down there and no one would hear.

She opened the door to the back stairs and recoiled as her nose was hit by a pungent odor of cooking. Obviously Glorious Foods had not been engaged to do the catering. The door to the kitchen stood open, and she could hear voices. She hesitated. She had not counted on having to pass an open door. If anyone inside looked out, she told herself, all they would see was an errant guest. If they accosted her, she would identify herself, say she had come to surprise Peter, and go out and join the party; then either try to sneak up the back stairs from the second floor or give up her plans entirely.

If, however, the denizens of the kitchen merely observed her passing, but made no move to stop or speak to her, she would proceed with her plans, bearing in mind that later they might remember having seen a guest where no guest should have been. Pity she hadn't had a contingency costume to change into, but really she couldn't be expected to think of everything.

The contingency didn't arise. When Susan tiptoed past the kitchen, the people inside, glimpsed only hazily through clouds of steam, were so engaged in argument that they would not, she fancied, have noticed a troupe of orangutans tap-dancing their way upstairs.

The door to the second floor was shut, as it should have been. She climbed to the third floor, opened the door to the back hall, and unlocked the back door to the big room. She crossed the room and unlocked the door behind the hanging.

By this time, Susan figured, Peter should be in the apartment with Zimwi, helping him put on his Santa suit. She listened, but all she could hear was the distant strains of the orchestra. Then, over the music, she could hear the clomp, clomp of footsteps coming closer. According to plan, this should be Peter, but it sounded more like Frankenstein's monster. Through the holes in the hanging she could see a figure approaching. But it was the wrong figure. Instead of pallid white skin with feathers, red plush with whiskers. Santa Claus was coming first. They must have changed the order. Why? Didn't Zimwi want Peter to introduce him? Didn't Peter want to introduce Zimwi? Had something happened to Peter? Had Zimwi, in a fit of pique at the inadequacy of the hospitality offered him, done something violent to Peter?

She would worry about Peter later. Right now she must act fast or miss her chance of cutting Zimwi down before he got out of range. She lifted her gun, aimed it, and hesitated. There was something wrong with Santa Claus as Santa Claus. He seemed strangely shrunken. The red plush hung around him in great flopping folds. Pillows had been pushed inside in an effort to remedy his lack of girth; instead, they called attention to their presence by slipping and sliding in a manner that was almost obscene. Could Matthew Zimwi have lost a couple of hundred pounds in the last two days? But that wouldn't explain why his boots didn't fit, or why the face above the white beard was equally white. And why was he wearing gold-rimmed spectacles? Matthew Zimwi did not wear gold-rimmed spectacles. Santa Claus did not wear gold-rimmed spectacles. But Peter Franklin wore gold-rimmed spectacles.

It was Peter who was approaching in the Santa Claus suit. She did not lower her gun. What a host of problems would be removed if she fired now. No more unwanted guests, no more intrusions on her privacy, no more screams from her manager about the Foundation's excessive disbursements. Best of all, no more Dr. Froehlich.

"Who's that behind the tapestry?" Peter demanded. "Come out, I see you."

She had made the holes too big. But it didn't matter. She could still shoot him, she thought, and make her escape as planned, possibly pausing at the apartment to shoot Zimwi as she left. Perhaps she could pot Dr. Froehlich on her way out and make a clean sweep.

It was a great temptation. But the Melvilles had been brought up to resist temptation. She lowered the gun and came out from behind the hanging.

"Susan! What on earth are you doing with that toy pistol? I hope you're not planning to squirt me with water. If I get spots on the plush, I might not get back the full deposit for the costume."

"I wanted to surprise you," she said, putting the gun in her holster with a sigh of regret.

"It's not like you to play such childish tricks. What if I had been Matthew?"

"I wouldn't have come out. I was watching through the holes in the hanging, and when I saw the Santa suit I thought at first it was Mr. Zimwi. Where is he, anyway?"

"Dead to the world," Peter said. "Don't get alarmed; he's just dead drunk. I've been trying to keep him sober, but somehow he got hold of a couple of bottles of whiskey—bribed one of the workmen, I wouldn't be surprised. Can't have Santa Claus staggering downstairs, I told him. I thought maybe we could wait and I could sober him up with a little coffee, but he kept insisting he was going to be Santa Claus right away and nobody was going to stop him. He picked up my spear. I was afraid he was going to attack me with it. Then—"

"You tore it from his grasp?" Perhaps she had misjudged Peter.

"Not exactly."

Still she gave him the benefit of the doubt. "You knocked him out?"

"Not that either. He passed out cold."

"Oh," she said.

"There was nothing left for me to do but get into the Santa Claus suit myself. I put it on as quickly as I could and left, locking the door behind me. I hope the guests won't be disappointed."

"Why should they be? All you did was promise them a surprise, and the sight of you in that Santa Claus suit would surprise anybody."

He looked at her suspiciously. "I'm sure they're expecting something more—well—dramatic." He wriggled and some of his stuffing slid, making it look as if he were about to give birth at any moment. "I'm aware that the suit doesn't fit as well as it might. I tried to eke it out with pillows, but there weren't enough on hand."

"Come back in here," she said, pulling him into the room behind the hanging. "As I was passing through, I noticed a pile of pillows back in the corner that should do nicely."

"Those are Madungu cushions. Very rare and valuable, since the Madungus are extinct."

"They won't be any less rare and valuable through having served as Santa Claus's belly and may perhaps gain added historical interest." Despite his protestations, she stuffed him with the Madungu cushions until he was round and tight.

"Poor Matthew," Peter said. "He will be so disappointed at having missed the party. I wish I could— no, I daren't let him out later because, even though he may have sobered up somewhat, there's no guarantee that he will be any less violent."

"You can tell him about it later," she said. If there was a later. She hadn't given up her mission. In fact, it would be much easier now. She'd let Peter introduce her; then, when Santa Claus was distributing his gifts, she'd slip upstairs, dispose of Zimwi, and return to the party. With any luck, that meant his body wouldn't be discovered until the party was over and the guests, including herself, long gone.

Peter offered her his arm. "Shall we make a grand entrance together?"

"Santa Claus and Annie Oakley?"

"Oh, is that who you're supposed to be? I thought you were an elf."

"An elf with a gun?"

"This is New York. Even the elves are likely to carry guns."

They stood together at the head of the main staircase that led down to the first floor. The guests— ancient Egyptians, cave persons, Eskimos, Hindu deities, and a variety of ethnic entities she could not identify, gathered below with expectant cries. There was a drumroll followed by a flourish of trumpets.

"Ladies and gentlemen . . ." Peter began and stopped. Obviously it had just occurred to him that the speech he had prepared would not work. It had been designed to introduce Santa Claus, not to be spoken by Santa Claus. Peter looked helplessly at Susan.

"Improvise," she whispered, hoping she would not have to make his speech for him.

But there turned out to be no need for a speech. At that moment a bloodcurdling scream came from the back of the building, a scream so terrible that it made Susan's flesh crawl; and if it did that to a Melville, what must it be doing to the guests clustered below? This was followed by a crash that seemed to shake the building to its foundations.

It took a while before anybody was able to find out what had happened. Apparently Zimwi had come to and, determined to go to the party, had set out in his dressing gown. He could not reach the stairs because the door to the apartment was locked, and so, forgetting the warning that had been given him, overlooking the sign outside (or, as Susan always suspected, unable to read it; she had never thought much of missionary schools), he had opened the door to the elevator and plunged down the shaft to the basement. A lighter man might possibly have survived, but for a man of Matthew Zimwi's weight, the fall was inevitably fatal.

"The medical examiner tells me that he died instantly," the detective in charge told them after the body had been cleared away. "He couldn't have suffered."

"Oh, I am glad to hear that," Dr. Froehlich, who had joined the executive group unasked, said, clasping her hands as if in prayer. "Such a sad end to such bright hopes!"

"I'm afraid your Christmas has been spoiled," the detective said.

Susan gave the sad smile that the police—a sentimental lot—would expect under the circumstances, but her heart was full of cheer. She had not, after all, had to break her rule of not killing anyone over the holidays, and although she felt a bit disappointed at not having killed Zimwi herself, still, there were plenty of other evil individuals she intended to dispatch as soon as the new year began. She was not going to begrudge an act of God, especially at Christmas.

"I guess this means the party is over," Peter said sadly.

"I don't see why," she said. "They've taken the body out through the basement, so the guests have been spared any actually grisly sights, although, heaven knows, in their profession they should be used to them. Anthropologists," she said, in reply to the detective's questioning look.

"Ah," he said.

"None of the guests was actually acquainted with him, and accidents are always happening at parties."

"They are, indeed," the detective said. "I could tell you stories of accidents at parties . . ."

She smiled at him. "So I don't see any reason why the party can't go on as planned—or almost as planned, anyhow. And I hope that you and your men will join us in a glass of eggnog or glogg or whatever seasonal libation the caterers have laid on for the occasion."

"There are reporters outside and it's snowing," Dr. Froehlich said. "Shouldn't I ask them to come in and join us?"

"This is a private party," Susan said. "Let them stand out in the snow."

If she was going to get adverse publicity out of this—and she knew she would—she might as well have a little revenge first. She wished she could tell Dr. Froehlich to go out and join them in the snow but it would mean a scene, and she detested scenes. After New Year's she would make Peter fire Dr. Froehlich. Maybe Susan would think of some way of saving Peter's face. And then again, maybe she wouldn't.

In Canada, crime writing is a fairly recent phenomenon, yet mystery writers are already being taken far more seriously by the mainstream literary establishment there than in many other countries. Eric Wright's first book won him a City of Toronto Prize for an important contribution to Canadian literature. Since then, he's received international recognition in a number of ways, but here's one that really takes the frosted bun:

The Globe and Mail, *Canada's most prestigious newspaper, ran an article lamenting the dearth of truly memorable characters in today's fiction. It asked how many readers could identify these landmark figures in literature: Uriah Heep, Mr. Micawber, Eliza Doolittle, Charlie Salter, and Fagin. Eric's portrayal of a Toronto policeman's everyday life in its many vicissitudes is far subtler than Dickens's or Shaw's splashy portraits, but no less unforgettable.*

You won't meet Charlie Salter in this story, but you'll see why Eric got put on the list.

198

ERIC WRIGHT

TWO IN THE BUSH

From the day The Boozer became my cell mate and first told me about Clyde Parker, it took us nearly a year to set him up. In the end, though, the long delay turned out to be for the best because when we did catch up with him, the timing, Christmas Eve, was perfect.

Clyde Parker was the owner of a pub on King Street East. The Old Bush was a beer parlor, not a "men only" parlor but not the kind of place that ladies felt comfortable in, either, and as the man said, those that came in left, or they did not remain ladies very long. It had graduated from being one of the worst holes in the east end of the city to being quaint, one of the last unrenovated survivors of the days when drink was as feared as polyunsaturated fat is now. The Old Bush was such a relic that it was discovered a few years ago by a wine columnist who wrote an article about it which brought in a few people who were looking for an authentic experience, but they didn't come back once they'd got it. The regular patrons stared at them.

If there was only one or two of these tourists they'd leave them alone, but if six or eight of them came in, someone would give a signal and the pub would go quiet as the regular patrons stared at them. They didn't like that. A lot of old-timers used the place, and you could generally count on finding a few rounders there on a weeknight.

It was The Boozer who put us on to the fact that Clyde Parker, the owner, might be whispering into the ear of the coppers. I say "might" because we weren't sure for a long time, which was why we didn't go for Parker in a heavy way as soon as Boozer had tipped us. We had to give him the benefit of the doubt.

The Boozer had just done a nice little job over in Rosedale. At the time he was paying a window cleaner to let him know of any empties he came across, and one day he reported that the inhabitants of a certain house on Crescent Road had gone on vacation, and access was relatively simple. The Boozer duly dropped by at 3 A.M. with a few copies of *The Globe and Mail* in case anyone was about, let himself in the back door, and helped himself to a sackful of small stuff—silver, jewelry, and such, including a real piece of luck, a twenty-ounce gold bar he found in a desk drawer. The Boozer claimed it was about the cleanest little job he'd ever done. He worked with Toothy Maclean on lookout. Utterly reliable, Toothy was. So when they came for The Boozer, three days later, he had a long think and the only one he could see shopping him was Clyde Parker.

See, the night after the job, The Boozer had called in at the Bush for a few draft ales, and to pay for his beer he off-loaded a few trinkets, cuff links and such, on Old Perry. Old Perry paid him about a tenth of what they were worth, which in itself was about a tenth of what you'd have to pay in a store, but The Boozer was thirsty and he had plenty of goods left. Old Perry made his living by having the money in his pocket when you were thirsty, and we'd all dealt with him. We'd have known years ago if he was a nark. The other alternative, Toothy Maclean, was unthinkable. Then The Boozer remembered that Clyde Parker had been hovering round when he passed the stuff over to Old Perry, so he began to wonder. He confided in me and the two of us did some asking around and we came up with three others who'd been fingered not long after they'd brushed up against Parker. So that's how it was; we didn't have any proof, but we were pretty sure.

The Boozer wanted to send a message to the outside to have Parker done, but I talked him out of it. Not too heavy, I told him, because we might be wrong, and anyway, let's do it ourselves, let's be there when it happens. I was beginning to get an idea; though, when The Boozer asked, I said I didn't know yet. We had plenty of time to think about it. I got The Boozer calmed down, but he said if I didn't get a good idea, then he'd torch the Bush as soon as he got out.

I wanted something a bit subtler than that. I wanted to hurt Parker in his pride and his wallet at the same time, I wanted to cost him money and make him look foolish, and, if possible, I wanted him to know who'd done it without him being able to do anything about it. It wouldn't be easy getting past all those pugs that Parker used as waiters to look out for him.

About three-quarters of the way through our term—me and The Boozer had both of us still a couple of months to do—I got an idea. Or rather, I got the last piece of an idea I'd been putting together for a few months. Ideas are like that with me.

The first part of the idea came from a cell mate I'd had at the beginning of my stretch. He'd got ninety days for impersonating a Salvation Army man. You know, going door to door, soliciting contributions and giving you a blessing with the receipt. What he'd done, he'd got a Salvation Army cap one night from the hostel when no one was watching, and another night he got a pad of receipts off the desk in the office, and with a black raincoat and a shirt and tie he looked the part perfectly. He said he picked up five hundred a night, easy, in a district like Deer Park. A lot of people gave him checks, of course, which he threw away, but he didn't count on them calling the office when the checks didn't go through. (A lot of people *deserve* to be inside.) Two months later the coppers were waiting for him. He should have worked it for a week, then stayed off the streets for at least six months, as a Sally Ann collector, I mean. There's plenty of other things he could have been doing. But he got greedy and silly and they caught up with him taking up a collection round the Bunch of Grapes on Kingston Road. So that's where I got a bit of an idea.

I got the second part of my idea at a prison concert. You had to attend, and there was this citizen on the bill, singing a lot of old-fashioned songs. "Sons of Toil and Sorrow" was one. "A Bachelor Gay Am I" was another. In prison, I ask you. Some of the younger cons thought he'd made the songs up himself. And it wasn't just the choice of song. He couldn't sing. He was terrible—loud and embarrassing, hooting and hollering away, the veins sticking out all over his neck as he tried to get near the notes. The others nicknamed him Danny Boy, which he said was his signature tune. I thought, you should stick to hymns, buddy, because he reminded me exactly of a carol singer who used to sing with a Salvation Army band when I was a kid.

Then I realized that I had it.

All I needed was a trumpet player and someone on the accordion, and we were all set.

Me and The Boozer were both sprung in October and we moved in together. My wife had visited me once to tell me not to try going home again, ever, and Boozer had no home, so we found this little apartment on Queen Street near the bail and parole unit where we had to appear from time to time.

We were both on welfare, of course, at first; then we both found jobs of the kind that offered no temptation, and that no one else wanted. The Boozer got taken on at a car wash, and I found a situation in a coal-and-wood yard, filling fifty-pound sacks with coal. Neither of us needed the work. Boozer had gone down protesting his innocence, so he still had his loot stashed away, but he couldn't touch it for a few months because they were watching him. As for me, I was always the saving kind.

Did I tell you what I got shipped for? I sell hot merchandise on the streets. You've seen me, or someone like me, if you've ever gone shopping along the Danforth. I'm the one who jumps out of a car and opens a suitcase full of Ralph Lauren sweatshirts that I am prepared to let go for a third of the price, quick, before the cops come. You buy them because you think they're stolen, which is the impression I'm trying to create, but in point of fact I buy them off a Pakistani jobber on Spadina for five dollars each. I'd pay ten if they weren't seconds and the polo player looked a bit more authentic. I've sold them all—fake Chanel Number 5, fake Gucci, Roots, the lot. Anything to appeal to the crook in you. Sometimes the odd case of warmish goods does come my way, but I prefer to deal in legit rubbish if I can get it.

So there I was, unloading a suitcaseful of shirts that had withstood a warehouse fire, good shirts if a bit smoky, and the fuzz nabbed me for being an accomplice to a dip.

I was working the dim-sum crowd on the corner of Spadina and Dundas on a Sunday morning and I was just heading for my car to load up again, when someone shouted his wallet was gone, and then another shouted, and then another. Before you knew it, two martial-arts experts grabbed me and the cops were called and I got twelve months. I never even saw the dip.

But to get back to my story. First I had to get a couple of musicians. That wasn't easy until I bumped into one in the lineup at the bail and parole unit, a guy I'd known inside, who played in the prison band. He played trumpet, or cornet really, when he wasn't doing time for stealing car radios. He found me a trombone player. Then I had a real piece of luck because right after that I ran into the original authentic terrible hymn singer from the prison concert.

At first he wouldn't hear of it, but I went to work on him and he saw the virtue in what we were planning and promised to think it over. The next time we met, he agreed. I should have known.

We decided we could manage without an accordion player.

Now we had to get some uniforms. All we really

needed were the caps. The trumpet player used to be a legit chauffeur and he still had his old black jacket, and he thought he could put his hand on some others. The owner of the limousine fleet kept a bundle of uniforms in his garage storeroom, and Digger Ray assured us that getting access to them would not be a problem. Digger Ray was the trombone player. He was Australian and his specialty was playing the fake sucker in crooked card games, but he'd done a few B and E jobs. Toothy Maclean lifted the caps for us while The Boozer created a disturbance during prayers at the Salvation Army shelter. (He started crying and repenting right in the middle of a prayer and Toothy got all the caps from the office while they were comforting him.)

Now The Boozer had to line up three or four cooperating citizens who would be unknown to Clyde Parker, fellas who didn't use the Old Bush. It wasn't easy, but Boozer came up with three guys who hardly ever drank—not too common among his acquaintance, I can tell you—and once they heard about it they were keen to be included. So we were set. Now I had to go to work. I had the trickiest job of all.

I was the obvious person to approach Clyde Parker because I'd only been in the Bush once, years ago. I hate the place, always have. It's the kind of beer parlor where there's a civil war being fought at every table and the waiters are hired to break up fights, and if you stay until midnight someone will throw up all over your shoes. I like a nice pub, myself.

So Parker didn't know me and when I approached him he was very wary, at first. I went in two or three times until I was sure who he was, then I got talking to him. Had he heard, I asked, of this fake Salvation

Army band that was going around the pubs collecting?
He hadn't, but if they came near the Old Bush, he'd be
ready, he said. He nodded to indicate a couple of his
waiters who were lounging against the wall, waiting
for orders. I don't know where he finds them, but they
look as if he has to chain them up when the pub is
closed. No, no, I said, there's a better way than that,
and then I told him.

People like Parker are born suspicious, but they are
also born greedy and very conceited. They think they
are smart. So the plan was designed to make Parker
feel smart, which it did, and to make him some money,
and when he saw the point, he was in.

It was a lovely night, Christmas Eve. About ten
o'clock the sky was black and clear with thousands of
stars winking away. It must have been like that the
night one of them started to move. I'd've followed it.

Danny Boy had the car and we were to meet at my
place. I drove after that. We reached the street behind
the Bush at ten-fifteen. Zero hour was ten-thirty. We
figured four carols, about fifteen minutes, then the
collection during one more, and out of there by
eleven.

They waited in the car while I slipped across to the
pub and made sure Hooligan was in place. Didn't I
mention Hooligan? His real name was Halligan, and
renaming him Hooligan tells you something about the
level of wit in the Don Jail. He was our ace in the
hole, the one Parker didn't know about. Because of
him we had to steal another cap, and this time I
couldn't get to one nohow. Then Toothy remembered
that a buddy of his had a dog that his kids had trained
to catch Frisbees. It got very good at picking them out

of the air, but the trouble was that when there were no
Frisbees to chase, he filled in the time chasing kids
and snatching their hats off. He was harmless, but
parents complained, and they had to keep him locked
up. The kids could get him to snatch anyone's hat by
pointing to it and whispering. As I say, Herman never
hurt anyone. He could take off your hat from behind
clean as a whistle without touching you, just one leap.
So we borrowed Herman one night and waited near
the Salvation Army shelter and pretty soon out came
an officer and set off down Sherbourne Street. A few
minutes later Herman lifted his hat. It fit Hooligan
pretty good, too.

I checked that Hooligan was in place, and in we
went. Parker had arranged a little clear space by the
door, though he pretended to be surprised when we
walked in. I approached him, very formal-like, and
asked his permission to play some carols and pass
round the collection plate. He acted up a bit by
shaking his head, then he seemed to change his mind.
"All right," he said. "Four carols." I looked grateful
and swung my arm the way conductors do, and off
they went.

A trumpet and a trombone wouldn't amount to
much, you would think, but these fellas made them
seem just made for the job. Very simple, just the notes,
no twiddly bits. They were *good*. And of course, there
was Danny Boy. He was as good as another trumpet.
He didn't wait for a cue. Just started right in, head
back, veins sticking out. He could be heard right in
the back of the room, right in the corners. They started
with "O Come, All Ye Faithful," which Danny Boy
gave a verse in Latin of, then "Good King Wenceslas"
and "We Three Kings," and finally, one of Danny's

shut-eyed ones, "O Holy Night." By then we had them. Danny was terrible, of course, but he was very sincere and you could recognize the tunes. I wouldn't say anyone was crying—this was the Old Bush, after all—but they were quiet. So now we went into "O Little Town of Bethlehem," very soft, "piano" they call it, and Toothy and I began the rounds with the money bags.

This was Parker's signal. We was getting something from nearly everyone, a dollar here, two there, a five, then another. There's a psychology to these things. As soon as someone puts in five dollars, that becomes standard, like the ante in a poker game. People stop fingering their change and open their wallets. After four tables, five was normal. Then Parker spoke. "Gents," he said. "Gents, this is Christmas Eve." He paused, looking sincere. "I want to announce that I will match all contributions made tonight toward this good cause."

"And a free beer all around," someone shouted.

One of the waiters moved to throw him out, but Parker only hesitated for a second. "Never mind the free beer tonight, of all nights," he said, implying that free beer was standard on other nights at the Bush. "Tonight is for the others out there." He waved at the door. "The ones with no beer," he said.

The arrangement was, of course, that Parker would get half, three-quarters, really, including his own money, but free beer could never be recovered.

The next voice, though, nearly took him off balance, I reached a table where The Boozer had planted one of his cronies, and Boozer gave him a wink from the back of the room, and he jumps up and shouts, "Then here's fifty dollars."

Parker looked a bit greasy for a minute, but he caught himself in time to shout, "Good for you."

Then the fever took hold. The biggest single contribution we got was a hundred dollars, but no one gave less than twenty, and every time I came to one of The Boozer's cronies he would whip up the excitement with a fresh fifty. We went round the room with Danny Boy crooning away in the background, and when we were done we went back to the counter and emptied the bags onto the bar. Digger Ray and one of the bartenders counted it and Digger made the announcement. "Two thousand three hundred and twenty-seven." Someone shouted, "Your turn now, Parker."

Parker turned to the barman and held out his hand and received a wad of money which he handed over to Digger. Digger held it up to show it was a lot of money, no need to count it on Christmas Eve, and he swept all the money back into one of the bags and we were ready to go. There was still three minutes on my watch, so I made a little speech, and then, right on time, Hooligan made his entrance.

He was got up like the rest of us—Salvation Army gear, and a little collection box.

We'd rehearsed the next bit carefully.

"Merry Christmas all, and God bless you," Hooligan says, while the crowd started to look a bit puzzled.

Parker looked at me in a panic. The smell of something fishy was now reaching into the farthest corners of the room and I would have given the patrons about ten more seconds. "Holy Jesus," I said to Parker. "It's a real one. What'll we do now? There'll be a riot if they find out."

The two musicians and Danny Boy slid out the door

and one of the patrons said, "What the hell's going on?"

"Give him the money," I said. "For God's sake, give him the money."

Parker couldn't speak, but he nodded, and I stepped forward.

"Coals to Newcastle," I said very loud and heartily. "Coals to Newcastle, sending two groups to the same place. But you're just in time, Captain. Here." I handed him the sack of money.

Hooligan's eyes rolled up in holy wonder. "Bless you, gentlemen," he said. "Bless you."

I was praying he wouldn't do anything silly like make the sign of the cross over the room, and I signaled to Toothy that we should be on our way. Then I heard a sound that made my blood run cold. Someone opened the door and "Joy to the World" came flooding through, played by all fifteen members of the Salvation Army's silver band.

Parker, of course, was not surprised. Hooligan was *his* surprise, and he assumed that the band was backup for him.

Now there was just me and Toothy—Hooligan could look after himself—so I put my hand on Toothy's shoulder in a brotherly way and we almost got through the door before we were stopped by Sister Anna herself. She looked at Hooligan, puzzled. Hooligan looked at me. Parker looked at us both, and I did the only thing I could. I took the money off Hooligan, put it in the sister's hands, said, "Merry Christmas, Sister," and took Toothy and Hooligan with me through the door.

The car was gone, of course—the motto with us, if a job goes wrong, is "Pull the ladder up, Jack. I'm in." But no one was chasing us, so we threw our caps away and hailed a cab.

*　*　*

We waited until after New Year's, then we got an educated friend of Toothy's to pretend to be a reporter for a news station doing a story on Christmas giving, and the Salvation Army commander told him what had happened. "Someone phoned us, here at the shelter," the commander said. "They told us if we would come to the Old Bush and play a few carols, we would get a major contribution. We gathered it was some kind of surprise, arranged by the proprietor."

We never knew for a long time who had done it; then, about six months after, The Boozer and I were stopped dead in Nathan Phillips Square by the sight of Danny Boy, eyes closed, head back, in the middle of "Abide With Me." He was in full uniform. Behind him was the Salvation Army silver band.

We waited for him to come round with the collecting box. We kept our heads down, and when he drew level I looked up sharply. "Hello, Danny Boy," I said. "How long you been with this mob?"

He looked surprised, but not for long. "I saw the light last Christmas," he said. "Brother." And he moved away, shaking his box. The Salvation Army were just being charitable, of course, welcoming the backslider, never mind that his singing hadn't improved a bit, not to sinners' ears, anyway. You could say that what mattered was that he was in tune with God.

The Boozer wanted to do him right then and there, but I held him off. As I pointed out, it had cost us nothing, but Parker was out a couple of thousand, and the boys in the Old Bush (to whom we'd slipped the story) were still laughing.

Even on a good day, you can't win every race.

*Mickey Friedman's "The Fabulous Nick"
provides a new slant on a familiar Christmas
figure who finds himself playing detective in
Greenwich Village.*

*Mickey says part of this story is pure wish
fulfillment. The house where "The Fabulous
Nick" takes place is a replica of the brownstone in which she lives with her husband, a
museum director. She has often fantasized
that their fireplaces, all nonworking, would
someday be repaired.*

*Mickey Friedman grew up on the Gulf
Coast in the Florida panhandle, has done
college public relations in Ohio, been a reporter in San Francisco, and spent a year and
a half writing in Paris. Always a fan, she's
been publishing mystery novels (six to date)
since 1983. Mickey says she writes about the
places she knows, and she's certainly been in
some interesting places. But chimneys?*

MICKEY FRIEDMAN

THE FABULOUS NICK

Nick gets a lot of mail, most of it predictable variations of "Gimme." These requests come with the territory like the red suit and the twinkly image.

Nick is not quite the bowlful of jelly the ads portray. Barrel-chested maybe, but solid. And he doesn't find life as hilarious as the constant braying of his imitators would have you believe.

This letter, for instance, addressed to Nick in a childish hand, is not funny. The kid gets right to the point: "I hate you! Stay away from us!" Signed Jason T. McGuire, with an address in New York City that Nick, having considerable knowledge of geography, recognizes as Greenwich Village.

Hm. Nick almost never gets "I hate you." Certainly not the week before his big night, when everybody is crazy about him. There has been a screw-up some-where along the line, which happens when you get so many, many conflicting needs. Nick is going to have to do something about it, busy season or no busy season.

* * *

Jason Thomas McGuire, age seven, is slumped in a chair in the principal's office at his Greenwich Village elementary school. Jason is a wiry child whose big feet are dangling a couple of inches above the floor. He is brown-haired, freckled, and until recently, when he became an utter hellion, he was a great kid. The principal, an understanding woman who knows something about Jason's problems, is talking to Jason's mother on the telephone. Jason will be going home as soon as his mother can leave work and come to get him.

Upstairs, in the corridor outside Jason's classroom, a custodian, with rag and bucket of cleanser, scrubs at an obscene suggestion involving Santa Claus that Jason scrawled on the wall in red crayon. Jason's teacher caught him in the act.

The principal puts down the phone. She says, "Your mom's on the way, Jason."

No answer. Jason slumps lower. On a table by the principal's desk is a small decorated tree. Jason considers knocking the tree over and running out the door, but rejects the idea because it isn't trees he hates.

"Sorry you'll miss the party this afternoon. We'll see you after Christmas."

Jason shudders and turns his head away.

"Let's hope for better times in the new year, all right?"

Jason shrugs. Who cares about the new year?

The next morning, a cold, gray Saturday, Nick strolls down a quiet residential street in Greenwich Village. Dirt-encrusted piles of snow from an early flurry or two lie in shadowy corners between the brownstones.

Some doors have wreaths on them, and every now and then a decorated tree is visible through tall parlor-floor windows. Pleasant. More the kind of neighborhood where kids request ecologically correct toys or the latest video games. What reason would a child in this neighborhood have for hating Nick?

Nick is not in uniform today. Instead of his signature garb, he is wearing a knitted watch cap, a down vest over a flannel shirt in the Royal Stewart tartan, grubby jeans, work boots. He is carrying a large toolbox. He finds the address, an Italianate house with a fanlight and leaded glass panels beside the green door. He studies the four doorbells and leans on the one marked "McGuire." Soon, a woman's voice yells, "Who is it?" through the squawk box.

"Chimney man!" bawls Nick.

"*What?*"

"Chimney man. Get the fireplaces working. Landlord sent me."

"The fireplaces in this building haven't worked in years." The woman's voice is scratchy and distorted through the box.

"Landlord sent me, lady."

"Just a minute."

While Nick is waiting, he extracts a dog-eared business card from the pocket of his down vest. When, through the leaded panel, he see a woman approaching, he presses the card against the glass so she can read it. Without opening the door, she comes close and squints at the card. She reads aloud, "Santos, Angeles, and Evangelistas. Chimney and Flue Specialists."

Nick points at himself. "Nick Santos."

The woman looks at him skeptically. "You'll have to wait while I check with the landlord."

"Okey-doke." The woman disappears again, and Nick lounges against the wrought-iron fence and whistles "Here Comes Santa Claus" until she returns to let him in. If he couldn't convince a New York landlord to rehabilitate a few fireplaces, he'd hardly be worthy of his job.

Carol McGuire, a fair-haired woman in a green velour sweat suit, looks too worried and wasted to be pretty, but obviously she used to be. She stands with her arms folded watching Nick, who is lying on his back in the McGuire living room with his head in the fireplace, shining his flashlight up the chimney. "How long is this going to take?" she asks.

"Hard to say. I've got to look at the other fireplaces in the building. Be good to have a working fireplace, won't it?"

"It makes no difference to me. We're leaving as soon as we can find another apartment."

A little boy comes in. He is drawn and pale, his sweatshirt hanging on his thin body, his shoulders drooping.

Nick twists around to look at him. "Hiya," he says.

"Hi."

Carol McGuire puts an arm around the boy. "Jason, this is Mr. Santos. He's going to fix the fireplaces."

Nick chuckles. "Just in time for Santa to come down the chimney, huh, Jason?"

Jason McGuire's white face turns mottled red. Pulling away from his mother, he charges Nick, still stretched out on the floor, and kicks him viciously in

the leg. He runs from the room, and his mother starts
to cry.

"You see, Jason's father is in jail, and Jason blames
Santa Claus," says Carol McGuire. She and Nick are
sitting at the dining table having a cup of tea, which
Carol has insisted on preparing by way of apology to
Nick. "It's the most awful thing, Mr. Santos—"
"Nick."
Carol wipes her nose with a paper napkin. There
are dun-colored circles under her blue eyes. "The
tabloids are calling it the Yuppie Slime case. I'm
surprised you haven't heard of it."
"I've been . . . out of the city."
"When they took my husband away, some idiots
were yelling,

> *Yuppie slime, yuppie slime*
> *Robbed his neighbor at Christmastime—"*

Carol breaks down in fresh sobs. Nick sips his tea.
"Bunch of jerks," he says.

When Carol McGuire gets her breath back, she tells
Nick the story:
Until six months ago, the McGuire family was doing
fine. Matt McGuire made two hundred thousand
dollars a year working on Wall Street; Carol sold real
estate. Jason was a model boy, and in the gifted
program at school. Then, like thousands of others
before him, Matt McGuire was laid off. At roughly the
same moment the real estate market dried up, and
Carol's income plummeted. Hard times set in.
In exchange for a reduction in rent, Matt became

superintendent of their building. Instead of analyzing data and making transatlantic phone calls, he spent his time replacing burned-out light bulbs, mopping the foyer, and throwing away the innumerable Chinese take-out menus shoved under the door daily.

"He was a good super. A really good super, Nick," Carol says. "His pride was involved. He was the best damn super this building ever had."

Times got tougher. Carol abandoned real estate and took a secretarial job. An un-merry Christmas approached, and that's where Santa came in. An envelope arrived in the mail, addressed to "The McGuires" with no return address. The envelope contained, with no explanation, three tickets to the Christmas spectacular at Radio City Music Hall. On the back of one of the tickets was written, "Merry Christmas from Santa Claus."

"Matt figured somebody from his old firm sent the tickets, and didn't want to embarrass him by signing his name," Carol says. "Anyway, it seemed like the only Christmas cheer we were going to get. We told Jason Santa had sent us a treat in the mail. I mean—we didn't think it was wrong to use the tickets. Do you, Nick?"

"Of course not," Nick says. He has a touch of heartburn. Carol's story isn't sitting well with him.

On the appointed day, full of excitement and good cheer, the McGuire family took the subway up to Radio City. As they stood in line to go in, their attention was caught by another family of three— mother, father, and hysterical little girl. Eavesdropping, they gathered that the family had driven in from Long Island City to see the performance, only to discover they had left their tickets at home. In a burst of generosity,

Matt McGuire offered to give the little girl his ticket, so she could see the show with Carol and Jason.

"They weren't sure whether to trust us at first," Carol weeps. "Matt convinced them. He said, it was the season for giving. He gave the girl his ticket, kissed me, and said he'd meet us at home. The show was wonderful. The children were enthralled. Her parents picked her up afterward, and everybody was happy. It was such a sweet thing for Matt to do."

After Matt gave away his ticket, he took the subway home again. When he entered the building, he heard someone moving around in the apartment above his, an apartment whose tenant was on vacation in the Caribbean and not expected back for another two weeks. He climbed up to investigate and found the door slightly ajar. Fearing the worst, he went inside. One of the French windows was open. Apparently, an intruder had heard Matt coming and retreated to the back balcony, from which it was an easy drop to the ground. To his relief, Matt found the television, the VCR, the stereo, and a collection of ivory netsukes still in place. The only (slight) disturbance was in the kitchen, where a metal canister of sugar had been spilled all over the floor.

Delighted that he had frightened off the intruder before anything was taken, Matt swept up the sugar and threw it away. Being extra conscientious, he went to the corner deli and bought more sugar, refilled the canister, and replaced it in the kitchen cabinet. He locked the apartment with his keys. Since no harm had been done, he decided not to sully the season by telling anyone, including the police, about the almost-robbery.

Such, anyway, was his story.

"I believe him, Nick. He's my husband. I believe him," Carol says.

All was well until a couple of days later, when the upstairs tenant, a Mr. Barnaby Gough, turned up, saying he'd gotten bored and sunburned in the Caribbean and decided to spend Christmas in New York instead. All hell broke loose when Mr. Gough discovered that the cache of gemstones—diamonds, rubies, emeralds, sapphires—which, being a child of the Depression, he kept in lieu of a substantial bank account, had been stolen from the canister where he kept them mixed in with five pounds of granulated sugar. The police fingerprinted everyone in the building, and found Matt's prints on the canister, the broom, the doorknob, and one of the netsukes.

To all appearances, the former Yuppie Slime had indeed robbed his neighbor at Christmastime, and he was duly arrested. The McGuires were unable to come up with bail, so Matt would be incarcerated for Christmas. And Jason McGuire blamed Santa, because it all started with those dumb tickets to Radio City.

What kind of a bozo keeps a fortune in gems in a sugar canister? Nick asks himself as he waits for Mr. Barnaby Gough to answer his knock. Barnaby Gough, however, does not look nearly as nutty as Nick expected. Although he is surely in his seventies, he exudes health and vigor. He is tall, rangy, still a bit sunburned, only slightly dewlapped, and has a shock of white hair to rival Nick's own, although unlike Nick he is clean-shaven. He wears shorts, running shoes, and a T-shirt emblazoned "Danger! Dirty Old Man."

The Gough apartment, while elegantly furnished, is

a bit of a mess. A huge evergreen wreath with a red velvet bow leans on the mantelpiece. There is a rowing machine in the middle of the floor. The netsukes are crowded on the coffee table next to a drift of what appears to be junk mail: catalogs; calendars with greetings from hardware stores and insurance companies; a foot-long cardboard stocking with slots for quarters to donate to a children's charity; a red-striped cardboard fruitcake box with the legend, "To Our Valued Customer."

Nick explains what he wants, and Barnaby Gough says, "Feel free." He settles himself on the rowing machine and strokes and wheezes while Nick conducts a detailed investigation of the fireplace. Finally Nick, gazing upward at the sooty bricks, says, "Sheesh."

Barnaby Gough stops rowing. Nick has the feeling he'd been hoping for an excuse. "Big job, eh?" Barnaby pants.

"One for the books."

What with Nick pointing out to Barnaby the details of the chimney job, it isn't long before they are discussing Topic A—the robbery.

"Pathetic," Barnaby says. "Poor McGuire must've snapped. So sad."

"He knew you kept your jewels in the sugar canister?"

Barnaby grimaces. "It's not something I advertised, Nick, I assure you."

"Then how—"

"Well . . ." Barnaby braces himself against the wall and begins doing hamstring stretches. "In September, on my birthday, I gave a party. Just a congenial gathering, you know—this year I served vegetarian pizza, tofu burgers, energy shakes. To avoid complaints about the noise, I invited the neighbors: the McGuires, Felicia upstairs, Gaston Duvivier on the top floor. Maybe McGuire was snooping in the kitchen and found the stones, and waited until now for a chance to take them."

Nick scratches his beard. "Couldn't anybody have done that? The other neighbors, the other guests?"

Barnaby stops hamstring-stretching long enough to waggle a forefinger at Nick. "Good point, except for one thing. It turned out not to be a break-in. The door was opened with a key. I gave one to McGuire because he was the super, and he's the only person in the world who had one besides me. I don't hand those babies out on the street corner."

"Hah." Nick is silent for a moment. Then he says, "Truthfully, though, wouldn't it have been easier to put the jewels in a safe-deposit box?"

"Don't trust banks. Never have. Got what you might call an obsession about it," Barnaby says promptly. "The insurance company knew that, but they still issued the policy. I thought those stones were perfectly safe. Why would a thief look for valuables in a canister of sugar?"

While Nick is considering the question, there is a knock at the door, and Barnaby bounds to answer it. To the person outside he says jovially, "Fifi the fair! Come in, come in."

A thin woman with a handsome, beaky-nosed face steps into the room. Her dark hair is pulled back by a wide headband, and she is dressed in a long, loose sweater over high boots and black tights. She looks about forty, but may be considerably older. She says, "Just got back from the health club, Barnaby. Thought

I might run into you over there." She notices Nick. "Whoops! I didn't know you were busy."

"No problem. This is a guy you have to meet. Nick Santos, Felicia Fairlie, my upstairs neighbor."

"Pleasure," Nick says.

Felicia gives Nick a practiced once-over, and Nick wonders if white hair turns her on. Certainly Barnaby seems smitten, inviting her to sit down, offering her herb tea, and generally hovering and beaming. When Felicia hears that Nick is going to rehabilitate the fireplaces, she claps her hands. "Ooh, that's wonderful! When do you want to look at mine?"

"Any old time," Nick says.

"You would not believe the change in Barnaby. You wouldn't believe it," says Felicia.

"Since his jewels were stolen, you mean?" says Nick. Nick is crouching in her fireplace, his head up the chimney.

"No! Since I got him to start living a healthy life. Would you believe it, Nick? The man used to drink a martini every night. *Every night.* Never exercised. And the poisonous additives he was ingesting you wouldn't believe."

Nick emerges from the chimney to find Felicia, who is sitting on the sofa with her shapely legs crossed, eyeing his waistline. He slaps his midriff. "Milk and cookies," he says.

Felicia howls as if he had said something really witty.

When she recovers, blotting her eyes delicately with a knuckle, Nick says, "I take it you and Barnaby are good friends."

Felicia gives him a woman-of-the-world look. "I'm very fond of Barnaby."

"You spend a lot of time together, huh?"

"A fair amount."

Nick, a master at extracting information, fixes her with a steady gaze. "Did you know he kept gemstones in the sugar?"

Felicia draws herself up. "Nick, if I had had any idea Barnaby kept *sugar* in his kitchen, believe me I would have taken it upon myself to throw the nasty stuff out immediately."

Then she looks embarrassed and studies her fingernails.

As Nick climbs up to inspect the fireplace of the top-floor tenant, Gaston Duvivier, a heavenly smell wafts toward him. It is the smell of chocolate, but somehow it is the quintessence of chocolate, and mixed with it are other smells more subtle and equally delicious. By the time Nick reaches the apartment door, where he pounds and yells, "Chimney man!" his knees are weak.

Gaston Duvivier is balding and squatty, with protruding green eyes. He is wrapped in a chocolate-smeared apron. In a heavy French accent he tells Nick to take as long as he likes with the fireplace, and he disappears into the kitchen. Nick inspects the fireplace, and inspects it again. The smells from the kitchen become more excruciating. Gaston Duvivier does not reappear.

At last, Nick sticks his head into the kitchen. "Hey, thanks."

Gaston is removing a sheet of fat chocolate cookies from the oven of a stainless-steel restaurant stove. "You are finished? Good."

Nick leans in the doorway. "Finished for now,

anyway." Gaston is removing cookies from the pan. "Christmas cookies, huh?"

Gaston shrugs. "An experiment. Something to do on my day off."

"Yeah? What kind of job have you got?"

"I am a pastry chef."

"Wow."

Nick gazes at the cookies. Finally, with a resigned expression, Gaston says, "You would like to try one, yes?"

"Try one? Sure."

Nick is a connoisseur of cookies, and Gaston Duvivier's chocolate cookie is the best cookie he has ever tasted. After some of Nick's heartfelt praise, Gaston offers him another. More praise and several cookies later, Gaston nibbles one himself and says, "It is perhaps not bad."

As they munch, Nick asks Gaston what he thinks of the theft of Barnaby Gough's jewels.

Gaston responds with a Gallic shrug. "I think nothing."

"Are you a friend of his?"

Gaston has brewed coffee. He pours a mug for Nick and says, "Not a friend, no. I was once in his apartment, for his birthday party."

"How was it?"

Gaston's eyes roll upward. "Horrible! The food! *Mon Dieu!* The worst I have tasted in my life."

"That bad, eh?"

"The dessert, Nick! The dessert!" Gaston leans forward to grasp Nick's arm. Nick notices tears in his bulbous eyes.

Another cookie melts in Nick's mouth. "What was the dessert?"

"Some sort of ghastly pudding made of tofu. Disgusting! Inedible! I had to slip away, into the kitchen, to search for the—the—"

Gaston falters. Nick says, quietly, "To search for the sugar, Gaston? To make it more palatable?"

Gaston recovers himself. "I was going to say, to search for the garbage can, in order to get rid of it discreetly." He blinks once or twice, and his eyes are clear. Nick leaves a short while later, when all the cookies are gone.

Standing in the doorway at the McGuires', Nick discusses the chimney-and-flue situation with Carol. Behind her, he sees a dart board. A picture of Santa Claus is pinned to the target, and Jason is throwing bull's-eyes at Santa's red nose. To Carol, Nick says, "One thing keeps bothering me. About . . . your husband's problem."

"What's that?"

"The person who stole the jewels had a key to the Gough apartment, right? Could somebody have stolen your husband's keys? Or borrowed them long enough to make an impression in clay or something?"

Carol shakes her head. "Matt was unbelievably conscientious. He kept those keys in his jacket pocket at all times."

"He never—"

"He and I discussed this question, actually. He did remember one occasion when trash had been strewn around out front. He was afraid we'd get a citation from the Environmental Control Board, so he was working madly to get it picked up. The weather was unseasonably warm, so he took his jacket off and hung it inside, on the newel post at the foot of the stairs. But nobody came in or out except the neighbors."

Nick leans closer. "*Which* neighbors?"

"He said he saw all three of them."

Nick walks to the corner deli and gets himself a cup of coffee to go. Next to Gaston's French roast, it's swill. Back at the brownstone, he leans on the fence while he drinks it. He has just tossed his paper cup in the garbage can, still has the lid off, when Barnaby Gough emerges from the front door in a camel's-hair coat and earmuffs. He is carrying a bulging plastic garbage bag. He waves cheerily at Nick and drops the bag into the garbage can. "Disposing of the Christmas junk mail," he says and walks briskly away, leaving Nick still holding the garbage-can lid, staring down at the bag. Nick has just realized something.

When Barnaby Gough returns, now laden with bags from the Integral Yoga Institute's health-food grocery store on Thirteenth Street, Nick is sitting inside on the stairs. He is holding a red-and-white-striped cardboard fruitcake box imprinted, "To Our Valued Customer." He holds the box out to Barnaby. "I rescued your fruitcake," he says.

Barnaby's eyes narrow. "So you did."

"I noticed it upstairs, and wondered who would send a fruitcake to a health-food nut. So I looked at the small print." Nick reads, "'To Our Valued Customer.' And down here below, 'From Your Friends at the Admiral Savings Bank.' If you never do business with banks, why is the Admiral Savings Bank sending you a fruitcake?"

"Who's asking?" says Barnaby contemptuously.

He starts to push by Nick, but Nick stands up. Somehow, in the half-light of the hall, Nick looks enormous. His face is craggy and grave. He says, "I think you'd better answer."

"I don't—it's a mistake—"

Nick shakes his head. "It's no mistake. I called the bank. They confirm that you have a safe-deposit box there. They also said all communication with you was supposed to be through a box number. There must have been a glitch, and the fruitcake got sent here instead."

"They can't give you information like that! It's privileged—"

"My guess is, the jewels are in your safe-deposit box, where you put them when you thought up your scheme to defraud the insurance company. Collect the money, right? Then go abroad and sell the stones sometime?"

Barnaby shrinks. He says, "Who the hell are you, Nick? Undercover cop? Listen, Nick—"

"You sent the super and his family tickets to Radio City to get them out of the way. You didn't imagine Matt McGuire would get into the spirit of the season, give away his ticket, and come back to hear you setting the scene upstairs."

"I've had difficulties, you know. Times aren't good. I didn't expect anybody to be arrested—"

"But when he was, you went ahead and let an innocent man be your fall guy." Nick shakes his head. "Not only that. You made his son hate Santa Claus."

Barnaby's lips move. He might be trying to say, "I'm sorry."

Once Barnaby is in custody, Nick doesn't stick around for Matt McGuire's homecoming. Time is short, and there's too much to do. He does have a brief talk with Jason McGuire. Nick can be persuasive, and by the time he leaves, he's pretty sure everything is okay on the Jason front. Oh—he'd better arrange for somebody actually to repair the fireplaces in the brownstone before Christmas. Nick hopes, he really hopes, that Gaston Duvivier believes in Santa Claus.

I'd be interested to know whether any scholar has ever done a Ph.D. thesis on why so many college professors take to a life of literary crime. Few have done so with more zest, skill, and sometimes malicious wit than Robert Barnard.

Bob could possibly do it in Norwegian, even. After having studied English at Balliol College in Oxford University, he went on to teach English in Australia, then in Norway, finishing his teaching career at the University of Tromsø. Tromsø is at the highest latitude you can reach in northern European universities, and Robert Barnard is about as high as he can get on my personal list of favorites . . . even if some of his characters do choose strange methods of solving their domestic problems.

ROBERT BARNARD

A POLITICAL NECESSITY

It must be rare for the first thought of a newly appointed government minister to be: Now is the time to kill my wife. Don't get me wrong—I'm sure many of my colleagues would like to, with that dull, insistent sort of wishing which will never actually impel them to action, and which is characteristic of second-rate minds. My thought was not If only I could but Now I can. It had my typical decisiveness and lack of sentiment, as well as that ability to get to the heart of a question and come up with a solution which I am sure was the reason the Prime Minister decided to promote me.

I was brought into the government in the autumn reshuffle, and my second thought was: Christmas is coming. Ideal.

I should explain that the post I was given was one of the junior positions in the Home Office. I doubt whether the thought would have occurred to me if it had been in Trade and Industry, or Environment. The Home Office, you see, has a great deal to do with

Northern Ireland, and everything to do with the imprisonment of IRA terrorists. Its ministers, therefore, are natural targets. Indeed, two days after I took up my post, I had a visit by arrangement from a high-ranking Scotland Yard terrorist officer who lectured me on personal security; elementary precautions I and my family could take, and little indications that might give me the idea that something was wrong.

Including, naturally, suspect packages.

He actually brought along a mock-up suspect package, showed me all the signs that should arouse my suspicions, and then proceeded to take it apart and show me the sort of explosive device that would be concealed inside. It was a real education.

I tried not to show too much interest. Indeed, I hope I gave the impression of a man who is trying to give due attention to an important matter, but who has actually a mountain of things he ought to be doing. In fact my mind was ticking away as inexorably as a real explosive device. A suspect package among her Christmas parcels—a sort of *bombe surprise*. How wonderful if it could have gone off while she was singing "Happy Birthday, dear Jesus" with the children. But of course that was out of the question. I had no particular desire to harm my children. Merely to render them motherless.

There are many reasons why the old custom of wife murder has not fallen into disuse in this age of easy—indeed practically obligatory—divorce. One is to get custody of the children. Another is money. Another is personal satisfaction that no divorce can give. My situation is peculiar. Normally even an MP can move out of the family home, make mutterings about "irretrievable breakdown," and in two shakes of a duck's tail be shacking up with his secretary, or Miss Bournemouth 1989, or whomever he has had his eye on. Not the MP for the constituency of Dundee Kirkside. My constituents, though Conservative almost to a man and woman, are tight-lipped, censorious, pleasure-hating accountants and small shopkeepers, people for whom John Knox did not go nearly far enough. Liquor never passes their lips, dance never animates their lower limbs—their very sperm is deep-frozen.

Divorce, for the MP for Dundee Kirkside, was a non-starter.

Equally, living for the rest of my life with Annabelle was simply not to be contemplated. If I had not known this before, I certainly knew it at a Downing Street dinner shortly after my appointment. As ill luck would have it, Annabelle was seated near to the Prime Minister, while I was someway down on the other side of the table. But of course I am all too attuned to her voice, and I heard her say, "Whenever I see my two little ones tucked up in their little bed, I always seem to see the baby Jesus there making a third!"

The Prime Minister's face was a picture. So, I imagine, was mine.

Not that Annabelle's style of conversation, apparently derived from Victorian commonplace books designed to be given as Sunday school prizes, hadn't been useful to me in the past. I'd be the first to admit that in private. For instance, being only half-Scottish (and on my mother's side at that) and having been educated at Lancing, I was not an obvious candidate for a Scottish constituency. Thank God we Tories still interview the wives as part of the selection procedure! I don't say anyone was melted by Annabelle's liquid

caramel smile, but they were enraptured by her expressed conviction that we (we in the Conservative
party) are on this earth to do the Lord's bidding, that
she prayed every night that her husband would do the
Lord Jesus's work, that we were the party of the
family, and the Christian family at that—and a lot
more balls along these lines. I got the nomination, and
we celebrated by going down on our knees beside the
twin beds in our hideous Dundee hotel room. It was
the least I could do. Luckily the curriculum vitæ which
I submitted to the selection committee had merely
stated that we had been married in 1985 and our first
child born in 1986—months not given. Being the party
of the family didn't mean they approved of women who
were in the family way when they went to the altar.

That happened, of course, before Annabelle got reli-
gion from a poisonous American woman evangelist at a
dreadful rally in Earls Court that she had gone along to
under the impression that it was *Aida* with elephants.

"I'm so longing for Christmas to come this year,"
burbled Annabelle, her eyes all fizzing sparklers. "Just
us and our two babies celebrating the coming of Jesus."

I looked at her with love in my eyes and Semtex in
my heart.

"It will be lovely. But, do you know, I sometimes
regret the Christmases of my childhood. Over in
Belgium the real celebration was Christmas Eve."

My family retreated to Ostend, in the manner pio-
neered by bankrupt Victorians, when I was five. This
was as a consequence of a disagreement my father had
with the Inland Revenue which was not sorted out for
many years. I have no idea whether the Belgians do in
fact celebrate Christmas Eve. It was bad enough
living with the clog-hoppers, without mixing with

them. But I do know that many Continental countries do, and Annabelle has no knowledge of habits and customs outside Pinner.

"How odd," she said in reply. "Before the baby Jesus was actually born. I'm not sure I'd like that."

"Don't be so parochial," I said. "God isn't just English. He's got the whole world in his hands, remember."

That set Annabelle off singing for the rest of the evening in her clear, bright Julie Andrews voice that can shatter glass ornaments if she goes too high.

I meanwhile was not neglecting the practical side. I never do, it's part of my strength. I've always been pretty smart at do-it-yourself, and to explain my evening hours in the garage I told Annabelle that I was preparing a little surprise for Gavin and Janet at Christmas. Which wasn't so far from the truth. I had already made an incognito visit (luckily for me I am still so junior that my face is not known, which will not be the case for long) to Tottenham Court Road, where I picked up one of the devices the inspector had so kindly demonstrated to me. Fortunately I had a very dodgy contact in the underworld (I had used him when I worked for Conservative Central Office, for a small job of ballot-rigging), and from him I got the modest quantity of explosive necessary to send Annabelle into the arms of the Lord Jesus.

All was going beautifully to plan.

While all this was coming to fruition, I was naturally fulfilling—very energetically fulfilling—my obligations and duties at the Home Office. I was also making routine preparations for Christmas, or getting other people to do them for me. I paid particular attention to getting the right presents for Annabelle. I meant her to die happy—or, if she insisted on leaving my presents till later, I intended to make much, in a thoroughly maudlin way, of what pleasures I had had in store for her to the Special Branch officers who would investigate her death. I bought a diamond pendant from Cartier's; I had one of the bookish secretaries from the Home Office scouring the secondhand bookshops of Highgate and Hampstead for a copy of *The Bible Designed to Be Read as Literature,* which she had expressed a desire for—everything, right down to the Thornton's chocolates that she loved. Thoughtful presents, though I say so myself. The presents of a model husband.

The children's presents I could safely leave to her. She loved shopping for them, and she was usually out when I rang home in the weeks leading up to Christmas, on some spree or other of that kind. I got one of the secretaries to ring Harrods, and by the eighteenth a large Christmas tree was in place in the living room. Annabelle, the children, and the Norwegian au pair decorated it the same day. They were just finishing it when I arrived back from Whitehall.

"Do you celebrate Christmas Eve or Christmas Day in Norway?" I asked Margrethe.

"Christmas Eve," she said promptly. "That is when the Christmas gnome brings all the presents."

I smiled at her more benevolently than usual and suppressed any comment about the Christmas gnome. Really, was it a Christian country or a European Disneyland?

"You know, I think we'll do that this year," I said to Annabelle later than evening. "Celebrate *our* Christmas on Christmas Eve, after the babies have gone to bed. Then we can give all our time and attention to them on Christmas Day itself. Their day, entirely and completely."

"Perhaps you're right," said Annabelle, smiling her melting-fudge smile. "When you come to think about it, Christmas Day should be just for the little ones, shouldn't it?"

Soon the packages began to pile up under the tree. Presents from grandparents, aunties, presents from constituents, especially from businessmen and property developers anxious to keep on the right side of me. Most of them were for Gavin and Janet, of course, but Annabelle and I soon had a respectable number. I began to separate the piles—the children's on one side of the tree, ours on the other.

On December the twenty-first I put the suspect package into the pile—a brown padded envelope, with a stamp and a fake postmark. It nestled shyly under bigger and gaudier packages.

Christmas is a very uninteresting time in politics. Nothing important gets announced (unless it is something dodgy we are hoping to slip past the public with little publicity), and so many of the MPs slope off home early that there is very little of the cut and thrust of political infighting which is what I excel at. Even in the department things slackened off. I was able to get home on two or three afternoons in the lead-up period. I found Annabelle out shopping and the kids in the charge of Margrethe. Margrethe proved very unresponsive to my suggestions of how we should spend the afternoon. Really, Norwegians are not all they're cracked up to be.

Once she had got the idea of a special dinner for us on Christmas Eve, Annabelle chattered on about what it should be. The damned kids insisted on turkey on

The Day, of course, though I can think of about twenty
meats I would find more interesting. We finally decided on a cold meal—light, but with a few touches of
luxury. Margrethe was flying back to Bergen on the
twenty-third, but she did some of the preparations
before she went. We really get quite a lot of work out
of Margrethe. I made one or two suggestions—not that
I expected to eat anything much, but in order that it
should look right to the investigating officers. I would
have been a superb stage director. Annabelle said she
could get some of the things at the delicatessen
around the corner, and she would get the rest at
Harrods. She also said it was going to be an absolutely
smashing evening.

The day dawned. The children ("the babies," as
Annabelle calls them, though they are no longer that,
thank God) were of course wild with pre-Christmas
excitement, so I escaped to the office for most of the
day. There was, after all, nothing left to do. Soon after
I got home I suggested it was time for the kids to go to
bed, and as they were confidently expecting a visit
from Santa Claus, they didn't make too many objec-
tions. Then I began setting the scene. I put the drinks
on the phone table at the far end by the door. I
intended to be over there when Annabelle opened the
package. I toyed with the idea of being rather closer,
to get the odd cut and scar from the debris, but I
rejected the idea. Annabelle began bringing on the
cold collation with a series of appreciative shrieks—
"Doesn't this look *scrumptious?*" and the like. The
room was beautifully warm from the central heating,
and I rejected Annabelle's suggestion that I light the
fire. In fact, I was feeling distinctly sweaty, and I
would have taken off my jacket and tie, except that I

hate that sort of slovenliness. Round about seven-thirty, I said,

"I think it's about time for a drink."

"Oh, goody!" said Annabelle. Getting God had not quenched her taste for dry martinis. I got her a large one with plenty of ice. Then I got for myself a gin and tonic that was mostly tonic and ice. Keep cool, George, keep cool!

"Now!" I said, and we looked at each other and smiled. We had agreed to open presents when we had our first drinks.

First of all we opened our own to each other. Annabelle oohed over the Cartier pendant ("You *shouldn't* have, Georgie boy! What must it have cost?") I tried to look pleased with a very expensive shaving kit.

"I really thought you should start shaving *properly*, Georgie. Electric razors are frightfully *infra*, and people are starting to comment on your midnight shadow. Look what harm that did to Richard Nixon."

I regarded my midnight shadow as part of my saturnine and macho image. Nobody ever found Richard Nixon macho.

"I promise, my darling," I said.

Then she opened her *Bible Designed to Be Read as Literature*.

"Oh, wonderful! How *thoughtful* you are, Georgie-Porgy. People say that reading this is an entirely new experience!" She opened it and read: "'There were shepherds abiding in the fields, keeping watch over their flocks by night.'"

I suppose I was lucky she didn't sing it. She sometimes takes part in those come-along-and-sing Messiahs which are so very matey and democratic—

practically the Labour Party at song. I opened a little square box and found a three-disc set of Luciano Pavarotti's greatest hits. Talk about things being *infra!*

"Perfect!" I said.

So we worked through our presents, eating chocolates and trying things on till at last she laid her hand on the brown padded envelope and took it up.

"What *is* this one?" she said.

My heart stood still. I tried with all the nonchalance my sweaty state would allow to take up one of my presents and open it.

"Haven't the faintest idea."

"I noticed it the other day. Did it really come by post?"

"How would I know?"

"Because neither Margrethe nor I took it in, so you must have done."

"Can't remember. I may have done, I suppose."

"If so, it must have been Sunday. It's the only day when you were on your own here. I didn't think they delivered parcels on Sunday. What did the postman look like?"

Normally this would have been a cue for a spurt of sarcasm on my part. I hoped Annabelle would attribute it to the Christmas spirit that it was not forthcoming.

"Good heavens, one doesn't notice what postmen look like," I said mildly. "If you're wondering who sent it, you'd better open it and find out."

She was looking at it closely.

"The postmark is all smudged. In fact it doesn't look like a real postmark at all." She got up. "Georgie, I think we ought to phone the police."

She walked over toward the phone. I felt my face

going red; our positions in my plan were exactly reversed. I forced myself to take up the package.

"Of course I see what you're getting at, darling, but I really do think that you're panicking needlessly. I don't see any of the things the inspector said should put us on our guard. It's not from Ireland, the name is spelled right—there are none of the signs. A smudged postmark is hardly unusual."

Her finger was poised over the press-button dial.

"Better safe than sorry."

"No!"

My voice had come out very loud. The police would almost certainly be able to trace the package back to me if they got it intact. Annabelle paused.

"No?"

"I mean . . . we'd look awful fools . . . disturbing them on Christmas Eve, for nothing."

"How unusually considerate of you, Georgie. But you've been unusual for quite a while now. I'm beginning to think that Paul is right."

"Paul?"

"A chap I've been seeing."

"*Seeing?*"

"He said that if I drove you too mad with my Pollyanna act, it wouldn't be divorce I drove you to, but murder. He's seen you on television from the House. He thinks you're mad."

"Annabelle, look, this really has gone too far. There's no need at all to call the police. I was told all about suspect packages. This one hasn't got the look of one at all."

She stood there, twenty feet away from me, her hand poised over the dial, very, very cool.

"All right, buster: open it."

It's no wonder Margaret Maron chose to write mysteries; her own mother is one of the world's great mystery fans. And it's not surprising that Margaret agreed to do a short story for Christmas Stalkings. She has always thought of herself primarily as a short-story writer, even though she's better known for her superbly crafted novels. Nor is it any accident that this one takes place in rural North Carolina. Her own roots go more than seven generations deep into its sandy soil, where she still lives on her family's farm south of Raleigh.

The only person who's privileged to read and critique Margaret's work in progress is her artist husband, Joseph Maron. She says they fight a lot, but her system appears to be working, judging from critics' acclaim and the number of times she's been nominated for awards in the mystery field. So far, only one of her novels, Bloody Kin, *has been set in fictional but very real Colleton County, N.C., but we understand more will be coming. In the meantime, here's your chance to spend New Year's Eve in that enigmatic land of the black-eyed pea.*

242

MARGARET MARON

FRUITCAKE, MERCY, AND BLACK-EYED PEAS

Marnolla's first question after I bailed her out of jail was, "What's a revisichist?" Her second was, "Ain't you getting too old for a squinchy little shoe box like this?"

"You wanted a Cadillac ride home, you should've called James Rufus Sanders," I told her, referring to the most successful black lawyer in Colleton County, North Carolina. I switched on the heater of my admittedly small sports car against the chill December air and helped pull the seat belt across her broad hips, an expanse further broadened by her bulky winter coat. "You mean recidivist?"

"I reckon. Something like that. Miz Utley said I was one and I won't going to give her the satisfaction of asking what it was. Ain't something ugly, is it?"

"Miz Utley never talks ugly and you know it," I said as I pulled out of the courthouse parking lot and headed toward Darkside, the nearest thing Dobbs has to a purely black section. "Magistrates have to be polite to everybody, but under the habitual-offender statutes—"

"Don't give me no lawyer talk, Deb'rah," she snapped. "I wanted that, I *would've* called Mr. Sanders."

"It means this isn't the first time Billy Tyson's caught you shoplifting in his store, and this time he wants to put you *under* the jail, not in it," I snapped back.

She leaned back and loosened the buttons of her dark-blue coat. "Naw, you won't let him do that."

It was three days past Christmas, but she still wore a sprig of artificial holly topped by two tiny yellow plastic bells that had been dipped in gold glitter and sparkled gaily in the low winter sun.

Marnolla Faison was barely ten years older than me, yet her short black hair was almost half gray and her callused hands had worked about twenty years harder than mine. In truth our families had worked for each other more years than either of us could count and it looks like it's going to go on another generation, even though Marnolla left the farm before she was full grown.

"What in God's name made you think you could walk out with all that baby stuff?" I asked. "*Two* boxes of diapers? Who's had a baby now?"

"Nobody," she said.

I stopped for the light and we waved to Miss Sallie Anderson, waiting to cross at the corner.

Miss Sallie motioned for Marnolla to roll down her window and she leaned in to greet us. Her white curls were covered by a fuzzy blue scarf that exuded a delicate fragrance of rose sachet and talcum. "Did y'all have a nice Christmas?"

"Yes, ma'am," we chorused. "How 'bout you?"

"Real nice." Her face was finely wrinkled like a piece of thin white tissue paper that's been crumpled around a Christmas present and then smoothed out by careful hands. "Jack and Caroline were down with their new baby, and he's the spitting image of his great-granddaddy. They named him after Jed, you know."

The driver behind us tapped his horn. Not ugly. Just letting us know the light was green and he couldn't get by with us in the middle of the lane, so if we didn't mind . . .

It was nobody I knew, but Miss Sallie thought he was saying hello and she waved to him abstractedly. "I better not hold y'all up," she said. "I just wanted you to tell Zell that we sure did appreciate that fruitcake. It was so moist and sweet, just the best I've had since your mother died, honey."

"I'll tell her," I promised, easing off the brake. "And that reminds me," I told Marnolla as she closed the window and we drove on. "Aunt Zell sent you a fruitcake, too."

"That's mighty nice of her. She still making them like your mama used to?"

"Far as I know."

Slyness needled Marnolla's chuckle. "No wonder Miz Sallie thought it was so good."

She always knew how to zing me.

"Never mind Aunt Zell's fruitcakes," I told her. "We were talking about you stealing baby diapers for 'nobody.' Nobody who?"

"Nobody you ever met."

Her face took on a stubborn set and I knew there was no point trying to pry a name. Didn't matter anyhow. Whoever the mother was, she wasn't the one who tried to walk out of Billy Tyson's Bigg Shopp with a brand-new layette. It wasn't that Marnolla *wanted* to steal or even *meant* to steal; it's that her heart was bigger than her weekly paycheck from the towel factory and sometimes she got impulsive. With her daughter Avis engrossed in a fancy job out in California and nobody of her own to provide for, she tried to mother every stray that wandered in off the road.

"What's Avis going to think when she hears about this?" I scolded.

"She ain't never going to hear," Marnolla said firmly.

Avis was a little younger than me, born when Marnolla was only fourteen. She was the first baby I'd had much to do with and I'd hung over her crib every chance I got, gently holding her tiny hands in mine, marveling over every detail, right down to the little finger on her left hand that crooked at the tip just like Marnolla's. I really mourned when Marnolla and Sid moved into Dobbs while Avis was still just a toddler. Sid split to California a few years later; and when Avis was fifteen and going through a wild stage in school, she took thirty dollars from Marnolla's purse and hitchhiked out to live with him.

Marnolla grieved over it at first, but eventually reckoned that Avis needed her daddy's stronger hand to keep her in line. Every time I saw Marnolla and remembered to ask, she had only good things to say about the way Avis had turned her life around: Avis was finishing high school; Avis was taking courses at a community college; Avis had landed a real good job doing something with computers, Marnolla wasn't quite clear what.

"Not married yet," Marnolla kept reporting. "She's just like you, Deb'rah. Working too hard and having too much fun to bog herself down with menfolk and babies."

I was glad Avis was doing so good, but it was too bad she couldn't find the time to come visit her own mother. Not that I'd ever said that to Marnolla, she being so proud of Avis and all. I couldn't help thinking, though, that if Marnolla had somebody she was special to, she might not keep trying to help more people than she could afford. Loneliness is a big hole that takes a lot of filling sometimes.

I pulled up and parked in front of her little shotgun, three rooms lined up one behind the other so that if you fired through the front door, the pellets would go straight out through the back screen. The wood frame house was old and needed paint, but the yard was raked and tidy and the porch railing was strung with cheerful Christmas lights. A wreath of silver tinsel hung on the door.

"I'd ask you in," Marnolla said, "but you're probably in a hurry."

"You got that right," I agreed. "I need to get up with Billy Tyson before all his Christmas spirit evaporates. Maybe I can talk him out of it one more time, but I swear, Marnolla, you can't blame him for being so ill about this after you *promised* on a stack of Bibles you'd never take another penny's worth from his store."

"Tell him I'm sorry," she said as she stood with the car door open. A gust of chill December wind caught the gold bells pinned to her coat and they twinkled in the afternoon sunlight. "Tell him I won't do it never again, honest."

She didn't look all that repentant to me and Billy Tyson didn't look to be all that full of Christmas spirit when I entered his office back of the cash registers at the Bigg Shopp. He gave me a sour glance and went on punching numbers on his calculator.

"You here about Marnolla Faison?"

"Well, your ad did say bargains so good they're practically a steal."

It didn't get the grin I'd hoped for.

"Forget it, Deb'rah. I'm not dropping charges this time."

He'd gained even more weight than Marnolla over the years, and the bald spot on the top of his head had grown bigger since the first time I'd stood in his office and talked him out of prosecuting Marnolla for shop-lifting.

"How come she always steals from me anyhow?" he growled. "How come she don't go to K mart or Rose's?"

"You're homefolks," I said. "She wouldn't steal from strangers."

"That's because strangers would've put her in jail the first time she tried it with them. That's what I should've done." He glared at me. "What I *would've* done, too, if you hadn't talked me out of it. Well, no more, missy. This time when the judge asks me if I've got anything to say, you're not going to hear me ask him to let her off with some piddly little fine. This time she gets to see the inside of a jail, if I have anything to say about it. And I will, by damn! As president of the Merchants' Association, I've got an example to set."

"And you set a fine example, Billy," I wheedled. "Everybody says so, but it's Christmas and a little baby needed a few things and—"

"Dammit, Deb'rah, you can't talk about Christmas like the Merchants' Association don't do their part.

We're civic-minded as hell and we give and we give and—"

"And everybody appreciates it, too," I assured him. "But you know how Marnolla is."

"What Marnolla is is a common thief and she's gonna go to jail like one! Every time she wants to act like a big shot with some poor soul, she comes in here and steals something from *me* to give to *them*."

"Oh, come on, Billy. How much did she actually try to take? Thirty dollars' worth? Forty?" I reached for my wallet, but he waved me off.

"Don't matter if it wa'n't but a nickel. It's the principle of the thing."

"Principle or not, you know she won't get more than a couple of weekends at the most."

"Not if Perry Byrd hears the case," he said shrewdly.

He had me there. Judge Perry Byrd adores the principle of things. Especially if the defendants are black or Hispanic.

"I expect you're just tired out with too much Christmas," I said. "You have a nice New Year's and we'll talk some more next week."

"You can talk all you want." He had a mule-stubborn look on his face. "You're not gonna get around me this time."

I made a quick walk through Bigg Shopp's shoe racks before leaving just in case something nice had been marked down. There was a darling pair of green slingbacks. I didn't have a single winter thing to go with them at the moment, but Aunt Zell had made me several floral-print sundresses last summer and they'd match those dresses.

Besides, they were only $18.50.

Billy had come out of his office to help out at the express lane. I smiled at him sweetly as I gave him the shoes and a twenty. "Unless you'd rather I shopped at K mart or Rose's?"

"*Paying* customers are always welcome at Bigg Shopp," he said and handed me my change.

But at least he finally smiled. I dropped the change into the crippled children's jar beside the cash register and went out to the parking lot with a happier heart, figuring if I kept working on him, I could maybe soften him up before Marnolla's case was called.

As I put my new shoes in the trunk, I saw the fruitcake Aunt Zell had sent Marnolla.

For just a minute, I thought about running back in the store and giving it to Billy. In his mood, though, he'd probably consider it a bribe instead of a present in keeping with the holidays.

For some reason, people like to poke fun at Christmas fruitcake and joke about how there's really probably only a hundred or so in the whole United States and they just get passed around from one year to the next.

Those people never tasted Aunt Zell's.

For starters, she uses Colleton County nuts. Not those puny dried-up English walnuts you get in the grocery store, but thick, meaty pecans and rich black walnuts. She goes easy on the citron and heavy on her home-dried apples and figs. When the dark dense loaves come out of the oven in late October, the first thing Aunt Zell does, before they're even cool, is wrap them up in cheesecloth and slosh on a generous splash of what she euphemistically calls "Kezzie's special apple juice." They get basted like that every week till Christmas.

(She says Kezzie hasn't run any white whiskey since Mother died and he moved back to the main farm. The applejack he brings her every fall is some private stock he's had stashed back somewhere aging all these years. Or so he tells her.)

I live in town with Aunt Zell, my mother's sister, and I'm touchy about discussing my daddy, but it *is* the best fruitcake in Colleton County and that's not idle bragging. The one time she entered it at the state fair ten years ago, they gave her a blue ribbon.

Dusk was falling when I got back to Marnolla's. The lights on her porch blinked colorfully in the twilight and the calico cat curled on the railing came over to meet me as I mounted the two steps and knocked on the door.

When Marnolla opened it, the cat twined around and through her ankles. She scooped it up and stood in the doorway stroking its sleek body.

Her own body was encased in a long woolly red robe that looked warm and Christmassy. "What'd he say?" she asked.

It was cold on the porch and I could smell hot coffee and cornbread inside. "Let's go in the kitchen and I'll tell you."

"No."

I thought she was joking. "Come on, Marnolla. I'm freezing out here."

"I let you in, you'll start asking questions and fussing," she said.

"What's to fuss about?"

"See? Asking questions already," she grumbled, but

she stood aside and let me step into her living room. It was dark except for the multicolored glow of her Christmas tree. Normally the room was neat as a pin; that night, in addition to the expected clutter of opened presents at the base of the tree, there was a stack of quilts folded at the end of the couch and a pillow on top.

"You got somebody staying here?" I asked, as the cat trotted from the living room on through her bedroom and out to the kitchen.

Before she could answer, I heard someone speak to it. The next minute, a young girl stepped into view and I suddenly knew why Marnolla had tried to steal baby items.

She didn't look a day over twelve. (I later learned she was fifteen.) Except for her swollen abdomen, she was slender and delicately formed, with a childish face. But her lovely almond-shaped eyes were the eyes of a fearful adult, as if she'd already seen things no child in America should have had to see.

"Her name's Lynette and she's going to be staying with me awhile," said Marnolla in a voice that warned me off any nosy questions. "Lynette, this here's Miss Deborah Knott. My daddy used to sharecrop with hers."

She nodded at me shyly from the kitchen, but neither joined us nor spoke as she picked up the cat and moved out of my sight. Marnolla was giving off such odd vibes that I briefly described Billy Tyson's determination to see her in jail, handed over the fruitcake, and edged my way out the front door again.

Marnolla followed me onto the porch and shut the door. "Lynette's why you can't let them put me in jail," she said. "She's just a baby her own self and she's got nobody else, so I need to be here, Deb'rah. You hear?"

"I hear," I sighed and drove home in the darkness through side streets still festive with Santa Claus sleds and wooden reindeer, although the Rudolph spotlighted on a neighbor's roof was beginning to look a bit jaded.

Aunt Zell had made chicken pastry for dinner and she was pleased to hear Miss Sallie's pretty words about her fruitcake, but worried over Marnolla.

"Maybe Billy Tyson's right," I said as she passed the spinach salad. "Maybe it *is* going to take a few days in jail to get her to quit taking stuff out of his store."

"But if there's a baby coming—"

Aunt Zell paused and shook her head over a situation with no easy solutions. "I'll pray on it for you."

"That'll be nice," I said.

While I did care about Marnolla's problems, she was only one client among many, and none of them blighted my holiday season.

Court didn't sit the week between Christmas and New Year's, so we kept bankers' hours at the law office. I made duty calls on most of my brothers and their wives during the day, did some serious partying with friends over in Raleigh by night, and, since I was getting low on clean blouses and lingerie, skipped church on Sunday morning so I could sneak in a quick load of wash while Aunt Zell was out of the house.

She swears she isn't superstitious; all the same, if I want to wash clothes between new Christmas and old Christmas, she starts fussing about having to wash shrouds for a corpse in the coming year. I've tried to tell her it's only if you wash bedclothes, but she won't run the risk. Or the washer.

Rather than argue about it every year, I just wait till she's gone.

She came home from church rather put out with Billy Tyson. "I entreated him in the spirit of Christian fellowship to turn the cheek one more time and give Marnolla another chance, but he kept asking whether the laborer wasn't worthy of his hire."

I looked at her blankly.

"Well, it sort of made sense when he was saying it." She grinned and for a moment looked so like my mother that I had to hug her.

On New Year's Eve, I ran into Tracy Johnson at Fancy Footwork's year-end clearance sale. She's one of the D.A.'s sharpest assistants, tall and willowy with short blond hair and gorgeous eyes, which she downplays in court with oversized glasses. I caught her wistfully trying on a pair of black patent pumps with four-inch stiletto heels.

Regretfully, she handed the shoes back to the clerk and slipped into a pair with low French heels. They were okay, but nothing dazzling. Tracy walked back and forth in front of the mirror and sighed. "When I was at Duke, I almost married a basketball player."

I tried to imagine life without high heels. "It might have been worth it," I said. "Most of Duke's players at least graduate, don't they?"

"Eventually. Or so they say. Wouldn't matter. Judges aren't crazy about tall women either."

Her eyes narrowed as I tried on the shoes she'd relinquished and I instantly knew I'd made a tactless mistake.

"I see Marnolla Faison's going to be back with us next week," she said sweetly. "Third-time lucky?"

Hastily, I abandoned the patent leathers. It was not a good sign that the D.A.'s office remembered Marnolla.

"Woodall plans to ask for ninety days."

Three months! My heart sank. I could only hope that Judge O'Donnell would be hearing the case.

As if she'd read my mind, Tracy gave the clerk her credit card for the low-heeled shoes and said, "Perry Byrd's due to sit then."

Layers of pink and gold clouds streaked the eastern sky as a designated driver delivered me back to the house on New Year's Day. I forget who designated him. The carload of friends that came back to Dobbs weren't all the same ones I'd left Dobbs with and I couldn't quite remember where the changeovers had come because we hit at least five parties during the night. I recall kissing Randolph Englert in Durham just as the ball dropped in Times Square, and I know Davis Reed and I had an intimate champagne breakfast with grits and red-eye gravy around 3 A.M. somewhere between Pittsboro and Chapel Hill. Further, deponent sayeth not.

I'd been asleep about four hours when the phone rang beside my bed. A smell of black-eyed peas and hog jowl had drifted up from the kitchen to worry my queasy stomach, and Billy Tyson's loud angry voice did nothing to help the throbbing in my temples.

"If this is your idea of a joke to make the Merchants' Association look shabby," he roared, "we'll just—"

Before he could complete his sentence, I heard Aunt Zell's voice in the background. "You give me that phone, Billy Tyson! I told you she had nothing to do with this baby. Deb'rah? You better come on over here, honey. I need you to help pound some sense in his head."

It took a moment till my own head quit pounding for me to realize that Aunt Zell wasn't downstairs tending to her traditional pot of black-eyed peas.

"Where are you?" I croaked.

"At the hospital, of course. The first baby was born and it's that Lynette's that's staying with Marnolla and Billy's saying they're going to disqualify it."

"Why?"

"Because it's"—her voice dropped to a whisper— "illegitimate."

"I'll be right there," I said.

Despite headache and queasy stomach, I stepped into the shower with a whistle on my lips. Sometimes God does have a sense of humor.

Every January, amid much local publicity, the Merchants' Association welcomes Dobbs's first baby of the New Year with a Santa Claus bagful of goodies: clothes and diapers from Bigg Shopp or K mart, a case of formula or nursing bottles from our two drugstores, a pewter cup from the Jewel Chest, birth announcements from The Print Place, a nightlight from Webster's Hardware, several pounds of assorted pork sausages from the Dixie Dew Packing Company.

Integration had officially arrived in North Carolina before I was born, but I was twelve before Colleton County finally agreed that separate wasn't equal and started closing down all the shabby black schools. I was driving legally before a black infant qualified as Dobbs's first baby of the year.

I had a hard time believing this was the first

illegitimate first baby the stork had ever dropped on Dobbs Memorial Hospital, but this was Aunt Zell's first year as president of the Women's Auxiliary and she has a strong sense of fair play.

She'd make Billy do the right thing and then maybe I could pressure him to drop the charges against Marnolla.

"Forget it," Billy snarled. "She's not getting so much as a diaper pin from us."

We three were seated at a conference table in the Women's Auxiliary meeting room just off the main lobby. A coffee urn and some cups stood on a tray in the middle and Aunt Zell pushed a plate of her sliced fruitcake toward me. I hadn't stopped for any hair of the dog before coming over and I wondered if my stomach would find fruitcake soaked with applejack an acceptable substitute.

Billy bit into a fresh slice as if it were nothing more than dry bread. "Anyhow, what do we even know about this girl? What if she's a prostitute or a drug addict? What if the baby was born with AIDS? It could be dead in three months."

"It won't," Aunt Zell said. "I sneaked a look at her charts. Lynette tested out healthy when they worked up her blood here at our prenatal clinic."

"I don't care. The Merchants' Association stands for good Christian values, and there's no way we're going to reward immorality and sinful behavior by giving presents to an illegitimate baby."

"Why, Billy Tyson," my aunt scolded. "What if the Magi had taken that attitude about the Christ Child? Strictly speaking, by man's laws anyhow, He was illegitimate, wasn't He?"

"With all due respect, Miss Zell, that's not the same as this and you know it," said Billy. "Anyhow, Mary was married to Joseph."

"But Joseph wasn't the daddy," she reminded him softly.

"Bet the *Ledger*'ll have fun with this." I poured myself a steaming cup of coffee and drank it thirstily. "Talk about visiting the sins of the father on the child! And then there's that motor mouth out at the radio station. Just his meat."

"Damn it, Deb'rah, the girl's not even from here!" Billy howled. "You can't tell *me* Lynette DiLaurenzio's a good old Colleton County name."

"Jesus wasn't from Bethlehem, either," murmured Aunt Zell.

I can quote the Bible, too, but I decided maybe it was time for a little legal Latin. Like ex post facto.

"What's that?" asked Billy.

"It means that laws can't be changed retroactively. In this case, unless you can show me where the Merchants' Association ever wrote it down that the first baby has to be born in wedlock, then I'd say no matter where Lynette DiLaurenzio is from, her baby's legally entitled to all the goods and services any first baby usually gets. And if there's too much name-calling on this, it might even slop over into a defamation of character lawsuit."

"Oh, Christ!" Billy groaned.

"Exactly," said my aunt.

As long as we had him backed to the wall, I put in another plea for Marnolla. "After all," I said, "how's it going to look when you give that girl all those things in the name of the Merchants' Association and then jail the woman who took her in?"

"Okay, okay," said Billy, who knew when he was licked. "But this time, *you're* paying the court costs."

Aunt Zell leaned across the table and patted his hand. "I'd be honored if you'd let me do that, Billy."

The three of us trooped upstairs to the obstetrics ward to tell Marnolla and the new mother the good news.

Lynette was asleep, so Marnolla walked down the hall with us to the nursery to peer through the glass at the brand-new baby girl. Red-faced and squalling lustily, she kicked at her pink blanket and flailed the air with her tiny hands. Billy's spontaneous smile was as foolish as Aunt Zell's, and I knew an equally foolish smile was on my own face. What is it about newborn babies? Looking over Marnolla's shoulder, I found myself remembering that long-ago wonder when she first let me hold Avis. For one smug moment I felt almost as holy as one of the Magi, figuring I'd helped smooth this little girl's welcome into the world.

Nobody had told Marnolla that the baby had won the annual derby, and her initial surprise turned to a deep frown when Billy said he'd call the newspaper and radio station and arrange for coverage of the presentation ceremony sometime that afternoon.

"It's going to be in the paper *and* on the radio?" she asked.

"And that's not all," I caroled. "Since it'd sound weird if people heard you were going to be punished for trying to provide some of those very same things for the baby, Billy's very kindly agreed to drop the charges." I tried not to gloat in front of him.

"No," said Marnolla.

"*No?*" asked Billy.

"What do you mean, 'No'?" I said.

"Just no. N-o, no. We don't want nothing from the Merchants' Association." Marnolla turned to Billy earnestly. "I mean, it's real nice of ya'll, but let somebody else's be first baby. You were right in the first place, Billy. What I done was wrong and I'm ready to go to jail for it."

I found myself wondering if the Magi would have felt this dumbfounded if Joseph had told them thanks and all that, but he'd just as soon they keep their frankincense and myrrh.

"What about Lynette?" asked Aunt Zell. "Shouldn't she have some say in this? You're asking that young mother to give up an honor worth at least three hundred dollars."

"More like five hundred," Billy said indignantly.

For a moment, Marnolla wavered; then she drew herself up sharply. "She'll be all right without it. I'll take care of her and the baby, too. So ya'll just keep those reporters away from her, you hear?"

I grabbed her by the arm. "Marnolla, I want to speak to you."

She tried to pull away, but I said, "Privately. As your lawyer."

Reluctantly, she followed me down to the Women's Auxiliary room. As soon as we were alone with the door closed, I sat her down and said, "What the devil's going on here? First you say for me to do whatever I can to keep you out of jail, and now, when the next thing to a miracle occurs, you say you *want* to go?"

"I didn't say I *want* to," Marnolla corrected me. "I said I was ready to if that's what it takes to get people to leave Lynette alone."

"Same thing," I said, pacing up and down as if I were in a courtroom in front of the jury.

But then what she'd said finally registered and I realized it wasn't the same thing at all.

"How come you don't want Lynette's name in the paper or on the radio?" I asked.

Marnolla cut her eyes at me.

"Who don't you want to hear? The baby's daddy? Has she run away from some abusive man?"

There was a split second's hesitation, then Marnolla nodded vigorously. "You guessed it, honey. If he finds out where she's run to, he'll—"

"You lie," I said. "She's not from the county, nobody outside ever reads the *Ledger,* and WCYC barely reaches Raleigh."

As I spoke, Aunt Zell came in uninvited. That wasn't like her, but I was so exasperated with Marnolla, I barely noticed.

"Deb'rah, honey, why don't you run home and look in my closet and bring me one of those pretty new bed jackets? Get a pink one. Pink would look real nice when they take Lynette's picture with the baby, don't you think so, Marnolla?"

Marnolla had always shown respect for Aunt Zell, but nobody was going to roll over her without a fight this morning. Before she could gather a full head of steam, though, Aunt Zell advanced with fruitcake for her and a stern look at me. "Deborah?"

When she sounds out all three syllables like that, I don't usually stay to argue.

"And take a package of turnip greens out of the freezer while you're there," she called after me.

Most of my brothers married nice women and they all seem real fond of Aunt Zell, but they sure were in a rut with giving her presents. I bet there were at least a dozen bed jackets in her closet, half of them pink, and all in their original boxes. I chose a soft warm cashmere with a wide lacy collar, then went downstairs to take the turnip greens out of the freezer.

After my overindulging on rich food all through the holidays, New Year's traditional supper was always welcome: peas and greens and thin, skillet-fried cornbread.

As I passed the stove, I snitched a tender sliver from the hog jowl that flavored the black-eyed peas and gave the pot an experimental stir. There was no sound of the dime Aunt Zell always drops in. Even if you don't get the silver dime that promises true prosperity, the more peas you eat, the more money you'll get in the new year. I hoped Marnolla'd cooked herself some. Her troubles with Billy were about to be over, yet worry gnawed at the back of my brain like a toothless hound working a bone and I couldn't think why.

When I returned to the hospital, I could tell by Marnolla's eyes that she'd been crying. Aunt Zell, too; but whatever'd been said, Marnolla had agreed to let everything go on as we'd originally planned. We fixed Lynette's hair and got her all prettied up till she really did look like a young madonna holding her baby.

Billy had rounded up the media and Aunt Zell got some of the obstetrical nurses to stand around the bed for extra interest.

My own interest was in how Marnolla and Aunt Zell between them had managed to keep everybody's attention fixed on the baby's bright future and away from the shy young mother's murky past.

As everybody was leaving, I heard Aunt Zell tell

Marnolla that by the time the baby had been home a week, people would've forgotten all about the hoopla and stopped being curious. "But the baby'll still have all the presents and she and Lynette will have you."

"I sure hope you're right, Miz Zell."

I drove Marnolla home and neither of us had much to say until she was getting out of the car. Then she leaned over and patted my face and said, "Thanks, honey. I do appreciate all you did for me."

I clasped her callused hands in mine as love and pity welled up inside of me. And yes, maybe those hands *had* stolen when they were empty, and maybe her altruism was even tinged by a less than lofty pride—which of us can plead differently before that final bar of justice? What I couldn't forget was that those selfsame hands had once suckered my daddy's tobacco and ironed my mother's tablecloths. And I remembered them holding another baby girl thirty years ago; a baby girl whose left little finger crooked like her own.

As did the left little finger of that baby back at Dobbs Memorial.

Aunt Zell must have remembered, too. I wondered what had really happened to Avis. The lost, scared look in Lynette's eyes did not bespeak a rosy, stable childhood. Drugs? Violence? Was Avis even still alive? I couldn't ask Marnolla how her pregnant granddaughter had fetched up here in Dobbs, and I knew Aunt Zell wouldn't betray a confidence.

"I hope you cooked you some black-eyed peas," I said.

She nodded. "A great big potful while I was timing Lynette's labor pains."

"Better eat every single one of 'em," I said. "You're going to need all the money you can lay your hands on these next few years."

"Ain't *that* the truth!" Her tone was rueful but her smile was radiant as she gave my hand a parting squeeze. "Happy New Year, Deb'rah, and God bless you."

"You, too, Marnolla."

"Oh, He has, honey," she told me. "He already has."